Philip Henry was born in 1974. sketches while studying Performing on to short stories and a couple of scripts. During long shifts at one of the more boring jobs he had, he began making notes for a novel, which he then wrote on his days off. That novel, *Vampire Dawn*, was released in 2004 and proved so popular it was extended into a trilogy with *Vampire Twilight* in 2007 and *Vampire Equinox*, due in autumn 2009.

Mind's Eye, a novel about the monsters of high school, was released in 2006 to great critical acclaim, as was *Freak*, the story of a boy like no other, released in 2008.

Philip continues to write novels, screenplays and short stories, all based around his home on the North Coast of Ireland.

Also by Philip Henry

Mind's Eye
Vampire Twilight
Freak

...and coming Halloween 2009

Vampire Equinox

VAMPIRE DAWN

PHILIP HENRY

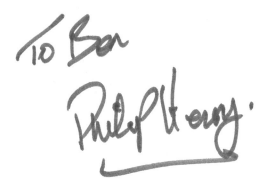

To Bon

Philip Henry.

CORAL MOON BOOKS
www.philiphenry.com

VAMPIRE DAWN
By
Philip Henry

Published By Coral Moon
www.philiphenry.com

Vampire Dawn Copyright © 2004 Philip Henry
This edition published 2009 by Coral Moon

ISBN: 978-0-9556556-3-0

Cover art by Ron McCann

10 9 8 7 6 5 4 3 2 1

love bites

They didn't believe the stories.

The gossip that spread around the school frequently turned out to be either an exaggeration or an outright lie. The story of what had 'really' happened to fourteen residents of the area started out sounding far-fetched and had now, with contributions from several hundred pupils, grown to be ridiculous. As a result, anyone who heard the evolved version of the story instantly laughed it off as a schoolboy's creation.

If either of the young lovers had given any credence to the rumours, they wouldn't have picked the darkest, most secluded spot in Castleroe Forest to 'park'. But as they made love their minds were on other things; she was thinking about Russell Crowe in full gladiatorial battle dress, while he was mentally doing his nine times tables. (All too) soon she screamed 'yes' and he screamed 'sixty-three', and they relaxed into each other's arms. The sounds of panting and mumbled calculation ceased and all that could be heard was the river lapping at the bank and the gentle whisper of the wind pushing through the trees…well, that and a Queen epic.

"Who wants to live forever?" Freddie Mercury's question bellowed from the speakers of the Ford Escort. It was the fourth, and final, Queen song on his 'sex tape'. The first three songs were chosen for their rhythm; *Breakthru*, *I Want It All* and *Don't Stop Me Now*, while the last song, which was playing, was to chill out to afterwards. Sometimes he felt slightly inadequate because his ninety-minute tape only had four songs recorded on it, but he was realistic: he was seventeen and knew he had a three-song limit.

He looked down at his naked girlfriend resting her head on his chest. He thought she was beautiful, though she would disagree. According to her, she was too fat and her earlobes protruded too far. It was true that she wasn't 'supermodel-skinny', but she wasn't fat in anyone's eyes but her own. She was genuinely insecure about her appearance—she didn't just put herself down to try to elicit a compliment like a lot of girls do—so, to show her that it didn't matter to him, he had tried to make light of the situation. Citing the Queen song, he had told her, 'Fat-bottomed girls, they make the rocking world go round'. This had not helped. Instead, it had resulted in a three-day break-up that she used to starve herself to the point of illness. After that he decided not to bother trying to convince her that her earlobes were fine.

He had heard this song many times before (twice a week, three times if she didn't have to baby-sit), but now, as Brian May's blissful solo began, he thought about the reply. Would he want to live forever? He reasoned it would depend greatly on how you would live. It sounds like the perfect eternity if you're on an island full of scantily clad Amazon women with nothing but carnal indulgence on their minds; but, if you were locked in a room listening to The Bay City Rollers Greatest Hits on a perpetual loop, death would probably be the preferable alternative. He took a long drag on his cigarette and considered a third option: eternity with his girlfriend. Instead of a lifetime with either of the two extremes, forever with her would be a balance of both. Equal amounts of pleasure and torment, each enhancing the other's effect. Taking the rough with the smooth was maybe the best way, or maybe the only way, to live.

He sucked on his cigarette again. She raised two fingers behind her head and he placed the cigarette between her knuckles. He closed his eyes and laid his head back, smiling. He knew that if his theory was correct he was due for torment sometime soon, but as the last bars of the song faded into silence, he decided he would enjoy the pleasure while he could.

She exhaled a long cone of smoke against the steamy windscreen. It was really uncomfortable lying against his chest, the hand brake was digging into her side and her legs were squashed up against the door. She took several quick, final drags from the cigarette before dabbing it in the ashtray.

Without looking at him she asked, "Do you love me?"

His eyes rolled back in his head. It sounded like the sort of question you could answer with one word but he knew he wasn't going to get off that lightly. His response would only reveal whatever it was she *really* wanted to ask him. He had no choice but to walk right into it. In a deadpan tone he answered, "You know I do."

Now she made eye contact. "Why were you talking to your ex last night at the gym, then?" she said in an accusing tone.

"What?"

She sat up quickly and started putting her bra back on. "I knew you'd lie about it."

He shook his head in bewilderment. "I'm not lying about it. I saw her. I said hello. What's the big deal?"

"The big deal is..." She paused as she pulled her T-shirt over her head. "...you didn't feel the need to tell me." She wriggled into her jeans.

"Because it wasn't important," he retorted, while pulling his own jeans and boxer shorts up from around his ankles. "Do you want me to keep a log of everyone I speak to? I could submit it for your approval at the end of every week. Would that please you?"

"You went out with her—slept with her—for over a year, that gives her a certain power over you." She punched her arms into her jacket sleeves and zipped up the front.

"You think she wants me back," he cried. "She's screwing half the football team."

"She wouldn't do it to pleasure you, she'd do it to hurt me. She's a cruel fuckin' bitch, y'know?"

He shook his head. "You don't think you're being a little paranoid? I only said hello to her."

"At the gym," she snapped. "She was probably standing there all sweaty in her two-piece spandex flaunting her big tits and her small ass and her normal earlobes at you—don't tell me you didn't think about it."

"Look," he said, loudly, "I broke up with her because I didn't like her. She has a mean streak the length of the San Andreas Fault."

"Everyone knows that! How come you had to shag her for a year before you realised it?" She sat back, confident that she had won the argument.

He took a few seconds to think of a counter-attack. "So I made a mistake—everyone does it. What about your last boyfriend?"

"Oh, don't try to turn this around."

He ignored her and continued, "You went out with him for nearly a year and he was a real fucking prince wasn't he? The school bully. Beating up kids four years younger than him and stealing their dinner money. Where was your great sense of right and wrong then?"

She slammed her back into the seat and folded her arms. "I just want you to be honest with me," she mumbled.

He put his hand on her shoulder and turned her towards him. "OK, the truth is: if I didn't want to be with you, I wouldn't be with you."

She smiled a little. "And you'd like it if a cyborg with an Austrian accent went back in time and erased your ex from existence altogether?"

He thought for a moment and answered, "No. I'm glad I went out with her."

The smile fell flat again.

"Glad, because going out with that vicious tart just makes me appreciate what I have with you even more."

The smile returned, and bigger than before. "Even though I have a temper?"

"I love your temper."

"Even though I have crazy earlobes?"

"I especially love your crazy earlobes." They kissed long and slowly.

Suddenly she was full of energy. "I want to dance. Put on some music," she said eagerly.

He smiled and picked a tape while she climbed outside and stood in front of the car. He switched the headlights on her and turned the music up loud enough to hear outside, then lit up another cigarette and slowly walked around to the front of the car. He sat down on the ground between the lights.

She smiled seductively at him and started to move her voluptuous body to the slow rhythmic grind of the music. Her hands roamed freely over her body, caressing herself like a lover. She unzipped her jacket and slid it teasingly down to the ground where she rested on her hands and knees and began a slow feline prowl toward him.

His lips soon forgot his cigarette. As she crawled toward him he could only think one thing: God she's sexy! She was sexier with her clothes on than most other girls were nude, even though her T-shirt *was* performing way beyond the call of duty and left little to the imagination. She edged closer to him with her eyes peeking through her dark, sweat-drenched hair. She was close now—close enough to kiss. He edged forward. She withdrew playfully and smiled at him. Slowly she retraced her steps backwards, always keeping her eyes trained on her prey.

She flung her head back, removing her long mane of hair from around her face and raised herself up on her knees. She felt good. She felt desired. Most of all, she felt loved. She looked at him—sitting with a catatonic grin on his face. She decided to see how long she could tease him before he'd crack. Sliding her hands down her torso slowly she rested them on her hips. On their return journey upward she took hold of her T-shirt and slid it off over her head. He began trying to raise himself, but moved like a man trying to smuggle a javelin through customs. She smiled, closing her eyes and letting her head fall backwards. Suddenly she heard him scream and opened her eyes to be greeted by a man's face.

The man's arm caught her solidly around the neck. She flung her hand instinctively at his head and grabbed his hair. She pulled hard. He didn't scream. He didn't even yield forward to lessen the pressure. She struggled wildly but his hold remained firm. She kicked at his shins. He didn't move. She clawed deep into his face. The scratches disappeared momentarily.

Oh fuck! She thought, The stories are true.

She punched and kicked him anywhere she could for what seemed like hours. Soon her limbs began to tire. She was running out of fight. In a last ditch attempt she drew her head forward and then snapped it back toward his face. He moved to the side and caught her by the hair. She was staring straight up at him. He looked down at her soft, naked throat. His cold blue eyes sparkled with a mischievous excitement. As he smiled she caught a glimpse of his incisors growing long and pointed before her eyes. She never had time to scream.

Immediately he pulled her head to the side and bit violently into her jugular in one smooth fluid motion. Blood began to drain from her body at an incredible rate. She felt dizzy and her vision blurred. She forced her closing eyelids apart and looked for her boyfriend and found him inexplicably still standing in front of the car. Using all her remaining energy she focussed on him, not wanting to miss a second of his impending heroic rescue. He would save her from this creature. He would die for her, of that she was certain. The seconds passed slowly as if time itself was a goulish spectator to this macabre scene. With each passing moment of inaction her faith grew as weak as her body. What the fuck was he waiting for? His expression said he was trying to decide whether to try to help her or save himself. She wouldn't have thought twice about it. Even if it meant risking her own life she would have tried. He didn't. She saw him turn and run into the forest as her eyes began to close. She felt so weak, so tired. He never tried, she thought, and the darkness took her.

The creature released her limp body and dropped it among the numerous fast-food containers strewn around the picnic site. As he turned he saw the boy's fleeing back disappear into the forest. He grinned wickedly.

The young man furiously beat his way through the trees and bushes trying to defend himself against the attacking forest. Don't look back, he thought. Everything else could be dealt with later; his only priority now was to make sure there *was* a later.

Inside his mind he asked the stupid question: What the fuck was that? It was stupid because he knew the answer. He knew because of the stories—the stories *were* true.

But if he actually admitted that a vampire had just killed his girlfriend and was probably after him now, he feared his legs might give up on him. Suddenly, a wave of calm passed through him and he stopped running. He felt light-headed and elated. Almost like being drunk without the problems of equilibrium. He turned and faced the other way.

A woman stood before him. She looked deep into his eyes—behind them—into his mind—into his heart. Instantly she knew him as well as any lover. She located where his desire hid and silently offered to satiate it. She stood with an unnatural stillness before him. The forest was quiet. She looked still deeper into his eyes. His mind was trapped between fear and longing, between what he should do and what every male hormone in his body wanted him to do. He knew that his impulse would destroy him if he gave in to it, but his mind rejected reason, he could think of no one else. He was here with her and she was perfect.

"Perfection has a price," she said aloud. She moved close to his face and looked deep into his eyes. "Immortality," she whispered, "it's a curse. Eternal youth sounds like a prize but all things have a dark side. With this the prize *is* the curse. It's the way things are. Without sorrow how could we tell when we're happy?" She kissed him lightly on the cheek. "All demons dream of being angels, but we can't sleep forever." Her accent was Irish, and although it strayed occasionally to Europe, America or any number of other places she had visited, it always returned home to Dublin.

As he was trying to fathom why he thought she should have been French, she grabbed the lapels of his coat and lifted him off the ground. They hovered just above the leaf-carpeted ground; it felt like a dream to him. Then, they shot upwards at unbelievable speed. He tried to remain focussed on her face, but his calm was leaving him quickly. Soon he became aware that there was no forest around him anymore. He looked down and saw the treetops getting ever smaller below him. This was the ticket that let him reclaim his fear. He screamed frantically.

She stopped their ascent and looked him in the eyes. "Life is *your* gift—mortality is your curse." She let go and watched him drop, his arms grabbing wildly for everything that wasn't there.

His heart beat faster and faster as the ground raced toward him. Even though he was falling at an incredible speed he seemed to have far too much time to think. He swallowed a bug and his mind shot off into this weird 'That was my Last Supper' conversation with itself, then into a more ridiculous train of thought about the protein content of winged insects. Why was he wasting his last seconds of his life? He should be making his peace with God, or Buddha, or Allah. He decided he should make peace with them all, just in case. Then he worried that maybe they'd get pissed off about divided loyalties. Nah, supreme beings don't get pissed off, do they? But there *was* something about 'Worshipping no other Gods but me'—whose book was that? He realised he should have thought about this earlier. He decided on a plan: Eenie, meenie, minie, mo. He babbled through the rhyme and Allah was the one to go with. That didn't feel right. Buddha would probably be fine with it because, believing in reincarnation, this scenario would be played out many times and He *would* eventually win. But the Christian God might not be best pleased to be eenie meenied out of the metaphysical running. He had to do something quickly. He was going to hit the ground any second. He shouted, "To whom it may concern: HELP MEEEEEEEE!"

The female vampire grabbed him four feet above the ground, stopping his momentum instantly. "Always amazes me what goes through peoples' minds before they die." She dropped him the last four feet and he lay there face down in the mud.

The reprieved mortal made a mental note to decide on a religion the next time he had a spare five minutes. He picked himself up and faced the woman. Even though his desire was heavily diluted by fear, he still felt a lingering attraction to her. She was beautiful—not an opinion—a fact. Her body was caged in a plain black dress from neck to ankle. There was no need for padding or support to accentuate her curves, for the unseen body within would conjure a desire in all men to set it free. Her long dark hair touched just beneath her chin framing her wanton red lips and striking green eyes on a white background in a perfect oval.

The male vampire strode up behind her, pushing his fingers through his thick disordered hair. The long dark tails of his coat flapped as if warning of danger. His statuesque presence was defined by a paleness which could have been mistaken for frailty had his chiselled features not exuded the kind of strength and confidence that demanded submission from all who looked upon them. He stopped behind her and put his arms round her waist.

"She does love a chase." He kissed her on the cheek. "Makes the heart beat faster—blood pump quicker—you can drink it more rapidly and get a better hit. A bit like Tequila slammers." The mortal boy noted his accent was more northern; he sounded like a local.

She took a step toward the mortal, looked at him and walked away.

"What's the matter sweetheart?" the vampire asked her.

"I'm not hungry, you have it," she said, rather embarrassed.

"Not hungry? But you haven't eaten all night. You only had that kid coming out of the science-fiction convention last night and there was hardly a pick on him."

"I just don't feel hungry," she replied.

"I'll bet it was that kid, he had far too much acne. I told you it would give you indigestion."

"It's not indigestion, Xavier," she screamed.

Xavier was a little taken aback; she never got angry. "Don't shout at me, Claire. You're cranky because you haven't fed." Xavier grabbed the boy's arm and held out his wrist to her. "Please, try to eat something."

"No," she said firmly.

Xavier felt tightness in his chest and rubbed it. He turned to the boy. "Did your girlfriend eat a lot of garlic?"

The boy nodded nervously.

The vampire burped and rubbed his chest again. "That's going to be repeating on me all night."

Claire was staring at the girl's body lying in the distance.

"You're not on a diet again, are you?"

Claire shook her head.

Xavier took her by the shoulders. "I've told you a million times, when you became a vampire your body became perfect. You can't get fat or have bad skin or dandruff or any of the things that mortals love to waste their time obsessing about." He looked her in the eyes. "You're beautiful and I love you."

"You don't understand, Xavier," she said softly. "I'm just sick of it. I'm sick of it all. Those two were in love and you just killed that girl without a second thought."

"What are you talking about? That's what we do. There are predators and prey; if we weren't the spiders, we'd be the flies."

Claire hung her head. "It just doesn't feel right anymore." She walked off towards the road.

Xavier turned to the mortal. "Can you believe that?"

He was frozen to the spot with fear but managed somehow to answer. "No. But, hey, if she's not hungry, she's not hungry," he said forcing a sympathetic smile.

"A hundred and six years we've been together, and I still don't know what goes on in her head most of the time."

The boy nodded nervously, trying to think of something to say. Something helpful. Something insightful. Something that would earn him his freedom. "Women!" he shrugged.

Xavier stared after Claire and shook his head, exhaling. "Yeah." He turned and quickly grabbed the boy's throat and broke his neck. The body dropped at his feet and was instantly still. Another garlic flavoured burp forced its way up his windpipe and he patted his breastplate to try to coax it all out at once, but it wouldn't come. Xavier stepped over the corpse and mumbled, "Women!"

He walked after Claire, but she was nowhere in sight.

soliss

It took Claire just over two hours to make her way to London, which was pretty good time for any vampire. She sat on the rooftop facing Ten Downing Street, watching the Blairs through a window putting Leo to bed. She often came here. She had brought Xavier once but he had said how easy it would be to kill the Blairs and throw the whole country into chaos. He had missed the point. They had power and stature but they were in love, still. Most other celebrity couples were phoney. Even if she hadn't had the ability to read their thoughts, she imagined it was obvious to anyone who took the time to think why they were together. As Claire saw it they all basically fell into three categories: Climbers, Clingers and Morons. The Climbers are the ones who marry someone as famous, or, if possible, more famous, than they are so the media can talk about it endlessly and give them both all the free publicity they need. The Clingers are the sad people who have *had* their fifteen minutes of fame but try to attach themselves to anyone who might extend it to a half-hour. The Morons (mostly footballers and glamour models) thrive on nothing but physical appearance. Their relationships usually last longer than the rest because they never think about anything, so opinions never conflict. Their marriage is solid until the looks go. They're all vampires—they just feed off fame, money and power instead of blood. She and Xavier were no worse than any of them.

Tony and Cherie were different. The fame and notoriety were incidental to the relationship and not the other way round. That's why Claire came here. Living proof that you could have both power and family. It was what she longed for, but vampires can't have children. Because they never get any older, the foetus never gets a chance to develop. Every female vampire in the world was probably pregnant with her baby frozen in time at the moment of fertilisation. Claire yearned to be a mother. The last time she'd mentioned it to Xavier was in 1980 and his only solution was to Make another vampire. It just wasn't the same. Apart from the emotional attachment of carrying it for nine months, there were all the things that a newly Made vampire wouldn't need to learn: walking,

11

talking—those were the moments she craved to know. When a human is transformed into a vampire—no matter what the mortal's age is—it's body becomes that of someone of approximately twenty-one years, and there it stays. Of course, there were things to teach it, but 'drink blood, hide from the sunlight and don't talk to strangers with wooden stakes' didn't seem appropriate for a newborn, yet, that was what it would have to learn.

Claire remembered her own first awkward steps as a vampire. She had wrestled with her conscience for weeks at the thought of killing a human. She had had a strict religious upbringing and had been told her whole life that killing was wrong; now she was told it was right. Not only right, but also necessary. Even after several kills, the guilty thoughts persisted. Thoughts that should have remained silent, because in giving them an audience she fell victim to the worst pain her life, mortal or immortal, ever suffered.

The other vampires, in an attempt to free her from her mortal ties, slaughtered her parents, her little brother, her friends and even the local priest. She was told it was for the best—she couldn't have contact with them and she would have outlived them all anyway. But all the logic in the world didn't banish the torment. It had stayed with her all these years, mostly to a lesser degree, but always there. The unrelenting anguish was reason enough not to force this existence on anyone else.

Her train of thought was interrupted as the lights went out in Number Ten. Claire smiled, remembering what Soliss, a vampire she met once, had told her so many years ago: 'Sleep. Dream the impossible is true, for when you awake this nightmare life will claim you once again'. She didn't know what he meant at the time, she had only been a vampire a few months when they had met. She was still adjusting to the change, forgetting the limitations of being mortal and embracing the hedonistic world of the undead.

Soliss had a gentle sadness in his eyes and seemed uneasy killing mortals. On the rare occasions when he fed on humans he hunted what he called 'the deserving'—thieves, muggers, murderers and rapists. He only spoke to other vampires when he needed to understand some facet of his being. On one of

12

these visits Claire had noticed him. His thoughts were not like those of his peers and this made him stand out in a crowd. In the brief conversation that Claire had had with him she sensed his regret and alienation. He didn't belong anywhere. He was a monster to his mortal friends and a stranger among his own kind. It wasn't until years later that Galen, the oldest surviving vampire in Ireland, had told Claire the story of Soliss. So tragically poignant was the tale that she remembered what he had said almost word for word:

"When a vampire decides to Make another, it is a very exclusive privilege. They will often watch their subject for many months, observing their personality and demeanour, to assess suitability. After all, eternity is a long time and anyone who Makes a vampire becomes their mentor and responsible for them and their actions. This was not the case with Soliss.

"He had been made a vampire by a Che'al, a demon who hunted and fed indiscriminately on mortals, immortals or even other demons. The Che'al were the most primal and sadistic creatures ever to roam the land and although humanoid in appearance they frequently moved on all fours and were classed as animals by all who knew of them.

"One night, in the spring of 1893, this particular demon added a vampire to his credit. By eating him and ingesting his blood the beast had acquired the traits of a vampire. The Che'al were not smart by any means; it never realised or cared who it had killed or what effect it might have. Its savage bloodlust was in overdrive when it came upon Soliss's farm.

"Soliss had put up a valiant fight against the beast when it had attacked his livestock. He had followed it into the cellar of his feed store where it had pounced on him and pinned him to the ground. Luckily his scythe was close to hand and he hit the creature several times in the neck and face and sent it into retreat, but not before some of its blood had found its way into him.

"The remains of the Che'al were found the next day in the middle of a field. It had fallen asleep unaware of its new vulnerability and had been cremated by the first rays of the dawn sunlight. Soliss had slept the day through in the basement where he had repelled the beast. He awoke that night to the to the sound of soft, cautious footsteps descending into the basement. His practical mind gave way to an irresistible alien instinct within him. A hunger unlike anything he had ever felt; a hunger for blood.

"He heard his name whispered softly by his bride but it meant nothing to him. He watched the candle's nervous flicker grow brighter, step by step, until she reached the bottom of the stairs. He could smell her fear and it was intoxicating. He imagined her blood, thick and warm, running down his now cold body. Unable to restrain himself, he leapt from the darkness with unexpected strength. His hands grabbed her throat and slammed her to the ground. She was about to scream when she recognised her attacker. Her body relaxed. Once she saw it was Soliss she no longer had any fear. She trusted absolutely that he would never hurt her.

"Soliss looked at her and remembered who he was. But the hunger—the hunger. Sharp pains stabbed his insides, trying to coerce his ravenous desire. He looked once more at the innocent face below him and released his savage embrace. Before she could speak he ran up the steps of the basement and into the night.

"The undead have a very distinctive smell, and he was found that same night by two vampires out feeding. They brought him before me. It was a unique situation. Nothing like it had ever happened before so no one knew what to do with him. It didn't take long to realise that he resented the life that had been forced upon him. He shunned all other vampires and was solitary and distant. He spent his nights watching his wife go through the mechanics of daily life and waiting on their porch every night in the hope that he would return. I heard of this and suggested the perfect solution was to make Soliss's wife a vampire as well. When this was put to Soliss he flew into a rage, attacked two vampires and almost killed me. He loved his wife too much; he wouldn't be so selfish as to condemn her to the waking nightmare in which he lived.

"He was seldom heard of after that. He returned to his wife and told her of the disease that had infected him. Her love for him was strong and true and after a time they resumed as normal an existence as their conflicting species allowed. He had all the blood, albeit from livestock, that he needed and the two lived happily for the next three years until his wife was taken ill. No potion, lotion or poultice could cure this mysterious affliction. In a few short months her sickness progressed to the point where she was completely bed-ridden and her every breath brought with it more pain.

"Ever since the local healer had expressed his pessimistic prognosis they had both been thinking the same thing; that Soliss had a cure, not only a cure but also a vaccination, against all illness and even death.

"As her sickness continued and the weeks turned to months they both thought about it but never mentioned it to the other. It was not Soliss who finally suggested it. He had been hoping that his wife's religious beliefs might have spared him the consequences of his decision, but her pain was not quelled by good so she made the same request of evil. Soliss had made his choice weeks earlier and though it pained him greatly he denied her. Her love for him soon became resentment and ultimately hate for refusing her that which she needed. Time and again when she pleaded, when she screamed, when she cried and even as she drew her final breath Soliss remained resolute.

"She died in the morning on a bright July day and when she did Soliss leaned down, kissed her and walked outside. The sunlight immediately attacked him and the exposed areas of his skin, his head and hands, burst into flame. Soliss slowly dropped to his knees and raised his hands to the sky as his soul begged for forgiveness. The rest of his body was now reacting to the solar execution. The fire burned rapidly and unobstructed for the few minutes that it took to consume him. Soon all that remained was a smouldering grotesque statue of blackened flesh, staring at the sky looking for redemption from a God to which he didn't belong."

Every vampire in the land, probably in the world, knew that story. It had become a parable, something to be passed on to all newly Made vampires. The warning was that prolonged exposure to mortals can confuse and contaminate but Claire didn't believe this. Soliss knew exactly what he was doing and now she thought she knew why. She stood up and began walking along the rooftops with her mind questioning every step that led home.

home

Xavier and Claire lived in The Arcadia, a disused dance hall in the seaside town of Portrush. The building was once home to teenagers clad in zoot suits and bobby socks, where music and laughter resided, where boy met girl and fell in love and the future was everything they wanted. Now the doors through which so many had passed and found what they were looking for were closed and bricked-up, as were the windows. In the cold darkness the dance floor was empty apart from a few tattered banners and streamers that had long since lost their colour. Silence waited uneasily in such a place, like an unwelcome visitor anxious for an opportunity to leave. The Arcadia was everything it shouldn't be: it was a tomb. It stood on the shore next to a small beach and paddling pool on one side and a car park and larger beach on the other. The town had a good tourist trade, which gave the undead couple quite a varied menu, though they rarely risked feeding in their hometown and instead travelled to the neighbouring areas at meal times.

Xavier stomped from one side of the small stage to the other holding the left side of his jaw. Where the hell was Claire? It was nearly sun-up; she was cutting it close. Not that he minded her staying out early, but his tooth was killing him and he was sure she would know what to do. The fight was still preying on his mind, though it wasn't *really* a fight, was it? He didn't think so but maybe she did. A sharp pain gripped his jaw; he yelled and began punching the corner of the stage-right wall. Several bricks came loose and skidded across the empty dance floor. There was a noise: the skylight opening and closing. Claire was home. He stopped punching, laid his back against the damaged wall, lit a cigarette and put on his nonchalant face just in time. Claire dropped from the roof-space into the middle of the dance floor. They stared at each other for a moment, each waiting for the other to set the tone of the conversation.

Because he really needed her help, Xavier spoke first. "Where have you been?" he said, trying to sound inquisitive and not accusing.

"London." She forced a small grin.

16

"Eating out in the West End?" She had gone to London without him even though she knew there was a little family in Chelsea who was Xavier's favourite blood group. Xavier had always been a little resentful that Claire had the ability to fly and he didn't. He couldn't swan off to England in a huff when he felt like it.

Claire smiled. "No, I took off to think. London is just where I ended up." She found it very funny that even after one hundred and six years of marriage *and* being able to read minds that Xavier still tried to hide things from her.

There was an uncomfortable silence. Neither knew what to say next. This was ridiculous, they knew each other beyond intimacy, they had been together for over a century and they were staring at each other like two shy teenagers on a first date. Xavier was sure he was not going to speak first this time but the pain in his jaw disagreed. He screamed loud and long, scaring all the silence from the room. He dropped to the ground and instantly Claire knelt down on the floor beside him.

"What's the matter?" she said with sincere concern.

"My bloody tooth is killing me." He winced, holding his jaw.

"We should get you to a dentist."

"A dentist?" he cried in disbelief. "Are you mad?"

"Not a mortal, a vampire dentist."

Xavier looked confused. "They have vampire dentists?"

"Of course; this is the age of political correctness. They're not allowed to discriminate. There are vampire doctors, accountants, police, managing directors, agents, lawyers..."

"They were always vampires." Xavier interrupted.

She looked at his wry grin. This was the old Xavier, the one she fell in love with, and she wanted him to know it. She bent down and kissed him with the perfect balance of passion and tenderness.

"Ow, fuck," she yelped and jumped backwards with her hand covering her mouth. "You bit my tongue."

"No I didn't, I swear."

Claire squinted at him. He wasn't lying. "Did you eat anything funny tonight?"

"I haven't eaten anything funny since the Edinburgh Festival," he laughed through his pain.

She smiled but composed herself quickly. "What *did* you eat tonight?"

"The girl at the picnic site, a guy coming out of a video shop with the remake of *Godzilla*—there was no point in him living—and a woman coming out of a chapel. She looked like her husband had beaten her. She was quite bruised. Still," he said smugly, "made the meat tender." He ran his tongue down to the tip of his right incisor

She moved towards him. "Let me look in your mouth."

"I'd like to see your qualifications in dentistry first, please." That smile again.

He opened his mouth and Claire examined inside, stretching his cheeks at the top and bottom until she found the cause. She carefully reached inside his mouth and very gently extracted two inches of silver chain with a small crucifix attached. She dropped it to the ground. Xavier moved his jaw around—the pain was gone. They both stared at the small cross. Xavier turned to Claire and smiled. "Catholics should carry a health warning."

Claire grinned. "What would my health warning read, then?"

He kissed her lightly on the lips. "Do not store in direct sunlight." Xavier put his arm around her waist and they walked off stage.

They had converted the two dressing rooms backstage into a living area. One as a bedroom, complete with wardrobes, dressing table and an antique mahogany double-coffin, and the other as a lounge with a TV, video and sofa. The Green Room already had a sink and small stove and so became the kitchen. The Ladies and Gents still had at least one working toilet in each and they stayed to their own to avoid arguments. Their material needs were small.

As they entered the lounge Xavier's gum was still smarting and he thought alcohol might speed up the healing. He raised the bottle of Bushmills Whiskey. "Drink?"

Claire vaguely nodded.

"I taped last night's Buffy and Angel, do you want to watch them before bed?"

"Can we talk, Xavier?"

"Evidently, or it would be quiet in here."

Claire's expression remained blank.

"Used that one before, have I?"

Claire forced a smile and nodded.

He took a deep breath then increased the whiskey measure, handed it to her and poured himself an equal one. They sat down on the sofa. "What's on your mind?"

"Do you remember Soliss?" she asked.

"That crazy bastard?"

"He wasn't crazy, he was tortured." She hung her head. "Stuck in the Purgatory between what he was and what he wanted to be."

That sounded too well thought out. Xavier needed to stop this. "Look, that story has been told and retold a hundred times; no one knows if it's true, no one knows if this guy Soliss even really existed. I mean, I heard Stoker made that story up one night when he was pissed on rum."

"He existed. I knew him," she said calmly.

Xavier paused, then gave the best argument he could think of: "Oh."

"It was just after I was Made, about a year before I met you."

"But you weren't there when he died, were you?"

She shook her head.

"You see that's what I'm talking about. Everyone fits the facts to their own story, so how could anyone know if he made this great stupid gesture?" He took a long drink. "It's just as possible that when his wife died he got so drunk that he forgot it was daytime, went outside for a piss and got toasted."

Claire set the whiskey on the floor and put her head in her hands.

"Yeah, that takes the whole romantic edge of it, doesn't it?" he added triumphantly.

"I'm not happy," she said, her hands still covering her face.

"You're just hungry. I'll bet you didn't feed at all tonight." He sounded like a parent telling her to eat her vegetables. "It's not too late, if I'm quick I could nip out and get you a postman or something."

19

She shook her head. "It's not that I'm unhappy tonight or last night or the night before." She paused before finally admitting the terrible truth. "I don't like who I am. I don't like what I do. I don't like this time, these people."

"I know what you mean. Remember how great we thought the year 2001 was going to be fifty years ago?" He remembered the youthful optimism of his early-hundreds. "Hover-cars and moon-bases. The great drug that would allow us to walk in daylight." With genuine pity he said, "None of it happened."

"Why not?" she mumbled through her hands, "In the eighties the humans seemed to be pushing themselves forward with such enthusiasm, how did they lose their momentum?"

Xavier smiled affectionately. "I miss the whole competitive thing of the eighties. Vamps used to kill each other over a Tofu-eating new-ager." He looked for a reaction but did not find one. He continued, "Some guys I knew back then had drunk enough blood to retire at one-hundred and thirty."

Claire's hands still masked her face. "It was Soliss that started me thinking and now I think I know what's wrong." She raised her head and removed her hands. Tears were streaming down her face.

Xavier's eyes became wide and his mouth dropped open. He pointed a disbelieving finger at her. "Oh fuck, you're sick!" he screamed and jumped back to avoid infection. "How? Who? What did you do?" He pulled the lapel of his coat over his mouth.

"It's been happening for a few months, pretty much ever since we came above ground." She wiped away the offending liquid. "I've been so scared, so confused, but tonight I figured it out."

"You're probably delirious, do you have a body temperature?"

"No, Xavier," she said defiantly, "you have to listen to me. I know what's causing this change in me...and you."

"Me?" Xavier lowered his protective lapel, jumped to his feet and started pacing in small circles. "I'm fine. I'm a totally normal vampire, I've still got all the drives I had when I was first Made."

"I know that isn't true, Xavier. Maybe it's happening to you slower than me because you're older, but it *is* happening. You are not all that you were."

He stopped pacing and defensively put both hands over his crotch. "What does that mean?"

Claire shook her head. "Your bloodlust, I mean. Can you truthfully say you felt the same rush killing that couple in the woods tonight as you did when we were first married?"

Xavier searched for an appropriate response but could think of none so settled for the truth. "No, it isn't as good. But we've gone through these feeding lulls before, you just gotta keep doing what you do until it gets better."

"And if it doesn't get better?"

Xavier dropped into the sofa and exhaled. "I don't know."

Claire moved close to him. "Like I said, I think I know what's causing it."

"Is it something we can fix?" he asked hopefully.

"I don't think so," she answered solemnly.

Xavier refilled his glass, turned to her and gestured her to explain as he sat back.

"The tainted ones, the first vampires, wrote in the Corpora Vampyre that they were born to create a balance. I know you don't believe in the ancient writings but stay with me, OK?"

Xavier donned a patronising grin and nodded.

Undeterred, she continued. "What the scrolls say is that Adam and Eve were born and grew to early adulthood in the Garden of Eden but the land suffered great upheavals; earthquakes, plants and animals dying without cause. With only good in the world, nature was out of balance. Mankind could not evolve if he had no choices to make; the purity needed a nemesis. The garden continued to incur the wrath of nature until one creature became the last of his kind, and facing extinction, fed on the flesh of its dead. An affront to the life He had given it, God banished the creature to live in darkness forever. But it restored the balance, and as it was the last of its kind, nature blessed it with the ability for asexual procreation."

"Yes, we all know the story, it's a great revelation to New-Mades, but what has this got to do with us?" he asked.

21

"Don't you see? Nature knew it needed evil as well as good. They're symbiotic; they feed off each other. That's what made me think of Soliss. Do you think that because he loved his wife so much that it upset the balance, maybe even made her sick?" Xavier looked sceptical. "We've awakened in a time where the only heroes are quiet ones and the only villains are cowards. There are no crusaders. This generation is apathetic. They talk on their mobile phones and their Internet but there's no personal connection, no real love exists because they've analysed it a thousand different ways and it's all psychology and pheromones. Politicians, religious leaders, teachers—they've all been caught doing the opposite of what they endorse. Slowly, everything mortals believed in has been taken from them, and their pride won't risk letting that happen again. The bottom line is; these passionless people are starving us to death."

Xavier thought for a moment and then said, "You're saying without extreme good there cannot be extreme evil."

Claire enthusiastically nodded. "And since no one these days gives a shit who lives or dies..."

"We're becoming redundant," he concluded.

"It's ironic, really. For centuries the mortals hunted our kind with such vigour and determination," she said quietly, "if they'd only known that all they had to do was stop trying and we'd die."

That morning Xavier lay awake in his coffin staring at the so familiar grain of the wood inches from his face. All the information was swimming in his brain as he tried to think of other vampires that might confirm or deny Claire's theory. Unfortunately, the last time they were above ground, in the eighties, a Slayer had dusted most of the old gang. She was the reason they never went out with other couples anymore. She had staked, severed or burned all of Xavier and Claire's drinking buddies.

The Slayer. Xavier never imagined an angel of death would look so good. She had equal amounts of demure devotion and playful exuberance, all wrapped-up in an almost naive sex appeal. She exuded the kind of subtle desire that left a little more of her to think about every time you met her.

Added to which, practically no one's ass looked well in shell-suit bottoms—but hers did. It was almost a shame to destroy something so beautiful. She was one of the heroes that Claire had talked about. Xavier had killed her purely out of self-preservation, not malice or hate. He admired her. She fought with tenacity and imagination. It was also quite distracting to see sweat running down her lithe body clinging her Wham! T-shirt tight to her pert breasts. *That* was probably the edge that had allowed her to kill so many of the undead.

Xavier's victory was far from easy. They had fought for over four hours when her hair-band had come out as she fell. While she was momentarily blinded by her unrestrained perm, Xavier saw his chance and broke her neck as she tried to get up from the ground. Luck, or destiny giving evil another chance to restore the balance?

He remembered as he looked down at the Slayer's lifeless body that he had felt regret. For the first time since he had been Made he was sorry. Now he knew why—it was the first symptom of the illness. It was a necessity of being a vampire to have no regrets about killing humans. Xavier didn't see that as 'evil'. Vampires were just higher on the food chain than humans and it gave no more guilt than a human eating a chicken, or at least it shouldn't. Vampires were evil to humans, but humans were evil to chickens so it all just depended on where you sat on the food chain. It was a valid point of view that mortals never wanted to entertain. Vampires were sentient and intelligent beings too and deserved the right to exist.

Of course it didn't help that most vampires were only interested in their own pleasure. Their singular base need gave them great freedom to indulge in getting high and having sex (never inter-species though, humans couldn't keep up), which is how most of them spent their nights. None of them had the slightest inclination to write an opus or paint their most introspective longings. In many ways they resembled university students. Xavier despised the frivolous nature of his peers.

Where the hell were the Slayers of this generation? They would shake things up. But they were probably sitting at home with their feet up, grinning smugly at the thought of a job well done. In the months that Xavier and Claire had been above ground they had seen no other vampires. They had looked in all the usual haunts—castles, graveyards, and rock concerts—but to no avail. Xavier wondered if it was possible that he and Claire were the last of their kind.

He looked over. Claire's side of the coffin was still open. He saw the candle flickering. She was sitting up, reading. She must be scared out of her wits, he thought. Imagine how scared a mortal gets when they catch a disease and multiply that by one hundred and seven years of being healthy—well, as healthy as a dead person can be—and you'd be pretty close. He had to think of a way out of this. He stared at the grain again.

Claire sat reading the problem page of a woman's magazine, trying to keep her mind off her own worries by reading about someone else's and at the same time gaining an insight into this alien time they were living in. She couldn't believe how stupid the world had become. They wrote to these problem pages and went on television shows to ask questions that any idiot knows the answer to:

'My husband beats me up at least three times a week and tried to kill me with an empty cider bottle. Should I give him another chance?' Claire shook her head and scanned further down the page.

'... and when I confronted him he said he does enjoy oral sex, just not with me. What should I do?' Claire slowly blinked in disbelief and moved across the page.

'He says that his fiancée doesn't understand him and the girl he's in love with is in New Zealand and only his girlfriend and I are in town. But he stays with me more often than her so do you think there is hope?'

How can you motivate people so content in their misery that when they run out of reasons to stay with their partner they ask a stranger if they can think of any? They seemed to be willing to tolerate anything—but for what? Not for happiness—they weren't happy. Status? Who could be proud of having one of these primates on their arm? Security? How secure was physical abuse and infidelity? She dropped the magazine to the floor. Her head was sore trying to understand the shape of this generation's thinking. She closed her eyes and tried to calm her mind.

"Ha!" Xavier screamed in joy. His side of the coffin flew open and slammed hard on the floor. He sat up excitedly and looked at Claire who had been torn from her serenity. "I've got it. You said there's a balance, good and evil are symbiotic." Claire nodded. "Then they need us as much as we need them. Don't you see? The same thing has happened to them. The evil has been dormant too long and heroism has been starved to the point of extinction."

Claire's face brightened. "Then the way to restore it is..."

Xavier smiled and interrupted. "Yes." He moved closer to her and looked into her eyes with a renewed intensity. "If this world isn't evil enough then, by fuck, we make it more evil."

higgins, e.

The old man sat in his cell unaware of the screams from the other prisoners to turn the television down. Between his faulty hearing aid and the constant hiss of the oxygen mask on his face he could barely hear anything but would have ignored them if he had. The television remote control was loosely held together with red tape. His arthritis-riddled hands prodded ineffectually at the buttons, he was stuck with the news. An earthquake had devastated a community somewhere in South America, and the bleeding hearts were asking for his money before the ground stopped shaking. Well, they could whistle for it. No one ever gave him a free handout. No one ever gave him anything that didn't come with a price. Maybe if someone had he wouldn't be here now. The next story the newscaster tried to grab his attention with was about the thousands of pounds they were spending on a new treatment to try to impregnate some species of bird that was almost extinct. Let them die, he thought, Let them die like you're letting me die.

He had signed a waiver months ago, when the doctors told him his time was drawing short, allowing them to try experimental drugs and treatments that hadn't been approved for public use. It was something that went on a lot in prison but was hushed up. He had regretted signing almost immediately; the drugs they put him on the first week made him so weak and violently ill that death would have been the lesser evil. After that he had tried to recant his permission but his cries went unanswered and the tests continued. Sometimes they weren't too bad and gave a brief abatement of his ailments, but when they were bad—they were *really* bad. On one occasion he had reacted badly to the drugs and had been ill just after lights out. The acidic liquid he had brought up had swollen his throat and he couldn't shout for help. He had lain awake all night covered in his own vomit, the sour smell stinging his eyes and the lumpy bile curdling on his chest and neck. He cursed his own infirmity, wishing he could exact revenge on his captors. He foolishly thought he might get a break from the tests after that—maybe even an apology—but the tests continued without interruption. Sometimes, when the drugs caused more pain than they took away, he wished for death, just so he wouldn't be used as a lab rat anymore.

He tried again to change the channel but to no avail. He hit the remote control with all his rage and just managed to knock it off the arm of his wheelchair onto the floor by his feet. He put his head in his hands, frustrated at his attempt to dissipate his rage. He was tapped on the shoulder and jerked his head around. The sullen-faced guard stood before him with a clipboard.

The guard moved closer. "I *said*, eleven a.m.—parole hearing for 100377, Higgins, E."

Higgins winced and nodded, signalling he had caught the gist of what the guard had said.

The guard smiled and moved close to his ear. "Just think, this time tomorrow you could be a free man, trying to jerk-off in an entirely different toilet. Lucky you, eh?" he laughed.

Higgins heard that perfectly; spite travels well. He looked at the guard's identification badge, he knew his face but his memory for names wasn't good anymore. He squinted and made out C. Maxwell. He would remember it this time. Just below his name badge he saw a pencil protruding from the guard's top pocket. He wanted to grab it and jam it deep in that bastard's eye socket. He would have given up his chance for freedom to have his revenge. Freedom—that was a joke. If he were paroled he would be moved to some God-forsaken retirement home. Just a different room with another crappy TV probably. The only real freedom he had was in his mind— where his darkest memories were still vivid. The twisted symphony of the violence he had inflicted. The women he had tortured, raped and murdered played over and over like a broken record. He stared at the pencil again. There was no way his arms could reach that high so instead he pulled the tube out of his catheter bag and squirted urine over the guard's trousers.

Maxwell leapt back. "You son of a bitch," he screamed. He pulled out his truncheon and raised it in the air.

"A-hem." The warden stood at the entrance to the cell. The guard lowered his weapon and put it away. "Is Mr Higgins ready for the panel?"

"Yes, sir."

27

"Then let's get him down there." He gave the guard a warning glance and strolled off down the corridor.

Maxwell reconnected the still dripping bag and roughly dropped his oxygen cylinder in his lap. "You better hope you get parole, old man, otherwise I'll make sure you don't live to see another episode of *Baywatch*." He pushed his wheelchair towards the gate and caught Higgins's arm on the way out. It's a cruel fact that when everything else deteriorates in the body, the sensitivity to pain is heightened. It hurt much more than it should have. But Higgins refused the guard the satisfaction of knowing that and stayed silent.

Xavier and Claire didn't get much sleep that day and awakened long before sunset. After watching Buffy and Angel they used the remaining time to decide on a plan.

"The old rules are out the window," Xavier said firmly. "We can't waste time observing and choosing those who would make the best vampires. It's all about quantity now. You and I can only sire once a week each. So, for the next few weeks, we have to Make vampires constantly and let them wreak whatever kind of havoc they want."

Claire looked uncomfortable.

"You do know that you're going to have to feed to have the strength to sire—are you OK with that?" he said, trying to be sympathetic.

"I guess I'll have to be." She smiled bravely. "We just have to keep doing what we do and get things back to the way they were."

"Any idea who you're going to Make?"

Claire shook her head nervously.

Xavier could see a hint of fear in her face—she was getting worse. "I think I'll go religious tonight."

Claire didn't acknowledge what he said. She was shaking and occasionally staring at the skylight, at the ever-darkening blue that would soon signal the time for her to do her duty.

Xavier tried to get her mind off it. "You know I've always been a sucker for siring religious nuts. It's the conflict, you see, that makes them insane. They remember their mortal beliefs and they clash with their vampiric urges and they're psychotic in a week. That's just what we need, isn't it?"

Claire watched the last seconds of colour disappear from the sky and closed her eyes tightly. "Right," she said loudly but not confidently, "let's go."

Xavier walked over and put his arms around her and she levitated them upwards, through the skylight and down to the car park outside.

The town was quiet for a weekend. She had secretly hoped that somehow someone knew of their plan and would be waiting outside to stop them. But there was no one. The majority of Portrush were spending the evening laughing with

29

their eyes closed at whatever sitcom was being repeated. Blissfully unaware of what was about to be unleashed on them.

"I'll meet you back here, then?" Xavier asked but didn't wait for an answer before adding, "Unless you want me to come with you."

She smiled at him. "No. I'll be all right. I'll see you later." He watched as she flew upwards and quickly disappeared.

Xavier knew he needed at least three mortals before he could sire anyone. They were not going to be easy to find in this town tonight. He walked for twenty minutes around the streets and saw no one. He finally decided to try Portstewart, which was only a few miles away. Although he couldn't fly, he had the ability to move very fast over land and reached the promenade in Portstewart in less than three minutes. This was more like it. Lots of drunken students were falling around and laughing on the streets. He saw three people exit a bar—two girls and a guy. He watched them stagger to an isolated part of the beach. They screamed hysterically as they ran in and out of the sea. Xavier approached them slowly. Before he had a chance to begin mesmerising them, one of the girls ran toward him.

"Hello," she said in an over-emphasised tone. "My name's Kelly. What's yours, gorgeous?"

"Xavier," he replied, shocked at the ease of his acceptance.

"Well, Xavier, I know we haven't known each other that long, but do you want to come back to our digs?"

The couple ran to her side. She was a hippie-looking girl with short hair. She wore a tie-dyed dress, which stopped halfway down her thighs. It drew attention to her pure, untanned legs and her bare feet moving slightly, tickling themselves in the sand. Her companion was a geeky looking guy. He smiled like someone who had won the lottery twice in the same night. He obviously couldn't believe his good fortune at meeting such 'liberal-minded' girls.

The hippie girl slowly scanned Xavier from head to toe while letting her hands wander freely over the geek. "Yes," she purred, "come back with us. We'll have a great time. Trust me."

Xavier, somewhat unsure of his motives, agreed immediately.

The flat was small and dank. It was carpeted wall to wall with beer cans, ashtrays, cigarette papers and half-eaten take-aways, which were no doubt intended to serve someone as breakfast. Xavier had slept in crypts that smelt better. Kelly ran quickly to a small green vase and poured half a dozen white pills into her hand. The couple were squirming eagerly on the sofa as they kissed. They paused just long enough for Kelly to throw one of the pills in each of their mouths. She then put one in her own mouth and walked towards Xavier. As she got close it occurred to Xavier that he had forgotten to check for mirrors—something all vampires should do on entering strange surroundings. He turned and looked behind him quickly.

"Slayer?" Kelly innocently asked.

Xavier backflipped into a corner and arose instantly in a fighting stance. "Where?" he cried urgently.

She slowly raised the pill balanced on her forefinger. "Here. They're called Slayers. Would you like one?" She blinked, as if unsure of what she had just seen.

This was a break for Xavier. He glanced across at the other two. The guy had his head inside the girl's dress—safe to say they didn't notice. He looked at Kelly with her finger still extended, offering him the pill. A new drug. Maybe it was worth a try. Every vampire is unique in what affects them and what doesn't. For instance, Xavier could get drunk on alcohol, but when he had tried cocaine and heroin in the eighties it had done nothing for him. Yet, some of his friends had indulged heavily in both narcotics and enjoyed them thoroughly. This drug must have been invented while they were underground. Xavier walked over to the girl and examined the small white tablet. It had a little stake carved into it. He put her entire finger in his mouth, closed his lips gently around it and slowly slid down to the tip, swallowing the pill. Her face rested somewhere between sleep and ecstasy.

The next couple of hours were very strange. In the first hour all the sexual energy disappeared and Xavier watched the three sit around staring blankly ahead. Each was fixated on their own certain point in space. Concentrating, as if a secret might be revealed if they thought about it hard enough. It was around this time that Xavier realised that the drug was not

31

going to affect him. Still, he remained seated. An hour later, while Kelly was licking the velveteen curtains and the other girl rubbed her naked breasts against a television screen of static, the geeky boy approached him.

"You having a good one?" he asked.

"Yeah, great," Xavier answered curtly.

"You just need to find something to do," he persevered. "Come with me." He dragged Xavier from his chair and took him to the kitchen. "Wash your hands—that's great, or your hair—that is *so* good. Your sense of touch is so heightened anything feels good." He looked in the fridge. "Want to put your face in a bowl of jelly?"

Xavier had stayed this long out of scientific curiosity (he told himself), but these people were pathetic. He didn't even have any desire to feed off them anymore. He patted the geek-boy on the shoulder and said, "Look, friend, I think I'll be going."

"No, no. We'll find you something. Oh, try this." He ran over to the ironing board. There was a plastic and glass object about a foot square, sitting upright on top of it.

Xavier looked quizzically at it. "What do I do?"

"Just put your face close to it."

Xavier complied and the guy turned the sun lamp on. Xavier screamed as his face burst into flames. He dropped to the floor immediately and slapped the fire into submission. As soon as he was sure it was out he jumped to his feet. The guy was frozen—smiling in a bewildered awe. Xavier's face was smouldering but the fires of anger were raging inside him. He lunged at the geek and ripped violently at his throat. He drained him completely and threw his body across the kitchen—smashing a stack of unwashed dishes—before coming to rest in its final inverted pose on the counter. Without hesitation he stomped into the living room and dragged Kelly from her private paradise world and gnawed angrily at her neck. She put up no resistance, like the boy. Either they didn't know what was happening or they didn't care. As he dropped her lifeless corpse he saw the other girl kneeling at the TV. She was now wearing a small tight angora sweater and a pair of black lace knickers. She watched him blankly for a moment, and then stood up fully, revealing her slender legs and toned stomach. She looked at Xavier with an unnerving serious intensity.

There was something different about this one. Xavier couldn't quite work out what it was, but there was definitely something—beyond her obvious sex appeal.

She softly said, "We hide inside the coloured paper walls of our chemically induced fantasy. Feeling safe only because of our ignorance of what waits outside. Sheltered from the cruel truth of illusion: that fantasy is vulnerable because reality has teeth."

Xavier walked towards her. "You know what I am?" he asked.

"I know," she answered without fear. "I didn't catch your name earlier, what is it?"

He had run across this type before: Goth chicks who wanted to be sired. They knew the history, which vampires came from their area. It wouldn't have surprised Xavier if she had heard of him; maybe she was even a fan. "Xavier," he answered with a conceited smile.

Her expression sobered. Xavier could sense recognition. He wondered if he could sire on the strength of two. She would make a great vampire. He looked at her dilated pupils staring intensely at the ground. Maybe he would come back for her later when she'd come down.

She took a step back and raised her head. "Die you bastard!" She stepped forward and kicked Xavier in the chest, sending him ten feet across the room into the corner, smashing the ceiling plaster. Gravity pushed him through the glass table below, cutting him numerous times on the face and neck. He quickly shook the disorientation from his head and looked up. The girl flipped a small wooden stool up in the air with her foot and punched it. It smashed, sending debris to all corners of the room, and left her with a crude stake in her hand. Xavier knew he hadn't the strength to fight. He'd been exposed to ultraviolet light and the blood he needed for siring was running onto this cheap orange carpet.

"My name's Lynda—that mean anything to you?" she asked. Xavier used his remaining strength and raced out the door. In a few seconds he was resting breathless in an alley. He suddenly noticed his chest was bleeding. She had gotten a dig at him as he passed. It wasn't deep enough to touch his heart, but it was in the right place. Damn she was fast.

I guess that's the new improved slayer, he thought. He looked at the stake-mark on his chest. It was already starting to heal but slower than usual. He heard a noise in the alley behind him and turned round to be struck in the face by a cricket bat.

The impact knocked him to the ground and two men in their late teens jumped on him and began searching his pockets. Even with his diminished strength, these two were no challenge. He broke free of them and grabbed a throat in each hand. As he fed on the one in his right hand, his accomplice screamed and struggled to no avail until it was his turn. When the two thieves lay still beside him he went through their pockets. He found £400 in cash—which he pocketed—and a few other items that were only useful to mortals: watches, pills, sunglasses and the like—which he left behind.

"Busy little fuckers, weren't you?" he said, disapproving of their lifestyle.

Xavier stood up, feeling the potent intoxication surging through him like electricity. He realised his nose was quite badly broken and straightened it as well as he could. He might not look his best, but he was ready to sire.

He waited, unseen, at the window. Inside the dorm room of the Catholic boarding school, the girls sat in their sensible nightdresses. Most of them were writing letters, brushing their hair or reading the non-corrupting literature that had been selected for them. One girl walked from the far right all the way down the dorm. She wore a dressing gown and carried a large towel.

"Bath-time," Xavier whispered.

He found the bathroom window quickly—cigarette smoke was being blown from it. He watched her take every guilty drag until she was finished and threw the butt outside. She left the window open. Xavier walked over and saw her lower herself into the bath. She had a decent body—not amazing—but OK. It was clearly visible through the untreated water. Bubble bath must be evil, he thought. Her long, light-brown hair was unremarkable as was her plain face. Treasures await

34

you, he thought, the Black Blessing will make you beautiful and adored by all.

She placed a wet flannel over her face and relaxed. Now was his chance. He silently moved in through the window and stood beside the bath. Unaware of his presence she gave a pleasured moan and slid further down so only her face was above water. He couldn't mesmerise her because her eyes were covered. He had to do it the less refined way and just grab her. But hold on. What were her hands doing? This might be worth watching. Xavier was smiling from ear to ear with expectation. Unfortunately her guilt and paranoia compelled her to give a final check before she indulged fully. She removed the flannel and saw Xavier standing, smiling down at her. She was about to scream—he lunged at her.

Claire was waiting back at the Arcadia for hours before she finally heard the skylight move. Xavier dropped the thirty feet from the roof and landed hard on his shoulder in the middle of the dance floor. Claire ran to him and knelt on the floor beside him. He looked terrible. His clothes were stained with blood, his nose was bent, his face was cut and burned, and huge blisters seemed to cover most of his body.

"What the hell happened to you?" she said with an ever-increasing pitch.

Xavier timidly touched a blister, which began on his cheek and ended pushing his left eye closed. "What kind of sick, paranoid, fuck...blesses their bath water?" Claire almost laughed the situation was so improbable. "Oh, yes, very funny. My near death is a subject of amusement." He tried to hold a stern face but cracked when he saw Claire trying to hold it in. They laughed together and he lay back in her arms.

She stroked his hair. "You didn't sire, then?" she asked.

"No, I've had a hell of a night. I got burned by an artificial sun, mugged, dowsed in holy water and I met the new slayer—she took an instant dislike to me."

"I sired." She smiled proudly.

Xavier raised himself up and turned to her. "Really? Congratulations. Tell me all about it."

"Well, you know how we can't really spend the time assessing everyone and some vampires, if they're Made while they're still young, can grow to resent what they missed out on?" Xavier nodded. "Well, I figured, give the old back their life instead of taking it from the young. I went to this old-folks home and found three that were so ill they wanted to die and then found one to sire." She nodded at the stage. In the darkness Xavier made out the figure of a handsome young man. He was sleeping in the foetal position on the floor in the corner. Claire smiled maternally. "His name's Higgins."

bells, books & candles

Christian Warke sat in his van for a long time staring at the vampire's lair. He told himself he was making a thorough check of the building, noting every possible escape route. He was, in fact, biding his time until he had consumed a sufficient amount of Bell's whiskey to fuel his stamina for the task at hand. He had been sent on a lot of these missions over the years and, lately, most had been wild-goose chases, but, on rare occasions, it hadn't been kids messing around or superstitious locals and this was what caused his hesitation. Christian had witnessed too many truths which most believe were fiction. Things most people would rather stay ignorant of and scoff at as ludicrous than believe the overwhelming evidence in their favour. This didn't bother him; he had long since stopped caring what anyone thought of him. *He* knew of the evil that waits in the darkness and *he* would stand against them—alone. This was his calling: to rid the world of these beings.

If anyone had been told of his heroic deeds, the creatures he had killed, the innocents he had saved and the sacrifices he had made, they would not have pictured Christian Warke. He blinked blearily at the bloodshot eyes staring back at him in the rear-view mirror. He raised his hand and brushed his straggly hair out of his eyes; it was unwashed and the grey seemed to be winning the battle for dominance. He looked a lot more than his forty-six years. He was skinny, unshaven and wore clothes so dirty that the most humane thing to do would be to burn them. This image was not caused by lack of food or money; it was just a by-product of years of revenge. His persona was fashioned by unceasing hatred mixed with sleepless nights, extreme physical exertion, too much alcohol and having experienced a fear that few ever know.

He took a long drink and finished the bottle. That was a sign, like finishing the last cigarette in the packet, that it was time to go in, though there was more in the back of the van. Maybe just a few swigs from a fresh bottle wouldn't do any harm. Time was on his side, after all, it was still morning—he had all day. He flattened out his left hand and held it before his face. It jerked slightly as if it was being pulled from above and below with *almost* equal force. He closed it into a fist to stop the shaking. He pulled down the sun-visor and stared at the faded photograph of his wife, smiling widely with her arms wrapped lovingly around the man he used to be. He touched her cheek, trying to remember the softness of her skin but feeling only the bland paper beneath his finger. With a fresh burst of rage he snapped the visor back up, grabbed the stake and crucifix from the passenger seat and jumped out of the van, slamming the door in his wake.

The inside of the structure reeked. The fettered smell of decay was everywhere. Christian switched to breathing through his mouth as much as possible to lessen his exposure. He found himself in a dark, narrow corridor decorated with out-of-date graffiti. As he edged forward, each footstep sent gentle ripples across the flooded floor. His heart beat at the inside of his chest like an insane prisoner desperate for release. The darkness was only interrupted by the occasional slithers of sunlight that dared to venture in. Still, it was enough for him to navigate his way forward without too much stumbling.

Suddenly his breath became visible and coldness passed through him. He dropped his stake and crucifix as he shivered. His fear threw him to the floor and quickly snatched his weapons back into his grasp. He sat kneeling in the dank water, waiting for it to happen again. Nothing. He felt a fear long since forgotten by him, but instantly recognisable on its return. He closed his eyes tightly and growled his frustration through his teeth. He opened his eyes and looked around again. He was alone. When he was content he was in no immediate danger, he moved to raise himself to his feet. Then something caught his eye. Three words had been scratched crudely into the lower part of the wall: SAVE HER CHRISTIAN. He moved closer to assure himself he wasn't hallucinating (which had happened many times before), and traced his fingers over the letters—they *were* really there. What did it mean, save whom? Wait, what was he thinking? It was probably just a coincidence. He scanned the other scribblings on the wall and guessed from the references to Guns 'n' Roses and Nirvana that the vandals hadn't been busy since the early nineties. He tried to think of something that happened in the early nineties that would urge someone to write those words. He could think of none—he couldn't even think of a famous 'Christian' from any period in history.

This was distracting and maybe that was its intent. He knew some vampires had the ability to read minds but he had never known one to go to these kinds of lengths to confuse their hunter. He decided he would make a more detailed examination of the writings once he had searched the building. He stood up slowly and walked on down the corridor. He had walked about one hundred feet when his pace began to quicken. He had seen no signs of vampiric activity and wanted to complete his sweep of the building and get back to those writings.

Then a whisper stopped him. One by one he silenced all the subtle noises he was making: his feet splashing the water underfoot, the rustle of his arms brushing his overcoat, the water lapping at his shoes. He held his breath. Dead silence. Only the erratic protestation of his heartbeat tried to invade the stillness. He was again unsure of whether or not to trust his senses. It could have been the wind whistling through the rafters or the swaying of trees outside. He stood motionless, waiting. Then he heard it. It was faint but distinct. He closed his eyes; trying to listen harder and determine what direction it was coming from. It was getting louder—like it was coming towards him. He opened his eyes and saw nothing but the noise was still getting louder. It sounded like a long drawn-out raspy breath, spitting incomprehensible orders at him. It was becoming too loud now. He covered his ears but the volume remained, getting still louder. Then one voice silenced the others—a woman pleaded, "Help her, Christian." With that, the noises ceased and silence was admitted to the room once again.

Christian was shaking. He cautiously released his hands from his ears. That was no fucking coincidence. That was—he hesitated before believing it himself—a ghost. He had never experienced a haunting before; in fact, to be quite frank, he didn't believe in them. Vampires were real, physical beings he could destroy, but ghosts? He hadn't a clue.

He slid his stake and crucifix into either side of his overcoat and strode forward just looking for somewhere to sit down and try to figure out what the hell was going on. As he neared the end of the corridor he noticed an orange light coming from a large room. It was candlelight. He heard a cough—someone *was* here. His curiosity was dismissed as his fear returned and he hurriedly grabbed his crucifix and stake back into his hands. He peered inside and saw, in the centre of the room, a circle of candles surrounding a makeshift altar made of old desks covered with curtains. The corners of the room were in darkness. In one of those corners lurked the source of the cough.

Christian quickly scanned the details of the room. He smiled and relaxed; the pressure was off. He exhaled as completely as his abused lungs could and after a very brief risk-assessment (he'd seen enough vampire digs to be ninety-nine percent sure), he stepped inside the room and shouted, "Hello!"

"Who dares disturb my slumber?" a startled female voice answered, from the darkness of the far right corner. "Thou shalt face the vengeance of the undead for this outrage," she added in an ever-changing accent.

"Yeah, I'm here to read the meter," Christian replied, trying to hold back a smirk.

"Meter! Canst thou mortal not see I use candles?"

Christian, doing a damn good job of holding back his laughter, continued, "Look, I got your new Jacuzzi in the van. How are you going to run it, by candle-power?"

"But I didst not order a Jacuzzi!" she cried. She walked into the light in the hopes her appearance might inspire some terror. She was slim, in her mid-twenties, dressed all in black with an uneven white foundation covering her face. Her shoulder length blond hair looked like it hadn't been washed or even combed in weeks. "Now, be gone," she commanded, "lest my bite find your neck."

He could take it no more and burst out laughing in her face. "Oh, thank you," said Christian when his laughter allowed. "You get so few laughs in this job." He laughed uncontrollably again.

"Dost thou doubt the power of..." She added a dramatic pause before her revelation. "...a vampire!"

Christian finally got his laughter under control and said, "You are *not* a vampire".

40

"Infidel!" she screamed. "Thou willst pay for this heresy."

Christian smiled and said, "Here's *why* you're not a vampire. One, you've got a sleeping bag over there, not a coffin; two, there are a stack of empty Pot Noodle containers lying by the door—not really vampire food, though to be honest, not really human food either; three, you've got a circle of blue and silver candles. In witchcraft, blue are used mainly for protection and silver for communication—two things vamps don't have a lot of use for; four, your teeth are sitting on that chair; five, nobody speaks like that anymore, in fact, I don't think anyone ever did; six, you were coughing—vampires don't get the cold; and last, but not least, you've been standing in a ray of sunlight for the last five minutes."

She hung her head for a moment and then raised it and looked at Christian. "I think you got me," she said, resigned to the fact and voicing her true, Scottish, accent. "I'm not a psycho—please don't think I am. I have very sane reasons for doing all of this," she added urgently.

"I'm sure you do," he replied in a patronising tone and sat down on a nearby chair while lighting a cigarette.

She walked over to him and pulled up a chair facing him. "I'm trying to put a little magic back in the world. A little mystery to tease the imagination. Have you seen the state of the human race?" Rhetorical, Christian assumed, so he remained silent. She continued, "Nobody goes out anymore. The streets are empty. Houses are filled with questions never asked, with dreams not allowed to bloom: pruned if they grow—not mourned if they die. It's a terrible thing that has happened. A huge thing, but is it on any TV shows or on the front of any magazines? No, because no one has noticed."

"How did you do the corridor thing?" he asked.

"What corridor thing?" she replied, shaking her head.

"The noises in the corridor, calling my name."

She smiled excitedly. "You heard them too. That wasn't me. There is a presence here; it's why I, sort of, let the vampire facade slip a bit. I found a *real* supernatural event."

"You don't have to keep it from me, really, I go out a lot and there is quite enough magic and mystery in my life," he said flatly.

"Yeah, I heard that reading electric meters can be one adventure after another."

"I don't read meters. My name is Christian Warke. I hunt vampires."

The girl's eyes became wide. She stood up and edged backwards toward the outer wall. "How could I have known your name or that you were coming?" She smiled.

Christian thought hard. Except for Kyle back at base, no one knew where he was going. He was almost certain no one could have told this girl. "I guess you couldn't," he finally admitted.

The girl reached the wall and opened the floor-to-ceiling curtains. Light rushed in and filled the room and immediately he knew where the girl's question had been leading. Completely covering the walls and ceiling of the room, in differing sizes, two phrases were scratched over and over: SAVE HER CHRISTIAN and HELP HER CHRISTIAN. The girl looked smugly at Christian and said, "It's for you-hoo".

After Christian had retrieved another bottle of Bells and lit another cigarette from the butt of the last, he sat on the bonnet of his van. In the five minutes since the girl—whose name, he had learned, was Audrey Wells—had opened the curtains and unveiled the scribblings, she had been beaming with a satisfied smile and talking constantly. It was almost like she regarded this as some kind of inter-dimensional modern art that Christian would appreciate. After all, he was experienced with the paranormal, so he *should*, in her opinion, have been as excited as some dour-faced, pretentious art-student in a black polo-neck who just discovered a lost Picasso in his basement. He wasn't. Christian was in a daze as she babbled on and on. Occasionally he heard random words like *etheric, ectoplasmic, cosmic* and various others he assumed she had heard in the movie *Ghostbusters*. In a brief pause in her diatribe (to inhale), Christian had managed to get his view across clearly and succinctly by saying, "Get your shit together, we're getting the fuck out of here." With that, he promptly exited.

He shook his head and stared at the old schoolhouse. It had obviously been a workhouse before it was (minimally) renovated, but it had kept its forbidding look through the years: three storeys, which looked down on everyone with the same disdain. The flat grey walls were completely out of place against the myriad of greens in the Scottish highlands, which surrounded it. It looked like a barcode slapped in the middle of a work of art. Still, unwanted and neglected as it was, it remained. Even when the sleepy hamlet of Charity, whose children it was intended to educate, had perished in flames and had never been rebuilt, it still remained.

This was too much for Christian. He didn't know what to do now. He was leaving; he knew that, but why? Why had he such a compulsion to go? There were people back at the base that would be able to deal with this better than him—but that wasn't why he was leaving. The building scared the hell out of him, but, strangely, that wasn't why he was leaving either. 'Help her.' Help who? How was he supposed to help if they didn't tell him who? Then it struck him—her, Audrey Wells, it has to be. Yes, that made sense; she was the only one in the place. The logic sated his curiosity.

He raised the Bell's and smiled at it in a 'Nice to see you again' way and twisted the cap slowly until he heard the familiar crack of the seal breaking, signalling the imminent liberation of the liquid inside. This was a ritual, a celebratory drink after a mission. In the beginning it had been a quick stop in the nearest pub for a pint. Now, however, it was a bottle before, a bottle after, and a bottle in-between if it was taking too long. He knew that by most people's standards this would be considered a problem, but he didn't have the same stresses as someone going to an office every day. Drinking because your supervisor said your productivity was below average was a pathetic excuse, but, having a job where, at any minute, bloodthirsty vampires might pounce on you and try to rip you apart—that, he thought, was a damn good reason.

He put the bottle to his lips and, like the familiar kiss of a lover, relished every second's pleasure while they were together. He lay back against the windscreen with the bottle cradled naturally in his arms. As he stared up at the ghostly clouds drifting above, a thought occurred to him: what if this girl is just plain fucking nuts? She may have scratched all those words herself as some kind of cry for help. OK, but how would she know his name or that he was coming? He racked his brains, but the only possible explanation he could come up with was that she was clairvoyant—which was pretty far-fetched. He'd met psychics and knew that premonitions were rarely so exact, they were usually cluttered with such obscure visual metaphors and symbolic imagery that they could only be understood after the event had happened. He turned and saw her stomping towards the van like a teenager with an unreasonable curfew leaving a party.

"I hope you know I'm coming back!" she shouted when she was close enough for him to understand that it wasn't a shout to cover distance but to show anger.

"Do what you like," he replied, knowing full well that as soon as he reported this to Kyle, a team would be all over this place and she would never get near it. He took a generous final drink before the drive (which was stupid, because he intended to drink *while* he drove as well).

"Should you be drinking if you're driving?" she said sternly.

"Yes."

She was momentarily knocked off-balance by the lack of excuse, but flippancy wouldn't excuse him either, she decided. "Let me put it another way: you *shouldn't* be drinking if you're driving."

Christian got into the van, slammed the door and started the engine. After a thirty-second standoff, he rolled down his window. "Get in," he said, clearly irritated.

Her stubbornness gave way to necessity: she was out of food and in the middle of nowhere. She had been lucky enough to hitch a ride with some hippies in a VW Camper van that had dropped her off, but she had no way back. She knew if she refused this ride it would be a hell of a long walk home or even to the nearest bus stop. She got in and silently stared straight ahead. Christian skidded the van one hundred and eighty degrees and drove off with a reckless abandon intended to unnerve his passenger.

They had been on the road for twenty minutes before necessity, again, compelled Audrey to speak. "It's the next turn off, Keybridge village," she said, so quietly she thought he would have to ask her to repeat it. He drove on just as he had been: smoking constantly and frequently drinking from the bottle gripped between his legs. Now what was she supposed to do? Her plan to make him speak had backfired because she truly didn't know if he had heard her. It seemed to her that most of his senses were numbed, so, why not his hearing as well? Damn. She decided the best thing to do was to let him drive on and if it looked like he wasn't going to take the turn off, *then* she would say it again. The silence was killing her, though. Even when she had been alone in the old schoolhouse she had talked constantly; she was just a 'talker'. This guy wasn't, though, he had obviously modelled himself on someone like Clint Eastwood—a tough guy and a man of few words.

They were nearing the exit and he made no indication that he was going to turn, but then, would he? This guy seemed to think there was one set of rules for the rest of the world and one set for him. She looked over at him and was about to speak when she noticed a police car drive alongside and look in his window. Christian looked out at them, raised his bottle, toasted them and took a drink. They rang their siren briefly and motioned him to pull over. Audrey couldn't help but feel a little satisfied. This guy was so arrogant he deserved to be brought down a peg or two.

When they pulled over, a portly policeman in his late thirties knocked on Christian's window. When he rolled it down the officer exaggerated a mild asphyxia as he caught a whiff of Christian's breath and waved his hand to diffuse the smell.

"Have we been drinking, sir?" he said (quoting page 1 of *The Clichéd Policeman's Handbook*).

"No, we've never met. I'd be happy to go drinking with you, though," Christian replied in his best Groucho Marx voice.

"Comedian are we, sir?" (Page 4, *Witty Retorts*, first published 1957.) He continued, in his single tone way, "Would you mind getting out of the car, sir?"

"Yes, I would."

Audrey couldn't believe the audacity of this guy.

"Sir," he began, in a much firmer tone, but failed to finish his sentence.

"Have you checked to see if this van is stolen?" Christian interrupted.

"Are you telling me how to do my job, sir?" (Page 14, under the heading 'What to say if your stupidity is exposed.')

Christian reached into his pocket and handed the officer his driving license. "Better check my criminal record while you're at it, who knows what I've done."

The officer snapped it from his hand and plodded back to his car. Audrey could tell by his face he was going to find something—*anything*. If Christian had returned a library book late, the cop would make sure he was serving six consecutive life-sentences for it by the end of the week.

Christian covered his face with his hands and massaged it briefly (until he realised there wasn't a cigarette in his hand or mouth). He lit another Marlboro and laid his head back as far as the headrest on the seat would allow. "So, what do you do in Keybridge?"

A personal question. As if whipped by a jockey, she reacted immediately and galloped at full speed in pursuit of conversation. "I run a little book-shop called Keybridge Books—it's a pathetic name, I know, but clever names are lost on people nowadays. It's had a few names; when I first opened I called it The Joy of Text, but that was attracting the wrong kind of clientele; then it was Bound and Bagged—I don't even want to tell you about the guys who showed up that month— so, that's why it got the more direct name. Keybridge is such a small place and, to be honest, anyone who reads anything more than a shopping list gets called professor, so you can imagine my turnover wasn't great for the first year, but, then, thank God for the Internet, the website was launched and I entered a more specialised market. It's very rare that anyone *actually* comes in to the shop, but they come in *virtually* in droves. I specialise in books on religion, demonology, the occult and witchcraft—that's how I knew about the candles—protection and communication—you were right, that's what I was trying to do. I also try to keep as many fiction novels on all that sort of thing, as well; it pays the bills. It more than pays the bills; it's a hell of a money-spinner, if you'll pardon the pun."

A full two-seconds without her speaking; he decided it must be his turn. "Do you need any help?" Christian asked, as delicately as he remembered how.

"No," she answered, bewildered. "But I think you will when that cop comes back. There's a little known law that they take very seriously around here: driving under the influence while Irish." She nodded eagerly and tried to convince him of her authenticity by adding the abbreviation. "D.U.I.W.I."

He ignored her ranting and got back to his original question. "Nothing *I*, specifically, could help you with?"

"Are you trying it on?" She tensed in her seat and looked discreetly for the policeman. "You're old enough to be my father and drunk enough to be my Uncle Stuart."

Christian shook his head—now he remembered why he enjoyed talking to vampires: he could kill them when they annoyed him. "No, I am not trying it on. I just wondered if the message in the schoolhouse referred to you."

"Oh." She relaxed and thought hard. "No, I don't think so. All I really needed was a lift home, and that wasn't even life or death; I *could* have walked if I got desperate. Besides, with all that scratching, they could have scratched me a bus timetable if that was the case."

The policeman appeared back at the window. He had the look of a fisherman whose line had snapped with his catch inches from his net. "Sorry to have kept you, sir." (From the seldom read 'Apologies' chapter), he grudgingly handed Christian his license back and walked off.

Christian shouted after him, "Hey, call me about that drink." The policeman ignored him and got in his car and hastily drove off. Christian smiled at Audrey. "Nice guy."

"How did you get away with that?" she asked in disbelief.

"Well, you see," said Christian, while restarting the van, "there's one set of rules for the rest of the world, and one set for me."

Twenty minutes later the van came to a stop outside Keybridge Books. They went inside and while Christian fulfilled his duty as courier between the bottle and toilet, Audrey slipped behind her desk and awoke her computer to check her e-mail. There were four hundred and six waiting for an answer.

Christian appeared behind her, drying his hands on his jeans. "That's a lot of orders; you wouldn't think there were enough books in here to give them all."

The inside of the shop was small and intimate at first glance, designed to look 'olde worlde' (for the Yank tourists). It was all decked out in wood panelling and leather that looked centuries old but had, in fact, been there less than twenty-four months. The books on display were also mostly for show, only the oldest were on the shelves. Anything leather bound and timeworn took pride of place at the front of the shop, covering the walls of the little maze of literature. The illusion was completed by the gentle orange glow of low-wattage light bulbs that gave the impression that the books were so delicate that even strong light would harm them. Taken all together they gave the desired 'first impression' when someone entered. The telltale bright colours and pocket-sizes of the more contemporary novels were out of sight in a large room at the back.

"They're not all orders," she replied, while reading the screen. "I get a lot of people e-mailing me just to ask me questions. If I know the answer I tell them; if I don't, I recommend a book that will." Still staring at the screen, she passed one of her business cards over her shoulder to him. He slid it into his hip pocket without looking at it and looked closer at her e-mail. "For instance, this girl says she has premonitions of a great evil about to awaken, and wants to know about how to read vision imagery. I don't know anything about that—but I know a book that does."

"You're right, it's a hell of a business."

"Look at this: no sender listed. *And ye shall tread down the wicked; for they shall be ashes under the soles of your feet in the day*. That's it—no question, no order. Odd."

"It's from the Bible."

"Really, which book?" she asked inquisitively.

"I can't remember exactly. It's Old Testament though; you can tell by the vengeful God—they made him nicer in the sequel."

Audrey leaned back in her chair. "I wonder who sent it?"

Christian decided to leave the mystery to her. "Do you have another line I can use to ring base?"

48

"Got to get those meters read." She sniggered at his pitiful job.

"Didn't I tell you I hunted vampires for a living?" he said, honestly not remembering.

"Yes, but you were just joking. You were just saying that because I was dressed as a..." The end of her sentence was trampled underfoot by unbelievable reality. For once in her life she was almost speechless. Almost. "You mean there really *are...?*"

He nodded.

"You really hunt...?"

He nodded.

"You came up there to...?"

He nodded.

Realising she had lost the contest for 'Who has the coolest job?' she pointed him to the back of the shop. "Phone's...in...the...office," she dithered, and watched him swagger unsteadily through the door. Audrey was looking at him in a whole new way now. She had him pegged as a pathetic drunk with some friends in high places but now she saw him in an altogether different light. He was a warrior, a crusader for the human race. He was an unappreciated hero, worn down by the daily fight against the forces of evil. She had always been attracted to men with a quiet, tragic dignity (though she had yet to meet one who existed outside the pages of a book or roll of videotape). She decided she should form an opinion about whether he was cute or not (it would complete the image if he were ruggedly handsome as well), and vowed to try to see past all the hair, dirt, grease and smell when he returned.

Christian got to the office and dialled the base and listened to it ring. He was confused by the last couple of minutes. He thought she had gone over that whole speech about ghosts and ghoulies because she knew he was in the biz. She hadn't. She had sincerely thought he was there to read the meter in a building in the middle of the Scottish highlands that not only didn't *have* electricity, but *never* had. The phone was picked up and, as usual, no voice spoke.

"Warke, Christian. Zero-six-one-two-one-nine-five-five." He waited as the computer checked his voiceprint.

Then Kyle spoke. "Christian, thank God. Do you know where your mobile-phone is?" Christian had completely forgotten that he *should* have a mobile- phone. He quickly patted the pockets of his coat and jeans with his free hand. "I'll take that as a no," Kyle added. "If you're looking for it, it's in the lost and found box in O'Neill's pub in Barnsley."

Time to change the subject, Christian thought. "Listen, that old schoolhouse was a bust. There was no vamp but I think there is a non-corporeal entity present. You should send Nicholl or Bradley up to take a look."

"Yes, I will," he answered quickly. "But that's not what I was trying to call you about." There was an ominous silence that lasted only a few seconds but, like a condemned man hearing the pause after the firing squad cock their rifles, it seemed to last forever. "We've had a call. A vampire has killed four in your hometown. Local lab results show the saliva traces left behind on all the victims came from the same individual. We compared it against all the DNA samples we have on file and we found a match." He heard the finger tighten on the trigger. "Christian, it's Xavier."

kaaliz

"Cl—ai—re," Xavier whined as he lay in his coffin convalescing (the elongation of names, a before unrecognised symptom of third-degree burns). Claire was impatiently pacing the corridor outside, waiting for Higgins to awake. Xavier's voice, which had taken a distinctly pathetic timbre, halted her and she stared upwards and tried to exhale her agitation. He was really milking it. He'd be fine in a couple of days and he knew it, but he was determined to play the martyr at death's door for all the sympathy he could get.

She opened the door enough to accommodate her head and looked in. "What is it now?" she snapped. She had been running back and forth all day getting him things. First it was some of the emergency blood (this was some of his own blood that he kept in empty sherry bottles left over from Christmas—vampires heal quicker with vampire blood to feed on), then a blanket, then a book, then the TV and video, then the radio and now...?

"I just wondered if you wanted to get in and try to make me feel better?" he asked coyly.

"No, I don't," she answered abruptly. "You look disgusting, honey. I don't think you could score on a 'lepers only' eighteen-to-thirty holiday."

"But I'm bored," he said, using his best little-lost-puppy-dog look.

"Read a book or do a jigsaw," she offered, with the last remaining scraps of diplomacy. The thought occurred to her that she could smack him on the head with a piece of two-by-four and bury him in the park. By the time he'd dug himself out he'd be fully recovered and not a snivelling hypochondriac invalid, but the remorseless killer she had married. But he was saved from this cruel-to-be-kind treatment by a sudden shift in the atmosphere. The air was noticeably cooler and the sky had darkened to conceal the deeds of the wicked. "Come and see if he's awake yet," she said excitedly. Xavier shrugged and got out of the coffin. After wrapping himself in a blanket he shuffled out and joined Claire.

Higgins was standing in the centre of the stage wearing a spare set of Xavier's clothes (Claire had decided his green cardigan, pale-blue shirt, high-waist trousers and carpet slippers didn't really fit the image). He touched the flesh and bones that had been reborn to him. Xavier and Claire appeared silently behind him. "I can't thank you enough for what you have done for me," he said, still with his back to them. Xavier was about to speak when he said, "That's very kind; I hope I don't disappoint you." He was replying to a silent statement— he could read minds.

"We should say things out loud," Claire said. "Xavier can't hear thoughts."

Higgins turned to Claire with a wicked, boyish charm glistening in his eyes. "But you can," he said, "and *you* were the one I was talking to."

Xavier didn't have to be able to read minds to hear the insinuation in that statement. He decided it was time to assert his authority and lay down the law before this little upstart got any ideas. He strode towards Higgins but, on his third pace, he stood on his blanket and fell forward, landing face-first against the hard, wood floor.

Claire winced. She knew what was in his mind and what he was trying to prove, so she didn't run to his aid. Xavier didn't want to get up. He knew the smug look Higgins would have on his face. The guy had only said two sentences and Xavier hated him already. He raised his head off the floor and noticed several teeth were lying in a small puddle of blood beneath him. Fuck. In his anger, his fangs had grown and, in his weakened condition, they had broken when he hit the floor. Xavier got himself to his feet and, in the hopes that there was some dignity to salvage, waddled back towards the side of the stage.

"Hey, look at this," Higgins cried. Xavier turned and saw him floating in the air. "I guess I take after my mum in more ways than one." He smiled.

Xavier looked at him with ever-increasing hatred. You can read my mind? he thought, Well read this: as soon as I get better... Higgins nodded at him—challenge accepted. Xavier shuffled back to his room.

"Don't mind him," Claire said, "he's just cranky because he's ill."

"I don't mind him," Higgins replied, with a savage calm.

His response made Claire a little uneasy, as did the fact that she couldn't read his intentions—he was blocking her. She put it down to nerves and changed the subject. "Are you ready for your first night as a vampire?"

"Absolutely." He smiled, appearing perfectly at home in his new life.

"We should pick you a new name before we head out. Any ideas? Please don't say Lestat; back in the eighties there were at least twenty of them living in the same area—it got very confusing."

"Well, I don't know. What sort of thing should it be?" he asked.

"You want something completely recognisable as not human. That usually involves using Zs or Vs or," she nodded towards the bedroom, "Xs."

"But you have a normal name, how come?"

"I didn't always. Claire was my name before I was Made; I changed back in eighty-six. I just got fed-up with the old one: Zigatta-Kaaliz—it's a bit of a mouthful."

Higgins pondered the name for a few seconds and then said, "Kaaliz: I like it. If you're not using it anymore, can I?"

Claire was flattered. She wanted to hug him, and pinch his cheeks, and tell him what a good boy he was. But she didn't—it just wasn't becoming of a role model. That's what she was, after all, Kaaliz's mentor. She beamed with pride. "That would be just fine," she said, trying to be off-hand, but failing miserably, "Kaaliz," she added.

"Shall we go?" he said politely.

Claire nodded and shouted, "Xavier, we're going now."

"Bring me back some blood," he bellowed from his coffin.

"I know," she whispered to herself through gritted teeth.

"No O-negative," Xavier added.

Claire turned to Kaaliz. "We've been married one hundred and six years: does he think I don't know that?"

"What's wrong with O-negative?" Kaaliz asked.

"Nothing, it's just him," she explained, "it makes him fart. And believe me, when you sleep in a coffin, that's one thing you don't need." She nodded towards the skylight and flew upwards before Xavier's one request became a shopping list. Kaaliz followed her eagerly.

53

Claire took him to a large housing estate on the outskirts of the town. She landed gently and turned to see Kaaliz drop clumsily and fall to his knees. "It just takes practice, don't worry about it," she said sympathetically. "Now, this is the dodgiest part of town. If we walk around here for a while someone should try to mug us."

Kaaliz got to his feet and walked to Claire. She was staring at the moon. For the first time he was able to look at her, examine her. She had such an allure, he could barely restrain himself from grabbing her and having his way with her right there and then. He wondered if all vampires had this trait. Maybe he evoked the same emotions and her desire was raging too, wanting *him*. Her dress teased his eyes, showing just enough to let him know that whatever he could see, was nothing compared with what he couldn't. He imagined what lay beneath her clothing. Treasures of the flesh, waiting to be plundered. Soon, he thought. Not now, but soon.

She turned to him. "Come on, let's find you some blood."

As they walked together, Kaaliz asked her, "So, blood. What do I need to know? Is young, innocent blood better? Does it have an expiry date, like milk?"

Claire smiled. "No, that whole innocent blood thing is just Hollywood bullshit. The difference between innocent blood and evildoer's blood is like the difference between water and vodka. It'll work, but for a really good hit, go for the bad guy every time."

"And, to make another vampire I would just do what you did with me?"

Claire was a little embarrassed. "No. When you were sired, you fed off me while I fed off you. I didn't have to feed off you." She hung her head.

"So why did you?"

"It creates a stronger bond. I wanted us to be close. Now, I live in your veins and you live in mine. I don't think you should sire for a while anyway," she advised. "I've been a vampire one-hundred and seven years and you're the first I've sired. That's the one thing you will learn: There's no longer any rush to do anything. You have, literally, all the time in the world."

"I suppose you're right," he agreed.

54

"But when you do, you need to drink from the blood of three before you can sire," she added.

Kaaliz smiled and nodded. She wanted him; he knew she did. He had seen movies; he knew vampires were not monogamous, even if they were married. They knew sexual fulfilment from many, not one.

"Which reminds me," she continued, "who were you in your mortal life?"

Kaaliz's first instinct was self-preservation and years of hiding the truth had taught him to lie on a moment's notice. "I was a house painter, why?"

"Your blood was as potent as anything I've ever tasted." She looked quizzically at him.

One-second, two-seconds, three-seconds, four... "I had so many blood-transfusions when I was in that place, I don't know whose blood is swimming inside me." He chuckled.

"Oh yeah, right." Claire nodded, satisfied.

From the darkness sprang a pasty-white youth, clutching a knife. He stumbled into a confrontational position and stood before them, twitching nervously. "All right, give me all your fuckin' money," he shouted.

Claire and Kaaliz stood still, unimpressed by the young man's threat. "These guys are good," Claire said, "Drug addicts—human waste, no one misses them."

"I fuckin' mean it, you bitch," he screamed.

Claire gestured Kaaliz forward with her hands. "Hors d'oeuvre?"

Kaaliz stepped forward and faced the youth. "If you want my money, you're going to have to take it," he whispered. The kid was clearly scared and twitching ever more erratically. "Don't deny your desires. I have what you need, take it from me," Kaaliz shouted. The kid lunged at him and Kaaliz stepped to the side. He moved so fast that he could have ran around the kid a dozen times before the knife got to his desired location. He stood waiting for the kid to notice that he had moved; eventually he did. He then waited for the kid's momentum to halt, but it was taking too long. He couldn't believe how acute his senses were. How fast his mind thought and how quickly his body reacted. He could wait no longer—he shot out his arm and grabbed the kid's elbow and yanked him backwards. A loud crack echoed through the streets. The kid's arm was bent ninety degrees the wrong way. He screamed briefly and Kaaliz pulled him close. To quiet him, he slammed his hand quickly below the kid's chin. Another crack signalled the kid's jaw was dislocated. Kaaliz was getting annoyed. This ham-fisted display was not making him look good. The kid flailed helplessly with his one good arm. He howled noises that would have been screams had his mouth been able to open. Kaaliz turned to Claire.

"Finish him," she said calmly. "Expose his neck, pull him close and instinct will guide you."

Kaaliz complied. He pulled at the kid's collar and ripped his jacket halfway off his back. As Kaaliz moved close to the kid's throbbing jugular, his eyes closed and his senses became even more heightened. He could smell the urine running down the kid's leg, the salt in his sweat and tears, the deodorant he had applied days before, cheap perfume, cigarettes, curry, cider and scores of other scents which were foreign to him. His lips were pressed on the kid's neck now. Instinctively, like an animal's innate knowledge of how to suckle, his head re-positioned itself. His tongue edged forward until it just touched the kid's main artery. He could feel the blood coursing, faster and faster. Nothing had ever come close to this feeling. Not sex, rape or even murder. He felt his teeth grow and dimple the kid's neck. Just a little pressure. Slowly. Make it last. Millimetre by millimetre his bite closed. Stretching the neck skin tighter and tighter. Blood pumping faster and faster. Then, with a rapturous climax, the skin punctured. Blood filled his mouth and Kaaliz shuddered with pleasure. It was like being electrocuted with delight. As the blood flowed down his throat his whole body tingled with satisfaction. It was pure pleasure in liquid form. He drank deeply. The world, all it had been and all it was, meant nothing now. This was all he would ever need. But all too soon the euphoria began to subside; he tried to hold on to the bliss as long as he could, but when he opened his eyes he was on the ground next to the motionless carcass of the kid, dizzy and disoriented.

"Can't keep drinking once the heart stops beating," Claire said, from somewhere in the real world.

A few minutes passed and Kaaliz got his bearings back. He was kneeling over the pathetic creature that had given him more elation that he had ever dreamed possible. He *had* given it to him, but then he had taken it from him. Rage boiled inside Kaaliz as he stared at the passive, dead eyes of the kid: they were laughing at him. *You'll get no more pleasure from me, you fucker!* Kaaliz drew his fist back and punched the kid in the chest. His hand went straight through the breastplate. Kaaliz pushed his hand on, further. It squirmed past the redundant organs effortlessly, reaching its goal. Kaaliz closed his fingers around the kid's heart and dragged it from his chest. He looked down at it resting in his palm, flesh and veins between his fingers, blood gloving his hand. He crushed it until it split and threw the remains in the kid's face. Kaaliz composed himself and stood up, facing Claire.

She looked worried, maybe even scared, but she did not berate him. "Let's go," she said solemnly, and walked away.

They made their way to Coleraine in silence. Claire landed outside an undertaker's with Kaaliz close behind her. His landing was better this time, though still faltering.

"What are we doing here?" he asked.

"We need to get you a coffin," she said practically, "and Mothercare don't have an undead section." She rang the bell and took money from her pocket.

"What, we're going to buy it?" he asked in disbelief. "Why not just fuckin' kill them all and take what we want?"

The large metal roller-door, where the hearses entered, rattled slowly upwards. It gradually revealed a beautiful woman in her mid-twenties, dressed in a black mourning-suit, standing looking out at the vampires. Kaaliz would impress Claire yet—he would get a coffin, feed on the girl and save the money. He charged at the sexy blonde with all his speed. The next thing he knew he was staring at the night sky with Claire slapping him lightly on the face. He jumped to his feet and realised he was still outside on the pavement. The blonde was standing, shaking her head at him. Cheeky bitch. He marched towards her and slammed into...nothing.

The blonde walked forward to within an inch of Kaaliz's face and whispered, "You're not invited, asshole." Kaaliz beat his fists against the invisible barrier separating him from his revenge.

"Kaaliz," Claire said quietly. "Don't make a scene, you won't be able to get in."

Ignoring her, Kaaliz leapt at the wall-of-air again and kicked, slammed and punched like some kind of demented mime-artist. "I will tear you apart," he screamed.

Claire walked to the barrier and said, "Sorry, it's his first night. We were just looking for a coffin." Kaaliz stopped his futile attack and watched the alternative approach. "Please," she added, "I have money." She showed the girl the wad of used notes.

The woman looked the unlikely pair up and down and then faced Claire. "What's your name, vampire?"

"It's Claire."

She looked at Kaaliz and said, "Claire may enter."

Claire walked past her host and Kaaliz again tried to force his way in, but gave up quickly. After a final kick at the barrier he admitted defeat and turned his back.

"I won't be long," Claire shouted to him, "just wait there."

The women walked into the showroom and the blonde said, "You know better than to try anything, don't you?"

"Oh yes," she laughed. "I tried to break-in here in forty-four and your grandfather taught me a lesson I never forgot." In the aforesaid year, when Claire had broken-in seeking some nice coffin-pillows, the girl's grandfather had cast a spell and made the light bulbs emit sunlight. Claire had been badly burned and did not try such a foolhardy endeavour again. "Is he still a practising warlock?"

"No, the closest he gets to that kind of thing nowadays is watching Charmed, and I think his devotion to that show has very little to do with the magical aspect."

Claire chuckled politely. "Tell him Zigatta-Kaaliz was asking for him."

"OK, I will," she answered agreeably. "So, you know the score, I guess you're all right. I'm Anna. What sort of thing are you looking for?" She cast her hand towards the dozen different styles of coffins on display.

"Just something plain, I think," she said, walking to the first casket. "You know, sixty-five percent of newly made vampires don't live more than a fortnight. They get it in their heads that nothing can harm them, and Kaaliz, well, he's a candidate for a quick death if I ever saw one."

"We haven't seen many vampires in the last few years—in fact, the last one I saw was in ninety-four. Did you know Vork?"

Claire had met Vork briefly at Galen's re-birthday party. He was a strange vampire, more interested in clothes and interior decorating than anything else. He made a big deal about 'coming-out' in the early eighties and expected everyone to praise his bravery, but vampires, being the self-absorbed creatures they are, regarded it with the same importance as the number-one single changing (or probably less). Vork struggled for the next few years to try to establish the Vork & Knife Theatre Company. A group of vampires to put on plays and puppet shows advertised by some impromptu street-theatre. The response was less than enthusiastic and he was forced to do one-man shows on Clapham Common. It was here, one night during his ambitious adaptation of *Ben-Hur*, that he found a group of men walking around the common who shared his love of sculpture, painting, opera and performance art (and rubber body suits). Unfortunately, they wanted to keep all productions private, so, with that, the Vork & Knife Theatre Company was no more. That was the last Claire had heard of him. "Of course I remember Vork, what was he up to?"

"He showed up one night outside our house with a guitar singing 'Fernando' by ABBA."

"To you?" Claire asked.

"No, my brother Derek," Anna replied, "he had seen him at the cemetery and took a shine to him."

Claire cringed, knowing this story was not going to have a happy ending. "What happened?"

"My dad is an ordained minister of religion. He blessed the water and turned the garden sprinklers on him." She looked almost apologetic. "I don't think he even tried to get away. He just lay there, with the water burning him like acid, until he dissolved."

Claire shook her head. "That was Vork: a hopeless romantic."

"I'll give you a minute to decide. I have someone else to look in on," Anna said and hurried out.

Claire could feel that Anna was sad about Vork. She respected the gesture, no matter how unrequited, that he had made. Vork had not died from the water—he could have escaped easily—he had died because he knew that his affections would never be reciprocated. It was something vampires and humans had in common: they both renounced logic when it came to love.

Claire ran a finger along the smooth surface of an elaborately decorated ivory-white coffin. It was really nice but would Kaaliz appreciate it? She didn't think so. There was something about him, something that made her uneasy. At first she thought it may have just been the way he defiled the body of the kid, but it wasn't—it was more than that. The feeling was just intuitive so she couldn't be sure if it was warranted or not. If only she could read his mind, then she could be sure. How had he learned how to block her so quickly? One thing she was sure of was that he had a lot of rage inside him. She had witnessed the violence that he was capable of and knew it would only get worse. Her concerns halted immediately when she remembered why they had chosen to Make others in the first place—this was the cruelty she and Xavier had lost, the cruelty the world *needed*, no matter how wrong it seemed. Kaaliz wasn't the aberration— they were. It made perfect sense, but it didn't make her feel any better.

Anna walked back into the room. "Have you decided?"

Claire shook her head quickly, remembering why she was there. "I'll take...just give me the cheapest one."

Anna nodded and walked to a plain, pine coffin. "This OK?"

Claire smiled. "Yes, that will be fine. You know what they're like at that age, he'll probably change it in a month no matter which one I get him."

Anna slid it on to a trolley and pushed it towards the doorway. Claire counted out the correct money as she walked behind her. As she put the excess back in her pocket she was ambushed by an idea: when they got to the door she should push Anna out to Kaaliz. He was being true to his nature;

instead of fearing how he acted, she should be trying to ape it. It was evil. It felt wrong, but it was what she *should* do. But Anna was nice, she had been friendly and courteous, there were plenty of other undertakers in the area who would have attacked the pair as soon as they realised what they were. She was torn between what was expected of her and what she wanted. But she was sick; she knew that, so maybe that was what was causing the dilemma. *We just have to keep doing what we do,* Xavier had said, but she was finding it impossible to think of harming this girl. No, she *had* to do it. This was the foul-tasting medicine that would make her better. Kaaliz would undoubtedly kill her before Claire could anyway; she *could* do this.

Anna stopped as they passed the viewing room. They looked through the glass and saw a middle-aged woman slumped over a coffin, crying passionately. "Poor woman," said Anna, "she's been in there all day."

Claire looked at the saltwater droplets running down the side of the coffin. Tears had been lost to her for over a century, but since they had returned she had re-discovered what they symbolised and embraced them like a long-lost friend. They were a physical manifestation of emotion that couldn't be denied. As if contagious, Claire began to feel her own eyes yearn to bleed the pain-releasing liquid. In an attempt to stop it she asked, "Is it her husband?"

"No, her daughter," Anna answered. "The girl and her boyfriend were found murdered out in Castleroe Forest."

Claire couldn't breathe. Fists of guilt and regret crushed her insides. That poor, broken woman—she and Xavier caused all of her sorrow. Claire's psychic powers reached out against her will and connected with the grieving mother, her anguish flowed into Claire like raging rapids. The mother blamed herself for letting her daughter go out with the boy. Her husband, with no other vent for his rage, blamed her as well. Her other two children hated everyone, including their parents. The love—so recently evident among the family—was poisoned now and forever more.

Claire could barely stand upright as wave after wave of desperate remorse from the mother hit her. Claire looked down quickly and drops of water fell from her cheekbones to the floor. She hadn't felt so alive since she *was* alive. She feared if she really indulged, and cried as much as she wanted to, she might never stop.

"Are you all right?" Anna asked. "I thought you guys couldn't cry."

Claire wiped the tears from her face. "Just a psychic link; I could feel what she feels." She turned, unsteadily, away from the woman and nodded Anna to go on.

Kaaliz was leaning his back against the wall-of-nothing when they reached the outer room. He turned quickly and stared.

He sent his thought clearly to Claire: *Push her out to me.*

Anna reached the threshold; the coffin was halfway out. Claire shouted, "Wait." Anna turned with a questioning look. Claire walked to her and pushed the money into her hands. "We can take it from here," she added.

Kaaliz looked at Claire with disgust. Claire lifted her end of the coffin and Kaaliz reluctantly took his. Claire walked out to the pavement and pushed the trolley back in.

"You are no longer welcome, Claire," said Anna, then apologetically added, "Sorry, it's the rules." She pressed a button and the metal roller-door trundled slowly to the ground and rested.

They stood in silence for a moment then Kaaliz said, "Why?"

"When you've been a vampire for a while you'll realise," Claire explained, "that not only *shouldn't* you kill everyone, but you can't. We may be a secret from eighty-percent of the world, but there are plenty of people who know we exist and know how to protect themselves." She wanted to go on but she was beginning to sound like some hapless employee trying to explain herself to the boss. Why should she be pandering to the likes of him? She knew more about surviving the nocturnal lifestyle than some vampire who wasn't even a day old. But it was the way he looked at her, like a predator trying to decide if she was food or a mate, which unnerved her. A car drove past and the driver gaped at them. Claire nodded upwards and said, "Let's get this out of sight."

The driver of the car was the second, albeit inadvertent, victim of the vampires that night. He had been sitting at home threatening God—who he was now convinced was a woman because of Her apparent refusal to have anything to do with him—that if She wouldn't answer any of his prayers he would come up there and present his demands in person. Needless to say, his job in a local chicken-packing factory had taken its toll on his sanity. He had got in his car determined to jump off the steeple of his church, after writing a suitably thought-provoking note saying 'There was no one to catch me'. His one-sided argument with God had continued in the car and he gave Her one last chance to give him a sign that his life was precious and he should live it to the full. This, of course, is when he saw Claire and Kaaliz holding a coffin. He snapped. While hurling abuse at the (in his mind sniggering) deity, he had driven straight into the River Bann. As his car sank he folded his arms, as if he had taken a seat in Death's waiting room, and tapped his foot impatiently. He was content in the knowledge that not only would the mortal world weep at the tragedy of a poor soul who had lost his faith, but also he would soon be asking Saint Peter for directions to the Complaints Department. Nothing is known about whether or not the latter happened, but the former did not. The ink in his self-penned epitaph had run and smudged in the water and by the time the police dragged his body from the river it was barely legible. What remained was: 'There was...no...catch.' This led the police to assume he was a frustrated fisherman. Therefore his legacy was not the crying Christians holding hands in some picturesque park as he imagined, but a fortnight's worth of jokes in the local pubs. Had he known this was not an omen but a couple of late-night shoppers, how different his death, or possibly his life, might have been. Had he been a few seconds earlier he would not have seen the coffin and God might well have come up with a cogent reason for living before he reached his church. A few seconds later and he would have seen Claire and Kaaliz flying upward into the night sky and that may have renewed his interest in life. Sadly, he was just in the wrong place at the wrong time which, when you're that unhappy, is a very easy place to find at any hour of the day.

Kaaliz and Claire flew back to Portrush. They landed on the roof of the Eglington Hotel, just a couple of hundred yards from the Arcadia. "Why have we stopped here?" asked Kaaliz.

"Because..." Claire searched desperately for a phrase that wasn't clichéd (and failed.). "...we need to talk. Kaaliz, I get the feeling you don't really trust me."

"Don't take it personally; I don't trust anyone, never have," he replied with a cold detachment.

"You *can* trust me, you know," she said. "I would never give you bad advice or tell you something that isn't true. Everything I tell you is to keep you safe." She smiled her maternal smile.

Kaaliz lowered his defences slightly and sat down on the coffin. "OK, talk to me," he said compliantly, "Tell me what I need to know."

Claire eagerly walked over and sat down beside him and took his hand. "I, well, we—Xavier and I—have such high hopes for you. I know you're going to make us proud."

"I hope I do," he replied.

Kaaliz and Claire spent most of the night sitting on the roof, talking. She told him the story of Soliss; the legend of creation in the Garden of Eden; tales of the times and places Xavier and Claire had lived in, the vampires they had known and how they died; vampire hunters; vampire slayers and on and on. Claire really believed she was forming a deep friendship with him. He was inquisitive and attentive, seeming genuinely interested in all aspects of his new life.

After an exhaustive Q & A session on all things vampire, Claire looked at the sky. "About an hour until sunrise," she said. "I'd better go and find someone for Xavier." She slapped the lid of the coffin. "Can you manage this the rest of the way yourself?"

"No problem," he replied. "Should I feed again?"

"Not unless you're really hungry; it doesn't sit well—eating this early and then sleeping."

"What about you? You didn't feed at all tonight," said Kaaliz, putting his hand on her shoulder. He thought she would interpret this as friendly concern, but he just wanted, needed, to touch her. No matter how platonic the gesture seemed to her, he was sexually aroused.

"I'll just share some of Xavier's," she said, standing up and gently removing his hand.

Kaaliz nodded. "I'll see you back at home, then."

"Yes, I won't be long." She wanted to make sure he could manage the coffin by himself, but he stood his ground, piercing her with those eyes, waiting for her to leave. Claire smiled half-heartedly and flew off.

Kaaliz glanced at the coffin. An hour—he could be back in time. He ran to the edge of the roof and leaped, flying off in the opposite direction as fast as he could.

home truths

Christian had run from Keybridge Books without explanation and drove as fast as his van would allow to Stranraer. There he had caught the first ferry to Larne. The journey gave him time to reflect and his initial propellant of rage was almost gone. Waiting to take its place was the slow, perpetual pace of fear.

Xavier was the reason Christian had this job and now he would finally face him. Even though this was scaring him to death, he took comfort in the fact that this would be his last mission, one way or another. Since the beginning he had said when he had his revenge, he would quit and find a normal day job. He wondered what job that might be now—what did twenty years of hunting vampires qualify him for?

He had decided on the drive that he would stay sober until he had killed this vampire, but this sailing was going to take another two hours and he was already nervously pacing the deck. He needed to calm himself so he lay on a padded bench and tried to rest. He needed to sleep but this was harder than it sounded—it was as if he had forgotten how to fall asleep, it had been so long since he had to try. He realised that, although he had been saying for years that there wasn't, there actually *was* a distinct difference between falling asleep and passing out. He finally conceded that if he were to get any sleep he would have to follow his normal pattern.

He found the bar. It was empty apart from four students sharing two pints of lager. "Bottle of Bell's," he mumbled to the barman.

The middle-aged barman looked him up and down but said nothing. He had been a barman long enough to know when to deliver the 'Don't you think you've had enough' line, and when to keep quiet and let them get on with it. The Barman sat the bottle and an ice-filled glass in front of Christian and said, "There you go, sir".

Christian gave a grateful grunt and threw some money on the bar, he didn't know (or care) how much, but the barman seemed more than pleased. He walked to a corner booth and began drinking until, sure enough, sleep found him.

He had the dream again.

He was in darkness. Not the darkness that comes with a starless night, but blackness more absolute than anything he thought possible. For all intents and purposes he was blind. The strange thing was he felt good, safe even, as he always did when he had this dream. In the unchanging blackness he knew it was summer: he smelt the freshly cut grass; he felt the sun on his face; he heard children laughing and he tasted the saltwater air of the beach. It was then that he became aware that he was moving—he was being driven somewhere. He felt gentle kisses on his cheek and comforting grips on his hand. He arrived at his mysterious destination and was laid on a bed and then wheeled down a corridor. The air was getting colder; summer was becoming winter. The safe feeling disappeared with the heat of the sun and a torturous feeling of déjà vu overcame him. A strong stench of disinfectant jogged his memory partially—he was in a hospital. He tried to raise himself from the gurney but was restrained. A plastic cup covered his mouth and nose and he began to feel his strength subside.

As he drifted, he heard a voice saying, "Nothing to worry about; it's an easy operation".

Then the dark wasn't so dark. It was getting lighter. Someone was unwrapping a bandage from around his eyes. With each revolution he could see the light a little brighter. Soon, blurred figures were distinguishable. Three people, one of whom was doing the unwrapping, were waiting. The last layer of the bandage was removed. Light attacked his unused eyes and he squinted. Quickly, they adjusted and he could see who stood before him. The doctor smiled at him. He turned and saw the nurse smiling. He turned and saw his dead wife, with her throat torn out, smiling. He looked back quickly at the doctor and nurse. They pounced on him. He saw their fangs grow. They took an arm each and began biting at his flesh. He screamed in agony. His wife watched, her tears cutting tracks in the dried blood on her face. He thrashed with all his strength but it was not enough, the nurse tore a long strip of flesh from his forearm. The doctor thrust his head at his chest and began to gnaw. He howled helplessly.

Christian woke-up and swiped his glass from the table as he instinctively drew his handgun. Sweat ran down his face as he waved the gun, searching for a target. Slowly, reality hit him and he realised it had been a dream—the dream. He put the gun away quickly but there was no one else in the bar anyway.

He wandered to the nearest window and noticed it was morning and they were in Larne harbour. He wiped the sweat from his face on his sleeve and walked back to his booth. He retrieved his coat and stared at the whiskey bottle, still a quarter full. He had revised his promise to himself; it now said he wouldn't drink when he got to Ireland. He walked a few paces from the table then turned and looked at the bottle, sitting like an abandoned child on a doorstep. He decided there wasn't that much left and he could have it drunk before he set foot on Irish soil. The child found a home.

When he got to the ferry terminal he phoned Kyle to get a contact name and number for the local investigative team. Kyle told him that there had been another violent murder and that the team was at the crime scene. Christian scribbled down the address and raced up the motorway towards Portstewart.

He found the house relatively easily; he had lived in the area for the first twenty-six years of his life and all the time spent killing his brain cells with alcohol had obviously not reached that far back yet. It was a modest little bungalow on the outskirts of Portstewart. It wasn't an upper-class area by any means, but you couldn't have got a house here if you were earning minimum wage either. Everything about it said 'comfortable'. The low picket-fence that wouldn't have kept anyone out; the windows left ajar—Christian bet himself that the doors weren't locked at night either. It all said that this guy had no cause to worry about his safety. Poor bastard didn't know about vampires; they don't need a motive.

A gruff, grey-haired policeman introduced himself as Detective Parry as he met Christian at the door.

Christian just replied, "Warke." No rank—no agency, just Warke. They knew better than to ask and he knew better than to volunteer anything more. Parry was overbearing and loud, and made it clear that he was ignoring the stench of whiskey on Christian's breath. He introduced Christian to his colleague, Detective Quigg. She was young and rather shy.

Christian noticed more than a passing glance from Parry as she shook Christian's hand and said, "It's Alana." She was around half his age but there was no doubt in Christian's mind, this was why Parry was showing-off his authority.

Christian knew it was better for him to take the lead in these cases. Most small town cops had never seen anything like a vampire attack before so it was up to him to assess the situation objectively. "OK, can I see the body?"

Parry looked at Quigg, who closed her eyes. Parry turned back to Christian and whispered, "Which part?"

Christian's heart sank into the pit of his stomach. He didn't need this first thing on a Monday morning, but he knew he had to verify it for his report. "Whatever his neck's still attached to," he said, grimacing.

Parry led Christian through the house and out to the back garden while Quigg, who was looking very pale, went for some air. The garden was flat and green, no plants, trees or flowers—just an immaculately trimmed lawn. In the centre lay a square of black plastic covering the head of the victim. Christian hesitated when they reached the plastic. He looked around for something, anything, else that might need his attention. He noticed a foul smelling liquid on the ground near the sheet; he crouched down and looked closer.

"Did you get a sample of this to forensics?"

Parry looked embarrassed. He mumbled, "That's... vomit. Our forensics officer threw up when he saw the...well, when he saw".

Christian knew he could delay no longer. He edged the corner of the plastic sheet up and looked under. His stomach tightened—had there been any food in it, he probably would have been sick too. The head looked as if it had been ripped off. The skin was torn, not cut. It looked like someone, or something, had grabbed his head and pulled until it came off. Several vertebrae of the spinal column were still attached to the base of the neck and the neck-skin looked as if it had been pulled taut before ripping. The head was lying on its side and no teeth marks were visible. Christian reached into his pocket and pulled out a latex glove and snapped it on his left hand.

"What are you doing?" asked Parry.

"I have to see the other side of his neck," replied Christian.

"I don't know if you should be moving it," Parry retorted, his confidence being overshadowed by revulsion.

Christian ignored him and put the palm of his hand on the cold, clammy forehead of the victim and raised it enough to see the other side of his neck. Two perfect circles had punctured his throat. Now he was sure. He gently lowered the head to the ground again and re-covered it with the plastic sheet. He remained crouching, collecting his composure until Parry spoke.

"Well, you ever seen anything like that before?"

Christian nodded. "I'm afraid I have."

"There's something else you should see," Parry added.

Christian stood up wearily and faced the Detective. "OK," he said.

Quigg walked across the garden and handed Christian a thick manila folder. "Case-files, sir. I thought you'd want to see them."

"Alana, why don't you show Warke what we found in the kitchen," Parry said.

Christian saw how they were playing it like a tag-team. One stayed until they were nauseous, then the other took over. It was a good system—Christian wished he had someone to tag. "Lead on," Christian said, putting a brave face on.

Quigg walked him across the lawn and back into the house. "It's in the kitchen," she said. "We don't know what to make of it—some kind of cult thing maybe."

"Who was he?" asked Christian.

"His name was Christopher Maxwell, he was a guard at Magilligan Prison. We're checking to see if anyone was released recently who might hold a grudge."

"Good idea." Christian smiled. If only, he thought, if only it was that simple. Quigg accepted the compliment and smiled like he'd just given her an A.

Quigg wiped the smile from her face and put on a more fitting sombre mask as she pushed open the kitchen door and revealed three words written in blood on the wall: HELP HER CHRISTIAN.

Christian's blood ran cold.

"It's the victim's blood," Quigg said in an officious voice. "We're checking his fingerprints to see if he wrote it. We're also checking his address book and talking to friends and family to see if he knew anyone called Christian, and members of the congregation of his church in case it meant *that* kind of Christian." Quigg turned to Warke to see if he was going to elevate her grade to an A+.

Christian tried to speak but no words were available. Quigg looked at him, waiting for his insights. Christian finally remembered how to speak, but had nothing insightful to offer. He turned to Quigg and said, "I have to go."

He rushed out and into his van. He fumbled with the ignition key until it found its home and brought the van to life. He reversed out of the driveway, causing traffic to screech to a halt on the road. He didn't care, this was an emergency; he had to find an off-licence that was open.

After visiting a local hotel and coercing a barman into selling him a litre of whiskey, Christian meandered around the streets he used to know so well. It had been almost twenty years since he had been there and a lot of things had changed but enough remained to remind him of happier times. He walked along the promenade up to the top of Main Street where he stopped and stared at the roundabout. It was the place where he had proposed to Carol.

For weeks he had been trying to find an opportunity—the right time (which was completely unnecessary because a woman knew if she wanted to marry or not. Waiting until after a particularly emotional episode of their favourite drama series about rural and rugged doctors was not going to make a difference). He found his perfect time at three o'clock on a rainy Sunday morning, when being drunk was the exception and not the rule. He had taken a break from trying to hail a taxi for the two of them and dropped to his knees and asked her to marry him. She had replied immediately that of course she would. He had always loved that; it was one of his fondest memories of her. He had asked her to give him everything he ever wanted and she had answered him as if he had asked for a Tic Tac. She later explained that she never had any doubt they would be married—they were too happy not to be. That was her logic. That was what he loved.

Christian walked on, drinking and remembering, glancing up occasionally when something caught his eye and refreshed a memory. He didn't know if he intended to or not, but soon he found himself standing outside their old house. The windows were still boarded up, the garden overgrown with weeds—but it still felt like home. He walked around the back and tried the key, which he still kept on his key ring. The door opened and let the impatient sunlight rush in. Christian stood in the doorway; it was just as he remembered it. He walked through the resurrected dust, dancing with the light, and up the hall. Pieces of the broken bedroom door had been kicked to the sides and forgotten.

He struck his lighter in the bedroom and lit one of the jasmine-scented candles that Carol always kept. She had burned one the first night they had made love and told Christian if they were ever apart to burn a jasmine-scented candle and the aroma would bring back the memory. It was working and Christian's eyes were welling. He sat on their bed and stared at the floor; the carpet had been lifted but the floorboards still showed traces of dried blood, covered by years of dust. He took a long drink and set the bottle on his bedside table. He lay down on the bed and pulled his knees up to his chest and wrapped his arms around them. Memories; too important to forget but too terrible to remember, were awakening and clawing at his insides. He knew these feelings would not be drowned by whiskey this time, so he didn't even try. Instead, he closed his eyes and faced his demons with excruciatingly accurate recall.

It was the winter of 1978 that it began. That was when he saw his first vampire. He had joined a local lodge called The Ministry of the Shield. He and Carol had been married for two years and, although they were very happy, he was aware that his excuses for going out with the lads were being invented ever more often, and losing credibility each time. It was nothing to do with Carol. It was to avoid stagnation, to feel free; but most of all, it was just because he was twenty-three years old. The rut of getting up, going to work, coming home, having dinner, watching telly and going to bed was getting really boring. He thought the Ministry, like most other lodges, would be concerned with drinking, watching adult movies and talking about football. It wasn't until he was initiated that he realised just how wrong he was.

72

Oliver Dwyer, the Witchfinder General, had established the Ministry in 1742. He had been called in to identify the source of the evil that was turning the townsfolk into demons that drank the blood of the God-fearing. Dwyer soon discovered that no witch was to blame, but being familiar with the legends of the old country he recognised that the problem was vampires. He immediately commandeered a local church, knowing vampires could not set foot on hallowed ground, and recruited local volunteers to assist him in the destruction of the undead. He trained them in the church, showing the locals how to fight and pointing out the creatures' weaknesses. But, skilled as the vampire hunters were, it seemed for every one they killed two more showed up in its place. Months passed and still the vampires kept coming. The priest gave up hope that he would ever get his church back and found other premises for the congregation to meet. Dwyer renamed the church The Ministry of the Shield and stayed there controlling the vampire threat until he died in 1768. On his deathbed he gave instructions that the Ministry should remain there forever, with the members passing on what they had learned to their sons.

Dwyer's wish was honoured and over the years the Ministry always maintained an active squad of vampire hunters. They gained government funding during a particularly bad uprising in the 1950's. After that threat had been contained the funding continued on condition that all Ministry operations were classified. A larger headquarters was built in the 1960's in a discreet corner of Yorkshire. The new building housed the largest collection of books on demons, vampires and the paranormal, and was where all field agents received their assignments.

Sometimes whole generations passed without incident and other times, like now, they needed every man they could get.

When Christian joined he was told of the scourge of vampires that was sweeping the land and that was why he had been accepted so quickly when a waiting list of years was usually the case. The vampires were becoming an epidemic. The Ministry had been there, as protectors of their community, for over two centuries, but they had never faced the kind of numbers they were now confronted with. Christian had been sceptical initially, thinking it was some kind of initiation for the 'new guy'. The other members had taken no time to try to persuade him, but armed themselves and headed out in a methodical search pattern of the town. Christian was grouped with two more senior men, both in their fifties, one with grey hair—Davis—and one who was bald—Patrick. Neither spoke on the car journey. The group arrived at a cave on a deserted part of the beach and stopped at its mouth. Davis turned to Christian and put a reassuring hand on his shoulder.

"Don't worry, son," Davis said, "most of the stuff you've seen in films is true." He pushed a wooden stake into Christian's hand. "If it comes anywhere near you, stab it with this, and don't stop stabbing until you hit the heart."

"The dark magic that preserves a vampire is stored in its heart," Patrick added. "Destroy the heart and the body reverts back to being a mortal body that died when the vampire took control. Understand?"

Christian slowly nodded.

"We ready?" asked Davis.

"We are," replied Patrick.

The three of them exited the car and headed into the cave, the torchlight sweeping from side to side like a blind man's cane. They walked for about five minutes until they reached a large chamber lit by candles on all the walls. In the centre of the chamber sat a dirty, battered coffin. Christian froze at the entrance. Davis and Patrick marched towards the coffin and flung it open without hesitation. It was empty.

"The bastard-thing's probably out feeding," Davis said. "We'll have to wait for it to come back."

Patrick turned to the terrified Christian and said, "Waiting is all part of..."

A vampire dropped from the ceiling and landed on Patrick's back and ripped at his throat savagely. The pair fell to the ground. He swung his stake blindly at the vampire that was holding him. His blood sprayed the creature's face. Davis was running towards his fallen comrade when another dropped on him. He grabbed its head before it could bite him, but had to drop his stake to do it. It was taking all his strength to hold the beast's fangs from his throat.

Christian was more scared than he ever imagined he could be. So much had happened in the last few seconds—what could he do? He raised the stake and looked at it—he knew what he had to do. He ran into the chamber screaming. He reached Davis first and kicked the vampire hard in the ribs, knocking it to the ground. Before it had stopped rolling he leapt on top of it and drove the stake into its chest. Its scream bounced around the walls of the cave for the few seconds that it took to die. It shrivelled up below him, decaying and decomposing in seconds. Davis was still catching his breath. Christian targeted the other vampire that was feeding from the now still form of Patrick. He ran at it and drove the stake into its back so hard that the point came out of its chest. It dropped Patrick and spun around, trying to grab the stake and remove it. It shrivelled quickly, just like the other, and it was dry and stiff as it hit the ground. Davis attended Patrick, but nothing could be done.

Despite losing Patrick, Christian was hailed a hero that night, and thanks to Davis's telling of the story, which improved every time, he was soon leading his own team and making a hell of a difference. It was exhilarating for him—to be part of a secret society that hunted vampires. He felt like Superman with his secret identity. He told Carol what he was doing almost immediately. She had always been very interested in the paranormal and accepted what he said readily and supported him.

Just over a year later Carol's brother, Jeff, approached Christian about joining. Since the vampire plague was still barely being controlled, Christian quickly explained the risks to him and asked if he was sure that he wanted to join. He said yes and was initiated that night. Christian took him with him that same night and they stumbled upon a nest of twelve vampires. Before Christian could tell him that they needed backup, Jeff rushed in and staked a vampire that had his back to him. Christian had no choice but to throw himself into the fray. Jeff was set-upon by five vampires almost immediately. He didn't stand a chance. Christian could not check on him until, somehow, he had killed the remaining eleven. He knew as he fought that Jeff was dead: vampires don't wound and they don't take prisoners. He had to call for help to have the body removed; it had been torn so violently that it would have fallen apart had Christian tried to lift him. Another body. Another reason to hate. Another boy who wanted to be a hero but became a martyr.

Christian was riddled with guilt. Could he have saved him if he had tried to escape and get Jeff to a hospital? It was unlikely, but it was something he would never know for sure. Carol took his death hard and wanted to get actively involved but Christian would not allow it; he would not risk losing her too. They compromised with her working at the Ministry's research library, trying to find new ways to defeat their foes.

Soon after, Carol fell pregnant. Her pregnancy seemed to advance quickly to Christian because he was rarely at home. Before he knew it, she was eight months gone. In the final month he got used to coming home to an extreme-up or extreme-down. Extreme-ups were not as good as they sounded, they didn't indicate elation or joy, but hyper-anxiety and panic-attacks about whether the baby would be all right, what if something went wrong, and all the other worries of an expectant mother. But it was an extreme-down that Christian came home to one morning, which changed his life forever.

He walked in an hour after dawn—he had given up his job at Punk Sounds; the Ministry was now paying him a wage—and found Carol sitting in the armchair, crying. He ran over and kneeled in front of her.

"What's the matter, Carol, is something wrong with the baby?"

She ran her hand gently down his face and cried harder. "I'm so sorry," she said.

Christian was confused. "What do you mean, what's wrong?"

She tried to speak but couldn't find a break in her tears. She hugged him tightly. He held her and let her cry without questions. When she ran out of tears she released him and began the story which she had been dreading telling.

"Do you remember a while back, I started researching a vampire called Xavier?"

Christian didn't remember but he nodded anyway.

"You remember he's local, we were trying to work out where his lair might be?"

Christian nodded again; it was sort of ringing a bell now.

"I found out about him, a lot of stuff about him, even who he was before he was Made."

Christian couldn't imagine where this was going.

"I found out his mother's name, and where she was buried. I thought he might show up on the anniversary of her death, so I went there and waited."

Panic hit Christian like a slap in the face. There were too many things to ask but before he could babble out any of the 'What if', 'How stupid' or 'What were you thinking?' statements that were amassing in his head, Carol continued.

"He did come; he laid lilies on her grave. But he heard me hiding in bushes." She started crying again.

Christian's eyes filled with tears. He gripped her hands, urging her to continue.

"I tried to stake him Christian." She cried and pulled Christian's hands close to her heart. "But he was too strong."

Christian wanted to wait for her sobbing to stop but he couldn't. "What happened, Carol?" he said.

Carol looked at him through her tear-filled eyes. "I don't want you to hate me," she cried.

Christian pulled her face close to his and said defiantly, "I could *never* hate you."

Carol considered his statement, wanting to believe it. Wanting more than anything to know that it was true. She loved Christian more than anyone else on earth. If anyone would understand, he would. In a fragile whisper, she answered, "It's his baby." She started crying again.

Christian let go of her and pulled backwards. His reason and fury mixed—each diluting the other. He looked at her with pity, contempt and rage all fighting for dominance. He tried to speak but the words didn't exist. He wished time would accelerate and carry him far from this moment, but seconds lingered like pedestrians at an accident. Whatever he was going to say to her, he couldn't say it now—he needed time to think. He stood up and walked towards the door.

"No, Christian, don't leave!" Carol shouted through her crying.

Christian walked on and slammed the door behind him.

As he walked up the driveway he still heard her crying and shouting, "He was too strong Christian, he was too strong!" Christian could barely see for tears himself but he walked on. Had he known that would be the last time he would see her alive, he would have turned and gone back in. Even if he had been angry, or said the wrong thing, it would have been better than the desertion she must have felt as he walked away.

"It can help!" she screamed after him.

Christian had replayed these events hundreds of times over the years and that final statement was the only one he didn't understand. He had been too confused and upset even to think about it at the time, but when he had it had puzzled him. What did she mean? What was she talking about?

Christian avoided her for the next nine days, then, as he and Davis sat in the Ministry's library, a message arrived. Carol was in labour. Christian stood up immediately and ran towards the door. He didn't reach it. He stopped, standing silently with his back to Davis.

Christian hung his head. "I don't think I can do it, Davis."

Davis knew this was a request, not a statement. "I'll do it, Warke." Christian remained motionless as Davis walked out.

Davis walked to the house and found Carol and her sister Janice waiting for the midwife.

"Who the fuck are you?" barked Janice.

"It's OK, Janice, he's a friend of Christian's," Carol panted, in a brief lull in her contractions.

"Why didn't he come himself? What is this, birthing support by proxy? Fuckin' asshole." Janice's lack of social diplomacy came from the fact that she had been living by herself in a remote area of Donegal for the past six years with very little human contact. She was writing a manifesto for independent women, which she described to her publisher as being like Germaine Greer's philosophy—with guns. (The book never was published; it was submitted to the publisher but when he suggested editorial changes, Janice dangled him from a fourth storey window. They got married a year later.)

The plump, red-faced midwife entered smiling and ushered Davis out, citing that this was no place for men-folk. Janice glared at Davis, preparing another barrage of insults, but he walked out before she could hurl them.

He waited outside until the screams of life-giving pain had subsided.

Carol was holding her baby when Davis strode into the room and took it from her arms—she didn't protest; she knew what he was doing. Janice and the midwife briefly fought with him until Carol told them to let him go. Davis walked outside, removed its blanket and held the naked infant up to the sun. It didn't burn—it shivered.

"Happy now?" Janice snapped. "Now give me that baby before it catches pneumonia." Davis complied.

Christian couldn't hide his joy that Carol and the baby were fine. He decided to let her rest and go and see the both of them the next day. Even though he wasn't technically a father, he felt like he was. He closed his eyes and saw an endless succession of perfect family days before them, like photographs waiting to be taken.

While on patrol that night they received news that Christian's home had been attacked. Davis and Christian rushed over and were met at the door by several other members of the Ministry. Christian knew what had happened by the look on their faces—the same apologetic look he had given relatives many times, but had to see for himself. As he walked inside, he heard someone say, "The baby's gone." That was the only thing he knew for sure. He walked on, hoping his other fear was unfounded. With every reluctant step that led him to the bedroom he prayed for a miracle—that this wasn't happening, that she was all right.

As Christian approached the bedroom he saw the pieces of the door strewn across the hall carpet, and the remains of the doorframe hanging off its hinges. His eyes closed as he reached the opening. He stood in the entrance for a moment, bracing himself, before slowly opening his unwilling eyes. Two white sheets covered two bodies. The amount of blood staining the sheets and the carpet was proof enough, but he needed to see. He lifted the first sheet: it was Carol's mother, her throat ripped out. Killed, he thought—the vampire didn't use her to feed, there was too much blood wasted. He lifted the second sheet. The innocent, repentant look on Carol's face would haunt him forever. He fell to his knees and hugged her.

He didn't know how long he lay there—it could have been minutes or hours. Voiceless faces tried to speak to him, but he would not hear them. Time passed. Familiar faces became strangers in white coats—he still would not hear them. For seven months he heard nothing but the voice of his own failure, shouting inside his head. Shouting the truth. Screaming for revenge, while whispering that he must return.

Christian raised his head from the musty smell of the mattress and watched the candle-flame spark and fizzle, fighting to stay alight. But there was nothing to keep it going so, eventually, it surrendered to the darkness.

dinner

Kaaliz had been sleeping soundly in his coffin, which he had placed it in the centre of the stage, when Claire had returned with Xavier's food that morning. She had peeked in to check on him and cross his arms over his chest (vampires don't do this just to look cool, it's to cover and protect their heart while sleeping). He looked so peaceful and content. She had been smiling from ear to ear with maternal pride as she gently slid his lid closed.

Xavier was looking much better when she woke him and took him into the living room. Claire still had to bite the victim's neck for him because Xavier's teeth weren't up to full strength yet. She had found a jogger for him on the beach. He was a man in his late forties and obviously married because he relished the opportunity of being talked to and not talked at. She had felt quite bad at first; he had said that today was the first day he had gone jogging and it was only because his doctor said it would increase his life span. But after ten minutes, when he grabbed a breast in each hand and tried to put his tongue in her ear, her guilt lessened enough to beat him around the head and bring his unconscious body back to Xavier.

After feeding (and after Claire had thrown the jogger's body in the sea), Xavier asked how the night had gone. She told him no lies, but left out quite a lot of the details. She told him of Kaaliz's failed attempts to attack Anna at the funeral parlour and how ridiculous he had looked slamming repeatedly against the threshold—that got a small grin. She could see Xavier had reservations about Kaaliz—she had too, but she was willing to work with him. She played on the 'he doesn't know any better' angle a great deal and tried to elicit some kind of empathy from Xavier, but he said little.

As Claire closed the lid on her side of the coffin that morning she looked across at Xavier, who was already sleeping. She felt bad about how much she had neglected to tell him. But she contented herself by reasoning that by the time Xavier was ready to go out feeding with them, all the things that troubled her about Kaaliz would be history. That was what she told herself. Her mind would not rest though—the niggling suspicion that everything wasn't going to be all right was growing. Somewhere between her imagination and her dreams she thought of Kaaliz, running around with an empty machine-gun. Harmless, until she gave him bullets.

Eventually sleep did find her. But it was polluted sleep, poisoned by the grief of the girl's mother. Unceasing remorse clouded her dreams; the only place where she could see blue skies was now as dark as her waking world. Good had found a more insidious way to attack than brute force and, possibly, more effective. Flesh wounds could heal, but memories lasted as long as their keeper did. Immortality had its own miseries.

Claire awoke that evening to loud thumping.

Xavier banged hard on the toilet door. "Fuckin' hurry up, will you?" he screamed.

Claire walked out of the bedroom, rubbing the sleep from her eyes. "I see you're fully recovered. What are you shouting about?"

Xavier turned quickly and pointed at the door. "He..."

"Kaaliz," Claire corrected.

Xavier didn't like that. He had taken her name (or part of it at least). Things had happened while he was recovering, bonds had been formed. Bonds that he hadn't been a part of. "Kaaliz," he sneered, "has been in there for fifteen fucking minutes!" He banged the door again. "What the fuck are you doing in there?"

"Use the Ladies," Claire diplomatically offered.

Xavier looked at her as if the idea was so off-the-wall that it didn't even deserve consideration. He pointed at the door again. "This month's copy of SFX is in there, I haven't finished reading it yet." He kicked the door. "You better not be dog-earing the pages," he added.

A muffled flush was heard and the door opened. Kaaliz stepped out and faced Xavier. "All yours, " he said nonchalantly and walked off. Xavier glared at the arrogant prick, hoping he'd trip on his ego and fall flat on his smug face. Unfortunately, he didn't.

Xavier stepped forward and was mugged by a foul stench that made him step back. "For fuck's sake!" He closed the door quickly and turned to Claire. He exhaled slowly, repressing his anger. He knew this was petty but it annoyed him nevertheless. "I'll tell you this, Claire, I pity the first fucker that crosses my path tonight." He stomped into the kitchen, leaving her waiting in the hall. "I've been cooped-up in this place for two days," he shouted from the kitchen, "plus I now have to share a bathroom with the Toxic Avenger." He walked back into the hall with a can of air-freshener and stood before her. "Added to which, I'm horny as hell and..."

Claire put her arms around him and smiled sleepily. "Well, that's one thing I can help you with, at least." She kissed him tenderly.

Xavier was pleasantly surprised. It had been weeks since they had 'rocked the coffin' and even longer since they had done it first thing in the evening. He smiled agreeably and ran his fingers through her hair until his desire hit a knot. He pulled back slightly.

"What?" she asked.

Xavier nodded towards the stage. "I can't do it while *he's* here."

"We don't have to change our whole lives because of him," she replied, smiling at his embarrassment.

Xavier reconsidered for a second then shook his head. "No, I can't. Why don't you give him some money and send him to the pictures." He held up the can of air-freshener and nodded to the toilet. "I'll meet you in ten." He walked into the toilet and sprayed until he closed the door.

Claire wandered out to the stage and found Kaaliz, dressed and ready to go. Xavier had recovered quicker than she thought he would—there was going to be no time to iron-out the wrinkles in Kaaliz's personality. Shit, what was she going to do? With Xavier so tetchy from cabin fever and Kaaliz being, well, Kaaliz, she knew that if they went out feeding together they would probably end up killing each other.

Kaaliz interrupted her thoughts by saying, "Claire, I don't want to seem ungrateful, but would you mind if I went out myself tonight?"

Had he been reading her thoughts? The idea quite unnerved her; she had always been able to conceal her thoughts from other vampires. No, it must be coincidence, but why did he want to go himself? She tried to read his mind and got the same nothingness as before. She guessed whoever he

83

was in his mortal life he must have had a lot of secrets that he hid very well and had carried the trait to his immortal existence. She asked him, "Why do you want to go out on your own?"

He shrugged. "I don't want to bother you every time I want to go somewhere. I just think I should get used to going out myself."

"Do you think you're ready?" she asked, trying not to sound like a fretting mother.

"Hey," he said, impersonating The Fonz. "I got nothing to be scared of, I'm the thing that scares other people."

He had that kamikaze look in his eye, like he was heading for destruction laughing. Claire felt quite happy that she wouldn't have to stand and watch his savage delight while murdering. On the other hand, what was she unleashing on the world? Without her to restrain him, there was no telling what he would do. But there was no sense in condemning him for things that he *might* do, and maybe last night got all that craziness out of his system. She had to trust that she had taught him well enough. He was receptive to everything she had told him on the roof, maybe; just maybe, he *would* be all right. "OK," Claire finally conceded, "but you keep an eye on the time."

Kaaliz was already floating up to the skylight. "I will," he said.

"And watch out for that slayer that got Xavier; don't try to fight her."

"OK," he answered.

"And if you get lost; ask somebody," she added.

Kaaliz nodded and was gone.

"Doesn't he know to close the skylight after himself?" Xavier said, from behind her.

Claire walked over and hugged him. "Ah, poor baby, are you cold?"

"No, I just think he should show some respect for the place he lives."

"It doesn't really matter, there's a nice full-moon tonight." She drew slow, playful circles on his chest with her finger. "It's kind of romantic, don't you think?"

84

Xavier glanced at the moon and smiled. "It's already sick and pale with grief that thou; her maid, art far more fair than she."

Claire kissed him and said, "How about a night in tonight?"

"Honey, I've got a lot of pent-up aggression," he said softly, trying not to kill the mood.

Claire understood. "OK how about this; I'll go and get some take-away while you take some, but not all, of your aggression out." She kissed his neck. "When you find your calm, meet me back here. We'll have a skinny dinner, some drinks, do some dancing and..."

Xavier nodded his approval of the plan, especially the unspoken ending.

As they kissed again Claire slowly levitated them up to the skylight and out into the night.

Xavier meandered around the streets of Portrush for nearly half an hour before he saw anyone. A bald-headed man in a brown tracksuit came jogging down the steps of the library clutching a piece of paper like it was the Olympic Torch.

Xavier approached him and said, "Is the library still open?"

"Yes it is," the man replied excitedly, "They're wonderful—these places."

"Really, why didn't you get a book while you were in then?" Xavier inquired.

The man looked left and right and moved closer to Xavier. "I'm a PE teacher at the local school."

"Oh right," Xavier nodded. "And they were all out of Sartre and Nietzsche?"

The man tried to hide his bewilderment. "No, you see, it's coming up to end of term and one of the other teachers told me about this book; Thesaurus—have you heard of it?"

Xavier nodded.

"I don't like writing the same thing on every pupil's report, so I looked up that book and got thirteen other words that mean the same as 'pathetic'." He waved the paper triumphantly.

Xavier had found his appetiser.

Back at the Arcadia, Claire was putting candlesticks down on either side of the unconscious girl she had tied to the table. She had put down the good tablecloth and laid napkins on either side of the table. It had been a long time since she and Xavier had a romantic evening alone together and she wanted everything to be perfect. The candlelight gave the appropriate ambience and although she didn't have Xavier's sense for detecting rare blood groups, she thought this one had quite an unusual, playful bouquet.

Claire had found the girl staggering along the beach. She was skinny, frail and, therefore, easy to subdue. Claire had waited in her path and watched every unsteady step she took. As she slowly approached, Claire scrutinised her appearance (she might be dead but she was still a woman). The girl's thin, white legs protruded from a black skirt that was so short that it could have been mistaken for a belt from a distance. She carried her shoes in her hands along with a small designer-copy bag. Her shirt was white see-through satin, which displayed a black lace bra, holding her small breasts beneath. To top her off, her 'blonde' hair should have been re-dyed at least an inch ago and the big, dangly earrings really didn't suit her. Then Claire noticed mascara had been applied to her cheeks with tears. She began to imagine the girl's problems and feel her emotions. Claire's psychic powers reached out. She was only seconds away from connecting to the girl's mind and knowing all her sadness. She fought the feeling, not because she wanted to but because she had to. This wasn't a sentient, caring being—this was dinner. Claire jumped to her feet and flew full-speed at the girl, knocking her unconscious and flying upwards with her all in one movement.

Dinner was beginning to twitch by the time Xavier returned. He dropped with balletic elegance from the skylight and bowed to Claire. She smiled, approving of his entrance. He spun quickly on his toes and when he stopped he had a bottle of wine in each hand. Claire clapped her hands lightly.

"I brought red and white, I didn't know what you'd get," he said.

"She's definitely a white, but don't worry we can drink the red later." She extended her arms and ushered him into the kitchen. Xavier walked in with Claire behind him. He paused momentarily, appreciating the effort that she had gone to, and then pulled out the nearest chair for Claire. She sat down and he kissed her temple.

"This is perfect," he whispered.

Dinner was really beginning to get agitated; she was hopping the table slightly and trying to scream through the gag (the good silk one that matched the tablecloth) that Claire had tied around her head. Xavier walked round the table and turned on the stereo before sitting opposite Claire. The familiar sound of *Love Bites* by Def Leppard began at an unobtrusive volume.

Claire thought she was the only one who had put any thought into the evening but Xavier had remembered the song that played when they got their wedding vows renewed in 1987. It reminded her of less complicated times when she knew who she was, and, what she was. "We should do this more often," said Claire.

"It'll be harder now that there are three of us," Xavier replied, and regretted it immediately. Tonight was supposed to be about Claire and him and he was making digs about the 'third wheel' already. He didn't like Kaaliz, and he wanted Claire to know it in no uncertain terms, but now wasn't the time. "Sorry," he added.

Claire smiled diplomatically. "Let's eat." They took one of the girl's wrists each and held them up. "What shall we toast to?" asked Claire.

Xavier had a lot of time to think over the past two days and he had arrived at the conclusion that Claire was right about their 'condition'. He had been feeling its affects for weeks and even though he kept telling Claire (and himself), that it had happened before and it would be all right, deep down he knew this was different, and he had no idea of its outcome. He didn't know whether or not to share his thoughts with Claire—he felt that he had to be strong enough for the both of them. But what would make her feel better? Would she be more comforted to know that Xavier was unaffected, or to know that she wasn't the only one? He decided the only way was to start talking and try to gauge her feelings as he proceeded. There would never be a 'right time' to broach the subject, so he began: "I still love you as much today as the day we met," Xavier said solemnly.

Claire was taken aback by this unusual display of emotion. She put the girl's wrist down and looked for signs of levity, but he was sincere. She opened her mouth to reply but Xavier continued.

"You were right—I am feeling this...thing, as well. It doesn't seem right to kill anymore, not natural." Xavier looked down at the girl on the table. "But, we do have to feed to survive."

Claire nodded slowly.

Xavier took Claire's hand. "I know as long as we're together we'll be all right."

The tears that had been imprisoned in Claire's eyes escaped down her cheeks and she swallowed hard. She raised her hand to wipe the tears away but Xavier stopped her.

"These are part of who you are, who *we* are, now. You don't have to be ashamed of them," Xavier whispered. He brushed her cheek lightly and she closed her eyes.

Claire couldn't think of the words that would adequately describe what she felt for Xavier at that moment. Finally, she decided their wedding vows had never been so relevant, and she said them aloud:

"From this beginning, two eternal loves shall travel as one.
Facing the sorrow and joy of the road that is yet to come.
I pledge my nights to you alone.
Blind to what has been and gone.
I belong to you; my infinite love, in death and beyond."

They leaned across the table and kissed each other. Not the kiss of a couple who had been married for over a century, but more like a kiss of newlyweds possessed with youth and desire.

Dinner had stopped trying to escape during this romantic exchange—she was quite intrigued. She was a big fan of reality TV shows (watching complete strangers cooking, making beds and folding laundry was a nice way to escape the daily drudgery of housework), and this one had her hooked. She even thought the male vampire (she had gleaned that was what they were), was quite attractive, but she would definitely vote the female out if she had the choice. This man was strong, but tender; dangerous, but loving; young, but wise; heterosexual, but enjoyed shopping for shoes (she stopped herself there, realising the fantasy was running amok). Of course, he was a murderer and technically not human but, hey, no one's perfect. She felt sure that most girls would agree with her and overlook those characteristics if they were out-weighed by other, more important, traits. She tried to get a look at his butt.

"Dinner's looking at my arse," Xavier said.

"Hey!" Claire slapped the girl's face and laughed. "I sees the way you is lookin' at my man," she said in her best American-trailer-trash accent. Xavier and Claire laughed heartily.

"fumph ya, gah shik bahats!" Dinner twisted her head, trying to loosen her gag.

Claire took her wrist and bit gently. She drank just enough to survive. It was like a Weight-Watchers meal—it didn't really fill her up, but it didn't taste good enough to want more. Claire looked down into the eyes of the girl, seeing consciousness slipping away. She thought of the life she was taking, the potential that would never be realised, the love that would never endure, the children that would never laugh and the mother who would cry. "Xavier, you've already eaten, maybe we can let this girl..." Claire's words trailed off as a dizzy spell washed over her. Instinctively she stood up and somehow managed to keep her balance. Her stomach was cramping. She put her hands on her belly and grabbed at the pain.

"Claire, what is it?" said Xavier, beginning to panic.

Claire felt sweat running down her cold skin. Shivers scraped their way up her spine. Her breathing laboured, she could hear herself wheeze. Her fingers numbed and she made fists trying to regain feeling, but nothing was helping. She screamed as the pain folded her body forwards. She lost her balance and fell onto her side. She had barely hit the stone floor when Xavier was by her side. He looked around frantically for the cause. Claire's body jerked as the spasms grew stronger. She was crying with the pain.

Xavier looked across at the dripping wrist hanging from the table. He shot over and touched his tongue to it. The bitter taste made him recoil immediately and he spat until the foul flavour lessened. He stood and looked down at the girl on the table.

She was almost unconscious but smiled weakly and tried to laugh. He was enraged and wanted to pummel her face. Claire howled in agony. Xavier ran to the bedroom and brought back the sherry bottle with his blood in it and held it to Claire's lips. Claire drank quickly and soon the pain decreased. Xavier looked back at Claire's unwitting assassin; ready to exact his revenge, but her body had stopped moving.

"What happened?" Claire croaked weakly.

Xavier pushed her hair back from her face. "The blood was infected; AIDS I think. Are you all right?"

Claire drank the remainder of the blood in the bottle and said, "I will be."

"Hang on, I'll get you more," Xavier said.

He ran down to the basement and fingered through the wine rack. Vampire blood was similar to wine in the respect that they both improved in taste and potency with age. Unfortunately, Xavier had bottled most of his emergency blood while he was either drunk or high (so when he drank it the feeling would return), and he needed an untainted bottle for Claire. Eventually he found a bottle of 1967.

They had spent most of that year chilling-out with Maharishi Mahesh Yogi at his retreat in Wales and had abstained from all chemical pollutants. Xavier never had such a feeling of calm and inner spiritual harmony and he, unlike the other guests, *could* bottle that feeling and did. It was lucky he bottled it when he did because The Beatles arrived the following week and he and Claire spent the next few weeks hanging-out with them, and various other celebrities, getting wasted. Considering the impact the Fab Four had had on popular culture, Xavier wished he could remember more about the time he spent with them. The only memory he had was a vague recollection of him and John Lennon filling Donovan's guitar with ants and watching him freak out when he played it and they ran all over his arms. It may have happened, then again, it may not have. His memory was near perfect except for

90

those few weeks; it had really messed up his mind. Xavier smiled nostalgically at the bottle and said, "Acid was great in the Sixties."

Claire was trying to raise herself to her feet when Xavier returned, but the pain, stabbing her like red-hot needles in her stomach, threw her to the ground again. Xavier rushed over and gave her the wine bottle of blood. She drank slowly from it and rolled it around her palate before swallowing. "Sixty-seven?" she asked.

"Yes." Xavier smiled. "Remember the Maharishi?"

"I remember trying to calm Donovan down for four and a half hours," Claire replied.

Xavier felt a little happier that his only memory of The Beatles actually did happen, but he was more concerned about Claire. "Drink some more," he urged.

Claire drank a little more and put the bottle on the ground beside her. "What I really want to do is sleep," she said weakly.

Xavier put his arms beneath her and lifted her. He stood cradling her in his arms for a moment; he knew the fear that had gripped him—the fear of losing Claire—scared him more than any disease that he might have. He carried her to the bedroom and laid her in the coffin as gently as he could.

"Stay with me," she said sleepily. "I have bad dreams."

Xavier ran his fingers through her hair. "I'll keep them away," he whispered, as sleep took her.

It was near dawn when Xavier awoke. He was still sitting on the ground leaning over Claire's side of the coffin. At first he thought the discomfort of the awkward position he was sleeping in had woke him, but then he heard a noise out on the stage. He checked that Claire was sleeping and went to investigate.

Kaaliz was aware of him as soon as he reached the stage. He turned and fixed Xavier with an unflinching stare. Neither of them spoke.

Xavier could smell the blood on Kaaliz's clothes and saw the unrepentant lust dancing in his eyes. He could hear Kaaliz's excited breathing.

Kaaliz was in the throes of trying to restrain himself from attacking Xavier. He was immortal. Nothing could harm him.

No one would defy him. No one would stand in his way, and one day; all would bow before him.

Xavier might have obliged him with a fight at any other time, but he had stopped for a quick drink of the '67 on the way through the kitchen and was feeling really mellowed-out and just wanted to lie back and listen to folk music. He shrugged at Kaaliz's unspoken challenge and walked away.

It was Claire who awakened first that evening. She had a dreamless sleep, visited by neither pain nor pleasure. She didn't feel one hundred percent healed, but she felt a hell of a lot better than the night before. Xavier wasn't in the coffin—or the bedroom. She prised her stiff body from the coffin, stretched, and went to find him. He was in the living room. He had fallen asleep wearing headphones and listening to a Bob Dylan CD. She shook him awake.

He looked up groggily at her. "What time is it?"

"Time to get up," she answered. "It's a brand new night full of surprises and possibilities."

Xavier's eyes focussed behind Claire. "You're telling me," he said.

Claire turned and saw Dinner standing in the doorway, no longer looking skinny and frail, but slim and radiant. Her hair was its natural brunette and cascaded over her shoulders to her breasts. She smiled, licking the tips of her newly grown incisors and said, "That wine sure packs a punch."

dhampir

Darkness. Was he awake or asleep? Was this a dream or was it real? Noises were teasing him. Whispering? Almost words—almost. Was he imagining it all? Did he really hear the words: 'Find her Christian'? He felt someone close. Familiar.

Torchlight making its way up the hall and into the bedroom interrupted Christian's solitude. The light shined in his face, blinding him temporarily. He raised his hand and shielded his eyes. The beam lowered to the floor. Christian blinked his eyes slowly until he made out the unmistakable silhouette of a man missing his right arm below the elbow, standing in the doorway.

"You look like hell, Warke."

"Time takes its toll on all of us, Davis," Christian said, getting up and sitting on the edge of the mattress. He tried to make it sound dismissive, like he didn't care, but he was straightening his clothes and pushing his hair out of his face. He didn't want Davis to see what he had become. He lowered his head and looked at the floor—at the bloodstain. He felt the tears well up in his eyes again. "How did he get in, Davis?" he whispered. "She knew better than to invite him. How did he get in?"

Davis exhaled deeply. When Christian had come out of the hospital he had been obsessed with finding Xavier. Davis had hoped after all these years Christian might have forgiven himself; but he hadn't. Davis decided, even though it would probably hurt him, to answer the question, "We think it was because the baby was his: some kind of parental loophole."

Christian kept his head down and nodded quickly. "Yes. Yes. I suppose that, sort of, makes sense."

Davis was genuinely worried at this stage. Christian was a wreck—he looked like he might fall apart, mentally and physically, at any second. "How are you doing Christian—being back?"

"Oh, I'm OK, you know," he answered quickly.

Davis walked over and sat down beside him. "Really?"

Christian was gently rocking back and forth on the bed. "I'll be all right, Davis, it's almost over. I'll get him this time." His voice was beginning to break. "Then it'll be over. It'll be

93

over when I get him." He turned to Davis and smiled to reassure him.

Davis looked at his face—scarred and weathered beyond his years—and tried to remember the fresh-faced boy he had been before the horrors of the world became part of daily life, before revenge was his only reason for living. He looked into Christian's eyes and hoped that somewhere deep inside Christian mourned the loss of that boy too. "There's a Detective Quigg looking for you," Davis said. Christian nodded vaguely and stared at the floor. "She phoned the Ministry. I told her you didn't even know where the new premises were; when you left we were still using the old building."

Christian was silent.

"That was a hell of a night—the night the vamps stormed the HQ, that's when this happened." He held up the stump at his right elbow but Christian kept staring at the floor. Davis kept trying to get through to him. "We knew they were coming, I even tried to get hold of you, but you were on assignment in New Orleans, they said." Davis looked at him for an explanation of what he was doing in New Orleans but he did not respond. "We lost a lot of good people that night. Fuckin' vamps burned the place to the ground."

Christian raised his head quickly and turned to Davis. "What about the Ministry's library?"

Davis shook his head. "A few volumes survived: those that members had at home for one reason or another."

"Did Carol have any?"

Davis couldn't understand what relevance this had. He shrugged. "I don't know."

"Could you find out?" Christian slapped his own forehead sharply. "Shit, I'm stupid. If she had any, they'd be here. We have to look." Christian jumped up and ran out of the bedroom.

"What are you looking for, Warke?" Davis shouted after him.

"I need to know what she was trying to tell me," Christian's reply echoed up the hallway.

After an hour of turning the little bungalow upside down Christian found a Post-it under the desk in his study saying:

94

dhampir?
The Dead and the Living
by Ezra Moorcroft

It was in Carol's handwriting. Christian and Davis searched the house, the basement, the attic and the garage but couldn't find the book.

"Maybe he took it—when he took the baby," Christian said. "Do you know what 'dhampir' means?"

Davis shook his head. "I've never heard of it."

"Do you have a phone on you?"

Davis handed him his phone and watched as Christian dialled, entered his voiceprint and asked Kyle if there was anything on the database. The response was negative and Christian spat air through his teeth angrily. Kyle caught his attention briefly again but a second later Christian yelled, "What's the point in asking Ministry Intelligence? Even if they did know anything, it would take them two weeks to decide whether or not to tell me." Christian hung-up the phone angrily without a farewell.

"Maybe Carol never found out what it was either," Davis offered cautiously. He looked at the concentrated scowl on Christian's face; he twitched like he was hurting his brain for alternatives. Davis attempted to calm him down again. "Christian, nobody but the Ministry would have access to that kind of literature. If your people across the water don't have it, then..."

"Ha!" Christian grabbed at his hip pocket and pulled out a business card. "I know someone who will."

Audrey Wells was leaving Keybridge Books for the day. She had a large stack of parcels in her arms, which she was steadying with her chin. She waddled under the weight like a saddle-sore cowboy to the door. The phone started ringing. She looked at it, hoping she could silence it with a severe look. She couldn't. She shook her head. "I'm not going to answer, so you can just shut-up right now," she said sternly to the attention-seeking communication device.

Audrey had a theory. She believed that all things; living or dead, organic or mineral, active or working for the Post Office, had inherent intents, good or bad, towards their keeper. She had come to this conclusion on the basis of a few instances when inanimate objects had, apparently, helped her.

The first was just after she moved to Keybridge. She was moving her books into the shop and turned on the radio for some music. She searched the three available wavebands from one end of the dial to the other and got nothing but static. It was a remote area and she put it down to interference from the surrounding hills. So, instead, she played her favourite Pink Floyd tape in the cassette deck and unloaded her books to the surreal soundtrack without giving it another thought. But later that afternoon the little old lady from the shop that sold yarn (imaginatively named The Yarn Shop), came to visit. She told Audrey that if she liked Pink Floyd the local radio station was playing their entire back catalogue arranged for accordion and bagpipes all day today. Audrey thought it a lucky coincidence that her ears had been spared this desecration of audio art and carried on unpacking happily. Yet, when she tried the radio the next day she could pick up local radio with perfect clarity.

Audrey failed to come up with a satisfactory reason for why this happened and added it to her list of unexplainable things she loved about planet Earth. Over the next few weeks she noticed other odd occurrences. Two Jehovah's Witness's arrived at the door one evening and as Audrey hid behind the religion section she noticed that the doorbell made no sound as they poked repeatedly at it. The pair gave up quickly and moved on to peddle their beliefs elsewhere. When she was sure they had gone, Audrey walked to the front door and tried the bell—it worked.

It was then that Audrey actively began cataloguing everything that her appliances did and whether or not it was helpful or not to her. To her surprise, most of the objects were trying to help and as she encouraged them they became even more helpful. The television would get stuck on a channel if it feared she had forgotten about her favourite show (and would only show *Baywatch* without sound); her video chewed the tape when she tried to watch *Star Wars: The Phantom Menace*; the kettle would only boil if she had decaffeinated coffee in the cup; the fridge would spoil unhealthy foods and the fire alarm and sprinkler system stopped her smoking in less than a week. The phone was unpredictable, though—Audrey thought it had a mischievous personality and got a second Internet line in to keep it company. This did not help. She was inundated with free phone-sex-chat numbers and all manners of free gifts were being offered to her by e-mail. The two lines were vying for her attention. She never got any junk e-mail or nuisance calls; the bank eventually had to send someone round to the shop because they could never get through to tell Audrey that her Small Business Loan was two months past due. Neither line would give her any bad news.

But recently the phone line had begun to rebel. In the last few weeks, market researchers, Tele-sales representatives and orders for Chinese food at all hours of the night, had bothered Audrey. She knew it was jealous of all the time she was spending on the Internet so she phoned her mother and, during the conversation, discreetly extolled the virtues of talking one-on-one. The phone had been good since then... until today. That morning she had, what she assumed to be, a prank phone call. She had answered the phone in the usual manner: "Keybridge books bought and sold. If you think it's an oldie, we think it's a must-y." Silence. (This was not uncommon—some people tried to work out her greeting.) Seconds passed with no response. She was about to hang-up when she heard a low whispering.

As the volume increased she made out four words repeating in a raspy voice, "Leave now. Don't go."

Audrey, a little freaked out by the contradictory grammar, slammed the receiver down hard. "I thought we had an understanding," she shouted at the phone. She squinted and could almost see a smirk, made by the *, 0 and # buttons. She shook her head at the phone like a disappointed parent and said, "No calls for two days." This is why she thought she could stop the phone ringing with a severe look, but she had forgotten that when Christian had ran from the shop she had turned to her appliances and said, "I want to talk to that guy if he tries to get in touch".

The phone, after a lengthy (0.22 seconds) deliberation, decided one of the conflicting orders had to be disobeyed. It also decided that if Audrey had amorous intentions toward this man it might make her happy to hear from him—and get the old phone back on ringing terms.

Audrey turned quickly from the shrill pleading of the phone and the top half of her tower of parcels fell to the ground. She screamed through gritted teeth and looked at the phone. Still it rang. She hurled the remaining parcels to the ground and stomped over and seized the trembling receiver. "What?" she screamed into the disobedient device.

"Audrey? Miss Wells? This is Christian Warke. I met you in the old schoolhouse. I'm the vampire... guy," Christian mumbled.

Audrey relaxed immediately and began acting her 'be yourself' persona that she had worked on studiously for two years. "Oh hi," she said, twisting her hair around her forefinger. "I'm so glad you called."

Ha, take *that* Internet line.

"Hey, listen," she continued, "you were right about that Bible verse; Malachi, chapter four, verse three."

"I need your help finding a book," Christian said in an officious tone. "It's called *The Dead and the Living* by Ezra Moorcroft. Do you have it?"

Audrey was kicking her left heel with her right foot and wishing she had some chewing gum to stretch. She scribbled the details down on a scrap of paper. "I'm sure I can find it." Inspiration struck her. "Maybe I could bring it to you when I find it."

"Don't you have to run the shop?" Christian asked.

"No, I was planning to take a week off to make crop-circles in Devon anyway. Where are you?"

"You can reach me through Portstewart Police Station, that's in Northern Ireland. Get that book here as soon as you can." Christian hung up.

Audrey put the receiver back in its cradle and added the name of the police station to her note. She didn't want to get her hopes up but couldn't help herself from smiling. She patted the phone and walked over to recover her parcels. She stopped and looked down at the wrapped books. "I need your help finding a book," she mocked. "I've heard some bad chat-up lines but that one takes the gateau. How bad could anyone need a book?"

"You shouldn't have done that," said Davis sternly. "Inviting a civilian into this situation is fucking reckless."

Christian shrugged and gave Davis his phone back.

"Goddamnit, Christian, don't you care about anyone else but yourself?" he shouted.

"I don't care about myself," Christian replied placidly.

"You just invited that woman into the middle of a blood feud: she could get killed. Didn't you even think about that?"

Christian pushed his hair out of his face and said, "I'd better go and see what that detective wants." He shuffled past Davis, staring at the ground and added, "Slam the door when you leave".

Davis felt guilty as he watched Christian leave. He had initiated Christian into the Ministry. He had made him a killer. Was he partly responsible? Did he destroy that boy? Did he create that monster? He walked over to the dust-covered wedding picture hanging on the wall. It showed Christian in a smart black suit, and Carol in a long flowing white dress, standing under an arch decked with bright, pastille blue flowers on a sunny spring day. He put his hand on the photo and wondered if that tragedy had befallen him would he be just like Christian? He prayed he would never know for sure, but he did know that Christian wanted revenge—it was all he wanted, and he deserved to have it. The man in the photo had a wife and a future filled with love and happiness to look forward to, that man bore little resemblance to the one that had just left. Davis decided then that he would use all his power to find Xavier, to help Christian end this once and for all. He was in his late-seventies now and missing an arm so he wouldn't be much good in a fight, but he could still pull a few strings with one arm. His fingers slid off the photo, cutting a line in the dust, dividing the doomed lovers once again. Davies hit redial on his phone, entered his voiceprint and said, "Kyle, it's Davies. I need to call in a favour. Who do you know in Ministry Intelligence?"

Christian arrived at the Police Station to the irate screams of a middle-aged man in a brown tracksuit. The man was holding a heavily bloodstained handkerchief to his neck and screaming that some "...psycho, faggot fucker..." had tried it on with him. Christian waited quietly for the Desk Sergeant to dismiss the man (which was the custom with unexplainable neck injuries). Eventually the sergeant had to call two constables to escort the man outside. As he was being dragged out he referred to a piece of paper and began screaming that the police were: "Incapable, incompetent, unhelpful, unskilful, untalented..." The remaining synonyms were lost as the door closed.

Christian approached the desk and asked for Detective Quigg. The sergeant looked at him suspiciously; he knew what Quigg was working on and the idea that this poor attempt at a human being was part of the investigation was mind-blowing.

"What's this concerning, sir?" the sergeant asked.

Christian was instantly annoyed. He didn't have time to dick around with this bureaucracy. He moved closer to the sergeant, who twitched at the smell. "It's concerning," he said angrily, "that poor bastard's neck. His won't be the last, or the most severe, if you don't get off your lazy arse and go and tell Detective Quigg that Warke is here."

The sergeant had enough experience of the chain of command to know that only someone who out-ranked him greatly would dare speak to him with such disdain. He nodded humbly and returned quickly with Quigg.

Quigg opened the security door and led Christian to her office. "Would you like tea or coffee?" she asked.

"No. What have you found out?" Christian answered curtly.

Quigg took a cardboard folder from her desk and opened it. "We've got a lot of facts dotted here, there and everywhere that don't make much sense."

"Tell me, perhaps I can join the dots."

"OK, well first we checked recent parolees and thought we were onto something when colleagues mentioned the name Edwin Higgins."

"Who's that?" Christian urged.

"A real piece of shit. Convicted in seventy-two on four counts of rape and two of murder. I spoke to the arresting officer this afternoon and he says they suspected Higgins of a lot more than that but could never prove it. Apparently there was a rash of sexually motivated murders from sixty-six until seventy-one, when they caught him. Twenty-four unsolved murders in all and, although Detective Murray could never find any evidence, he's convinced that Higgins did them all. He says Higgins as much as admitted it to him at the courthouse, taunting him about how he couldn't pin all the murders on him because the crime-scenes were always different." Quigg shook her head slightly and said quietly, "The bastard changed his MO just enough each time to avoid a connection being made. He knew what he was doing."

"This is our guy," Christian said.

"That's what I thought too until I spoke to the doctor at the prison and the nurse at the home where he stayed for two days after his release. They said there was no way he could kill anyone. He was sixty-eight years old. Life-long smoker and, consequently, wheelchair-bound. Severe clogging of the arteries in both legs; two mild heart attacks; advanced arthritis in his right arm; extremely diminished lung capacity— apparently he couldn't change TV channels without getting out of breath, and…well, the list goes on and on, but the upshot is: he was dying. The doctors gave him two months at most—it's the only reason he got parole. There's no way a man in that condition could kill anyone—if he tried to stand up straight it would probably kill him. Which leads us to our first puzzle. He was released to The Golden Slumbers Retirement Home and disappeared the second night he was there. Three other patients died that night under suspicious circumstances, which were hushed-up to save the families the distress, but nobody saw what happened—to those three, or Higgins."

"Three," Christian mumbled, putting his head in his hands. "He's been Made."

Quigg waited for an explanation of what that meant but when it was not forthcoming, she continued, "Parry's at the prison now. We're checking Higgins's visitors for the past five years; and the prison keeps a log of who all his outgoing mail was addressed to: we think he must have had an accomplice on the outside. It could be a relative, maybe even a son we don't know about, or, of course, it could just be some crazyfuck who found his name on the Internet."

"Don't waste your time: Higgins is who you should be looking for. See if you can find a picture of him when he was about twenty-one and give it to every police officer in the area. That will be what he looks like now…but with pointier teeth."

Quigg's mouth was hanging open in quiet awe. "You mean he's been…?"

Christian nodded solemnly. "I have to get out there and try to find them before nightfall." He stood up quickly.

"Another thing we can't explain is that message at the victim's house," Quigg said, halting his exit. "HELP HER CHRISTIAN."

Shivers tingled up Christian's spine. "I can't explain that either," he answered nervously.

"No, it's not *what* it says—it's *how* it was written. The coroner says it was written by the victim's left hand—he was right-handed by the way—after he was dead. There are signs of clumsy fingernail scrapes in the lettering, consistent with a heavily rigored hand being held by someone else."

Christian shrugged and shook his head. "I take it that's all you had to tell me."

"Actually, no." Quigg smiled confidently and began rummaging in her desk drawer. "The first murders that we alerted you about: the students in the flat." She pulled a videocassette from her desk and ran over to the TV and video behind Christian and hurriedly jammed the tape in and pressed play. "The ATM security camera down the street caught this."

Christian watched closely as the figure of a man appeared suddenly at the doorway to the student accommodation. Quigg froze the image as he turned to the camera. It was Xavier. Christian had never actually seen him in the flesh but he had studied enough descriptions and drawings to be sure that this was the vampire he sought.

"That's him," Christian said, "I have to go." Somehow the image of the vampire standing on a street that he himself had walked that very day made the danger closer and more immediate.

"There's one more thing," Quigg said as he ran to the door. She released the image on-screen and watched as Xavier disappeared in a blur into the night. Christian stared impatiently at the empty doorway on the screen with one hand on the door-handle. After a few seconds a young girl burst from the entrance clutching a makeshift stake. She looked up and down the street and then ran off in the same direction as Xavier. Quigg rewound the tape and paused on the clearest picture of the girl's face.

"I need to speak to that girl," Christian demanded.

Quigg smiled smugly and said, "Interview Room Two, down the hall."

Christian and Quigg looked in at the girl through the one-way mirror. She sat in a defensive posture with her arms folded. She was dressed in a short, loose dress, which had various shades of blue and purple melting into each other. Her feet were dirty and Christian noticed there were no shoes in the room. Her eyes were sad, accentuated by the dark make-up she had applied. But there was something about her, something Christian couldn't quite put his finger on.

"Who is she?" he finally asked.

"Her name is Lynda Walls. We got lucky with the image on the camera. I showed it around the station and a lot of the constables recognised her." Quigg opened the file again and flipped through to the relevant section. "She's been picked up dozens of times. Mostly possession: Cannabis, Ecstasy and Acid. A couple of Drunk and Disorderly's and a few Assault charges, none of them ever amounted to much but she's well known around the area. We've contacted her Next of Kin, she's on her way—it's an aunt, name of…"

"Have you asked her about the night of the murders?" Christian interrupted.

Quigg closed her file, annoyed that all her work was being ignored. "Yes, but she's not talking. She says she won't say anything until her aunt gets here."

"And when will that be?" Christian asked.

"She had to drive here from Inishowen, we called her a couple of hours ago—she shouldn't be long now."

"I'll wait," Christian said and sat down. "I'll take that coffee now."

Quigg didn't appreciate being treated like a maid. She had initially admired Christian for his single-minded approach to his work but now she realised it left little room for social niceties. She left defiantly, without asking him if he wanted milk or sugar—that would show him.

Christian stared at the girl through the glass. Her presence taunted his mind like a half-remembered dream. What was it about her that felt so…familiar? He moved closer to the glass and examined her. He was able to stare as intensely as he liked, hidden by the reflective surface on the other side. He lowered to his knees to put himself in line with her blank gaze. He looked into her eyes and wondered what dark burdens had been given asylum behind such innocent blue. She blinked and slowly pushed her chair back. She walked calmly over to the mirror and crouched down. Her face was only inches away from Christian now. She smirked and raised her fist in front of her face. Quickly she extended her middle finger and thumped the glass before Christian's face. He jumped back, losing his balance, and fell on the floor. He raised himself up and watched as she strode back to her chair and resumed her previous posture.

The door opened and Quigg walked in with a paper cup filled with coffee in her hand. She stared at him on the ground, silently asking for an explanation. Christian clambered unsteadily to his feet and brushed himself off, saying nothing.

"She's here," Quigg said, pushing the coffee into his hand and 'accidentally' spilling it on his wrist. She wasn't going to waste any more time trying to impress this asshole. She would do what he asked her to do and no more. She turned and walked out with Christian following her, sipping the foul-tasting beverage.

Christian was spilling coffee all the way down the hallway as he attempted to keep up with the brisk stride of Quigg. "This is…the mother, right?" Christian asked, trying to slow her down.

Quigg gritted her teeth, realising he hadn't been listening to her. "No, mother and father are both deceased—this is the aunt."

They reached Quigg's office and she opened the door and motioned Christian inside with an overly servile gesture, which he didn't pick up on.

"Christian?" the woman in the chair cried.

Christian looked at her; past the grey hairs and conservative dress, past the wrinkles and jewellery, and found the young girl he had known. It was Carol's sister. "Janice?" he said in disbelief.

Janice exhaled deeply, closing her eyes as she did so.

"Your first name is Christian?" said Quigg, angry at his neglect to mention that little titbit which had a major bearing on the case.

Christian ignored her, fixated on Janice.

Janice unclenched her eyes and looked at him with sympathy for what he had become. "Oh God, Christian, look at you."

"I'll leave you to it," said Quigg and discreetly left.

Christian sat back in Quigg's chair and pulled a beat-up cigarette packet from his jacket and flicked one into his mouth. He pointed the packet at Janice.

"I haven't had one in twelve years." She smiled apologetically.

Christian withdrew the pack.

"Oh, go on then," she added quickly.

Christian lit her cigarette, then his (for some reason being in the company of Carol's sister had revived some of his manners). "So, tell me," he said, "What the hell's going on?"

"OK," she answered, and reluctantly began: "That day that Carol had the baby, after your friend had been and gone, she begged me to take the child back to Donegal with me. I wasn't to tell anyone, only her and…mum knew. She said that the vampire would come for the baby as soon as the sun went down. So I took the child home with me. Carol named her just before I left: Lynda, after your grandmother. That's who you're holding for questioning—Carol's daughter.

Christian rubbed his pounding head. "But, we always thought Xavier took the baby. Why the fuck didn't you ever say the kid was still alive?"

"Carol knew the life you lived. She thought it would be safer far from Xavier, and far from you." Janice gulped, realising how cruel that sounded. "There's something else; Carol gave me a book when I took the baby called *The Living and the Dead*." She leaned forward. "Do you know what a dhampir is, Christian?"

Christian shook his head quickly.

"A dhampir is a child born of a vampire father and a mortal mother. The child has great strength and some psychic abilities. They are natural warriors against the forces of evil."

"Like a slayer?" Christian asked, not believing that he was unfamiliar with this aspect of vampires.

Janice nodded. "Of course, vampires don't want to produce progeny who are going to grow up to destroy them and this is why there aren't too many around. But I'm betting our man Xavier didn't know about the dhampir legend, or he would have attacked Carol during her pregnancy when she was most vulnerable."

"*It can help,*" Carol had said. Christian realised now that she knew what it would become. He pulled the cigarette packet from his pocket and lit another from the butt of the last. Janice puffed lightly on her cigarette.

"How long has she known?" Christian said in a low voice.

"The traits of a dhampir began when she was eighteen. She was able to see things—people in trouble. The first I heard of it was when she disappeared about a month after her eighteenth birthday. When she got back she told me she had a vision of a vampire attacking a Youth Club in Sligo. She didn't know how she knew, but she was sure it was real. She had hitched to Sligo, tracked it down, and killed it before it could hurt anyone. It was then I told her who she was and let her read the book. She knew then; it was her responsibility to save these people—she got the visions and felt like she couldn't refuse to act upon them. Every so often she would go off on another crusade to save some helpless soul from some unspeakable evil—I got used to it. But the burden became too much; she was getting visions of people in trouble all over the country and she couldn't get to them all. And when she didn't make it in time, the vision showed her the people dying. She became even more distant and barely even spoke to me. She couldn't take it anymore and that's when she decided she had to find Xavier. But she said she felt he was underground, waiting for a different age. She waited, trying her best to help as many people as she could, but all the people she saved didn't alleviate the guilt of those she lost. She started drinking and taking drugs to try to forget. She became unrecognisable from the girl I had raised. They were dark days.

"Then one night about seven months ago, I woke up and saw a silhouette at the end of the bed. I was about to scream when she raised a quieting finger to her lips. It was Lynda; I hardly recognised her because she'd cut her hair short. She looked at me with a vacant, emotionless stare. At first I thought she was sleepwalking but then she spoke: 'He has risen,' she said. I wasn't sure what was going on—I was half-asleep, but then she turned toward the door and said, 'He sleeps in a blue building by the sea. I'm going to end this.' By the time I had put my slippers on and ran downstairs after her she had already gone. I haven't heard from her since. But when I thought about what she said, I guessed this is where she had come."

"She must hate him as much as I do," Christian said.

"I think that's part of it, but not the main part." She leaned forward and stubbed out the cigarette. "I think what she wants more than anything is a normal life. Ever since these powers manifested themselves she's lost all her friends. They're scared of her. Boyfriends are worse: they don't understand why she should rush off to save some stranger's life when she should be having a burger and a beer with them. One ex-boyfriend tried to physically restrain her from leaving to help someone and she threw him sixty feet in the air without laying a hand on him."

"She has telekinetic powers?" he asked excitedly.

"You've seen that movie *Carrie*?"

Christian nodded.

"Multiply by a hundred." Tears welled up in Janice's eyes. "I can see why they fear her, but still, it tears me up. For such a kind heart, she's such an unhappy, lonely girl. Do you know if she's still taking the drugs?"

He nodded regretfully.

"Is that why she's been arrested? Will she go to jail?" Janice said, panicking.

"No, it's not that, and don't worry, I'll get her released within the hour," Christian said, rediscovering his empathy.

Janice choked back her tears. "I know why she does it—it's to belong, if only for a night. I've even written a book about it: *Collective Isolation*. If she'd only accept who she is and try to integrate it into her life instead of chasing Xavier in the hopes that the escape clause works."

Christian's brow furrowed in confusion. "What escape clause?"

"Sorry, I forgot, you don't know the dhampir legend." Janice explained, "According to the myth, the only way to remove the powers of a dhampir, is to kill the vampire that fathered it."

knight of the living dead

Portstewart, 1218 AD

Degore ran into the woods. He saw no bravery in fighting impossible odds and his retreat would serve to bring reinforcements. He would have his vengeance. A noise caused him to stop running and turn. His horse, that he had left crippled and lame, was screaming. Dark shadows scurried from the tree-line and tore at its flesh. The vampires had found him. He bolted deeper into the woods, stripping off his chest-armour as he went—it would only slow him down and would offer little protection against this foe if he were caught. He checked his quiver and found only seven arrows. The nest had contained more vampires than he could count. He didn't know how many were chasing him now but he prayed he could reach help in time or evade them until dawn, because he could not defeat them alone. The trees began to thin and he saw rocks ahead. He ran to them, thinking that maybe a cave would offer him sanctuary. It seemed the better alternative since the villagers he had met were unwilling to fight...even alongside Knights of the Round Table.

Sir Degore had landed on the shores of Ireland only four days before with Sir Dagonet and Sir Lamorak. King Arthur himself had dispatched them on their quest. He had said there was a threat not only against man, but also against God and all that was holy. They were to make haste to Ireland and fight the evil that had corrupted the land. As they were about to leave Merlin had summoned Degore to his chambers and given him an amulet.

"This will help stop the scourge from spreading, Degore," Merlin said. "It is enchanted and will give you the strength and abilities to destroy the evil."

Degore picked his way carefully through the rocks and wondered what Merlin had meant. How could this amulet stop the vampires from spreading? In this area he guessed they outnumbered men at least ten to one. The savages howled behind him. They were closer now. Perhaps the villagers' superstition was not as foolish as they had assumed.

When their ship had docked in Stewart's Port the men in the local tavern had refused to accompany the knights to fight, or even to guide them.

"The devil has many soldiers here," one man had said. "They know a man's mind, his weaknesses and his fears. Go north and trouble us no more."

As the three knights rode out of town Lamorak had said the villagers were uneducated and superstition ruled their lives. Dagonet was more interested; saying even the tallest tale is grown from a seed of truth.

For the next two days the knights travelled north, stopping in the small settlements and being fed by kindly locals. They heard stories of creatures with the faces of men that drank human blood, feared the sun and could only be killed by puncturing their hearts with arrows or decapitating them. Many had advice for the travellers but none wished to join the fight, scared to bring the devil's wrath upon their families. It was clear that they all wanted these creatures banished: some donated arrows and one old priest gave Degore a vial of holy water, saying the creatures could not cross a threshold blessed by God. It was on the evening of their third day that a young peasant boy, orphaned by the vampires, told them of an evil place where it was said the dead breathed again, and God did not hear those who entered. The knights were confident that they had found their quarry and, after obtaining directions, set off to confront their enemy.

They found the place with ease and made camp. The night was without incident for many hours; then, just as they were about to give up and move on, the vampires came. They were not the animals that some of the local folklore had described. They walked as men and spoke the language of the king. Five of them approached the three knights. Lamorak drew his sword and Dagonet loaded his bow.

Degore stepped forward to the nearest vampire and said: "We are here by order of King Arthur of England. You and your kind are trespassing on God's land."

The vampire spoke harshly, "No one here will bend their knee to your king or your God. I will scatter your bones across this land that you hold so dear, knight."

The vampire lunged at Degore. Degore stood fast. Before the creature reached him Dagonet's arrow plunged into its chest. The vampire fell to the ground and shrivelled to half its previous size. As Degore and Dagonet—and the remaining vampires—watched this happen, Lamorak took the opportunity to sever the head of the vampire standing closest to him. The head dropped at Lamorak's feet and he kicked it at the three remaining vampires. It hit one of them in the chest and he turned and ran, closely followed by his two companions.

"We should track them to their lair," Lamorak said impatiently.

"We don't know how many of them there are," Dagonet replied. "The one thing that is constant in all the stories we have heard is that they cannot walk in daylight. We should wait until sunrise."

"Agreed," said Degore.

Lamorak threw his sword to the ground and paced the camp. He hated having to wait. The fight had got his heart pumping. He felt the thirst to kill, to rid the world of these godless beings once and for all. He looked at the sky; dawn was close, but not close enough.

As soon as the morning sky began to be tinged with orange the three knights set off on horseback. The vampires were clumsy and, for an experienced tracker, gave away many telling signs of their direction but the easiest to follow was their unusually long strides, which left heavy footprints in the soft mud. The knights estimated that the creatures could travel as fast as any horse. They did lose the trail several times but Dagonet always picked it up again. They rode most of the day and finally came to a castle where the trail ended.

Degore turned to Dagonet and asked, "Do you know to whom this castle belongs?"

Dagonet shook his head. "No nobleman dwells within. The ramparts have no sentries and no flag flies. I believe we have found the vampires lair."

Lamorak jumped from his horse and drew his sword. "We must hasten our attack while the light is still with us."

Dagonet spoke hesitantly, "Tomorrow morn would offer us a greater time to discover the weaknesses of the castle and allow us to…"

"No!" Lamorak shouted. "I will not cower from these animals for another night. Each moment takes the sun closer to the horizon. We attack now."

Reluctantly Degore drew his sword and nodded. Dagonet drew an arrow from his quiver, crossed his chest with it and uttered a brief prayer before loading it into his bow. The three walked through the open gates. There was no moat so they left their horses grazing at the castle wall.

The courtyard of the castle was eerily quiet. Lamorak marched ahead to a door at the far end, which should have led to the main banquet hall. Degore and Dagonet followed, looking to all sides for an attack.

Lamorak swung the doors to the banquet hall open. The knights gagged at the smell of rotting flesh. The light was before them so it was not cast through the entrance.

Lamorak reached inside the door and pulled out a torch from its holder on the wall. "Dagonet, light this quickly," he said.

Dagonet took the torch and dropped to his knees and brought out two pieces of flint and some straw that would serve as tinder. He struck the rocks together repeatedly until a spark jumped into the straw and caught. Dagonet carefully arranged the other straw and blew gently on the small flame until the small ball of straw had nurtured a strong flame. He put it in the torch and luckily it caught easily.

Dagonet walked into the darkness, the torch only illuminating a few feet before him. Degore and Lamorak flanked him with their swords drawn. They were only about ten feet inside the room when the doors slammed shut behind them. The three turned but saw no one. They braced themselves, each facing a different direction.

Two hands seized around Dagonet's neck and pulled him upward in an instant. The torch dropped to the ground and the flame died. Lamorak and Degore heard Dagonet's cries for help high above but they could do nothing.

"We cannot prevail in these conditions. We must retreat," Degore said to the darkness where Lamorak had stood. There was no response. "Lamorak?" Degore heard the sounds of a fight in the nearest corner. There was no way to help; if he rushed in swinging his sword he might hit Lamorak. He looked around and saw a thin strip of orange under one of the long drapes that covered the window; the sun was still out. He ran to the window and pulled the drapes apart. The light entered the room and three vampires jumped off Lamorak as if scalded. Degore looked in disbelief at the vampires crawling up the walls and across the ceiling to escape the sun's rays. There were scores of them, maybe hundreds. He looked across and saw Lamorak was hurt and bleeding. Degore ran to him and dragged him to the doors and shot the bolt from its keeper. The vampires were cautiously making their way to the window; they would have the drapes closed again soon. Degore knew he had little time, even outside there was precious little sunlight left. He put Lamorak's arm around his shoulders and rushed him through the door and across the courtyard. They reached the horses quickly. Lamorak said he was strong enough to manage on his own and mounted his horse. Degore couldn't see how badly wounded Lamorak was, but he had a lot of blood over his face and he appeared to have been gashed on his left side. The two horses set off and quickly broke into a full gallop.

"We have to find somewhere safe to wait until sunrise," Degore shouted. Lamorak didn't respond; it seemed to be taking all his concentration just to stay on his horse. Degore looked behind him and saw the sun disappear. He whipped his horse harder. They rode hard until the horses, which had not fully rested from the long day's ride, began to tire.

Lamorak shouted, "I have to stop." He was clutching his side.

Degore pointed. "The trees, over there."

They both trotted over to the cover of the trees and dismounted. Degore set his exhausted horse to graze and walked over to Lamorak. "We can't stay here long. I'll tend to your wound and then we have to be off again." Degore removed Lamorak's armour and searched for his injury. "I can't see where you're hurt."

"I am healed." Lamorak said and drove a dagger into Degore's stomach. Degore stepped back and pulled the dagger out quickly. Degore looked at the dagger and threw it to the ground. Degore drew his sword. He saw the devil in Lamorak's face, in his pointed teeth and evil, unrepentant eyes.

"Lamorak…?"

"I have tasted their blood, and now I will dine for all eternity on you and your kind," he rasped. "Unless you join us."

Degore knew what he had to do—he could not let this creature live with Lamorak's likeness. "If any part of my friend still exists within you, know that I am sorry for what I must do."

"You are outnumbered, Degore. We are many and you are one: you cannot prevail alone."

Degore lowered his head and quickly raised it. "God is with me." He stepped forward and swung his sword. The creature's throat was deeply cut and it dropped to its knees and tried to hold the wound closed with its hands. The blood gushed from the wound, looking almost black in the dusk light. It tried to scream but no noise came from its open mouth. Degore walked to its side and swung his sword again, this time removing the head. The body thudded to the ground. Degore lowered to one knee and said a prayer over his friend's body.

He would grieve later, now he had to elude the vampires for the remainder of the night. He mounted his horse and continued at a brisk pace.

The surroundings seemed familiar and he realised that his travels had taken him in a circle and he was close to Stewart's Port where they had landed. He made for the coast and hoped there would be a boat that could take him back to England and gather reinforcements. He must have made it at least another two miles before his horse threw a shoe and fell. It could not continue and Degore ran into the woods on foot. He wasn't far from the port now.

In the rocks beyond the trees Degore found a small cave and crawled inside to rest. The vampires were close; he could hear their gleeful wailing. He felt inside his tunic and brought out the vial of holy water. He held it close to his chest and said: "God, protect me from evil this night." He poured the water on the ground; across the threshold of the cave and pushed his back against the wall. Only now did he notice how badly he was bleeding. Lamorak's dagger had cut him deeply and blood was pooling where he sat.

A vampire lunged at him and was deflected. The holy water had consecrated the entrance of the cave and it could not enter. Degore managed a thin smile.

"You cannot hide in there forever. When you emerge we will feast on you," the vampire shouted.

Degore was unsure of his chances against an enemy that was this strong, especially with his wound, but tried to speak with conviction. "The morning will send you into retreat and I will return to my king, who will waste no time in sending a legion of his best soldiers to destroy you." He was breathing heavy and feeling dizzy.

The vampire leaned close and whispered, "You will not live until the morning".

"I will outlive you, believe me."

The vampire turned in disgust and walked out of sight but Degore sensed he was still close. Degore took the amulet from the pocket of his tunic and held it tightly in his hand. He had to survive because Merlin had said this amulet would stop the vampires from spreading and Merlin was never wrong. He was tired and wanted to sleep but he had to stay awake. For Merlin, for his king and for God, he had to stay awake. He had to overcome this evil. Merlin really *was* never wrong. Degore held the amulet to his chest and waited—now he was confident that what he had said to the vampire *would* come true. He watched the entrance of the cave for the sunrise but never saw it, or any other sunrise.

Portstewart, 12:18am

Chloe ran into the woods. Her eyes were still stinging and tears were running down her cheeks. From the corner of her eye she caught a glimpse of a blue flashing light. She crouched down behind a tree and looked back at the road. The police were inspecting the moped she had stolen. She had watched enough car-chase reality TV shows to know you ditched the vehicle before they sent the helicopter after you; once the helicopter got a fix on you there was no escape. She had thought she would have had more time before they caught up with her—damned efficient police force, why couldn't they be the more stereotypically slow-witted doughnut chompers? She was in trouble and she would need a lot of luck to get out of this one. She headed further into the trees as quickly and quietly as she could, silently cursing the two Daves as she went. Chloe had planned the robbery herself and, although it had not quite gone to plan, it would have been a lot less of a disaster if her accomplices hadn't been a pair of stoner fuck-ups.

A week earlier she had been on the phone trying to explain to the Social Security Office that she had no money. According to some government minister (no-doubt on a salary of £400, 000) the ordinary Joe-on-the-street could live on £53.95 per week. With bills for electric, phone, heating and credit card debts that she had had before losing her job, Chloe was asking them how she was expected to eat. In their usual robotic manner they fobbed her off with ideas about loans that could be paid back by being automatically deducted from her social security cheque—now that was a bright idea; of course, she could clear her debts easily if they gave her less money every week. After a string of obscenities, Chloe slammed the phone down and tried to think of a way out of her predicament. The TV in the corner caught her attention for a second as it laughed and then groaned, like a terminal patient who is briefly amused and then remembers his situation. TV Licensing were also demanding their money and threatening a £1000 fine if Miss C. Knight didn't pay immediately.

Less than two months ago she had been a police officer, now she was about to embark on a life of crime. It was kind of funny, but she wasn't laughing. The one and only time she had tried a line of cocaine at a party was enough to get her fired. She wondered if PC Wilkins had known they were having a drug test the next day; he didn't take any. Wilkins had asked her out and she had turned him down flat, but such a point wasn't even worth airing at her hearing, even though it probably *was* why he did it. Chloe walked over to the mirror and looked at herself. She had dyed her shoulder-length hair traffic-light-red, something she had always wanted to do but the police wouldn't allow. She stroked her hips, she was still in good shape and if the amount of date-requests was anything to go by, she was quite attractive. So why would no one hire her? Could it be Wilkins, still? Chloe ran her fingers through her hair and shook her head quickly. Paranoia wasn't going to help; she couldn't go on blaming Wilkins for the rest of her life...even though it probably *was* his fault.

Chloe had only ever stolen one thing in her life: a lipstick she couldn't afford from a chemist's shop. Although it was exhilarating at the time she had not been able to live with the guilt and had covertly returned it unused a week later. She had been fifteen then. Now, ten years later and thanks to an apathetic government, she was considering theft again. This time, though, she would need to steal a lot more than a lipstick.

The intended target of her larceny was garage/ minimarket called 24-Hour Services. A guy known locally as Old Joe ran it. He was a notorious skinflint: it was said that when his wife died he tried to sell her clothes to a charity shop and, after two hours of haggling, the seventy-year-old shop-assistant had initiated a fist fight. Another story was that he took his wife out of the coffin just before she was buried and sold it second-hand in the local paper with the advertisement FOR SALE: Coffin, one lady owner, hardly used.

Old Joe may have been a cantankerous old git to most of his customers but he was always smiling and courteous to attractive young women. Luckily Chloe fell into this category and one cold day she had gone in to the shop wearing a tight top. As Old Joe had been inspecting her nipples like she was a Tic Tac smuggler, she had spied that his till was being held closed by a piece of tape. Maybe it was just a coincidence that she noticed the makeshift lock or maybe her subconscious knew that when her savings dwindled to nothing she would need to take drastic measures. Time was a factor, though—Old Joe would put off paying for the till to be repaired for as long as he could but it would only take one robbery to force him get it sorted. Chloe decided there and then that she would carry out that one robbery.

She planned it at home and that was how the two Daves got involved. The two Daves lived in the flat next to hers and spent their time (and their dole money) getting stoned. When 'the munchies' forced them out of their own flat they came round to Chloe and emptied her cupboards. There were no character traits by which to differentiate them: both had dark scruffy hair, were average height, wore the same charity-shop-grunge clothing, were paranoid about the government and spent all day getting stoned and watching TV. Chloe only let them in on it because she needed a getaway driver and one of them (she forgot which) had a car. Both Daves seemed excited about 'sticking it to The Man' and agreed to the robbery immediately.

Sunday night arrived and the two Daves waited in the car as Chloe ran in dressed all in black, including boots and gloves, and wearing a balaclava. She went unnoticed when she burst through the door because Old Joe was arguing with a large housewife at the counter over the price of a box of crackers.

"This coupon says twenty-five pence off," said the woman.

"But they've already been reduced by twenty pence because they're out-of-date. I'm not knocking another twenty-five off them!" Old Joe screamed at her.

"Then give me the other five pence off them."

"I will not. Fuck off."

The woman put the crackers down and pocketed her coupon. "You ignorant old bastard, I'll take this to the highest court in the land." She turned quickly and saw Chloe standing with her plastic gun.

Chloe strode towards her and said, "Hands up and don't move!" She waved for Old Joe to come out from behind the counter and he reluctantly did. "Over beside the woman," Chloe instructed. Old Joe shuffled over and Chloe jumped the counter and pulled the cash drawer open and began filling a carrier bag.

The two Daves were both smoking with the windows up. Dave in the passenger seat was intently watching the progress of a drop of water trickling down the windscreen. Dave in the driver's seat had his right hand clenched on the steering wheel and his left poised over the gear stick—he knew he was positioned like this for a reason and as he toked the remainder of the joint hanging from his lips he desperately tried to remember why. The anticipation was growing with Dave in the passenger seat; the droplet had almost made it to the bottom, he was glad he had come out to see this and would tell that cute red-haired girl next door all about it when they got home.

Inside the service station the woman picked up a can of deodorant and asked Old Joe what was the best price he could do it for.

"Read the price tag, you dumb bitch," Old Joe replied.

The woman started going through her bag for a coupon that might lessen the price. Chloe double-bagged her haul of cash, jumped over the counter and looked outside.

Passenger seat Dave wiped an emotional tear from his eye as the water drop made it to the bottom. He felt great, moved by the feel-good factor involved. "We should go and buy some ferns," he suggested quietly to Dave.

"Yes, that's it!" screamed Dave. He shoved the car into gear and slammed the accelerator to the floor.

Chloe watched helplessly as the car screeched out of the forecourt. Old Joe rubbed his glasses and looked closely at Chloe's gun. Chloe started to get a bad feeling. Old Joe walked closer to Chloe.

Chloe waved the gun. "Stay back, I'm warning you."

Joe continued and looked at the gun. "It says 'Super Agent Hero 500—do not squirt directly in eyes' on your gun."

Shit.

Old Joe lunged at the bag of money and wrapped both arms around it. Chloe pulled hard and Old Joe fell to the ground but still kept his grip on his beloved money. Chloe dragged him a little way across the floor, heading for the door. The woman rushed her and sprayed the deodorant in Chloe's eyes. Chloe let go of the money and Old Joe scuttled away with it immediately. Chloe's eyes stung like crazy. She rubbed them with her gloved hands trying to get her blurred vision to clear. She turned her gun on herself. The housewife gasped. Chloe squirted water in her eyes, soothing them. In the distance she could hear police sirens. Old Joe must have made it to the alarm. She had to abort; she dropped the water pistol and ran outside.

Old Joe stood up in aisle three clutching the bag of money to his chest like a baby. He looked at the brave woman with the can of deodorant in her hand and said, "You do know you have to buy that now?"

Chloe ran down the road as fast as her impaired vision would allow. She couldn't believe those two idiots had just driven off. She heard a high whining noise and saw a single headlight coming slowly towards her. A moped, it had to be— the kind that teenage boys use to annoy other road users. She pulled her balaclava off and showed her bright-red hair, hoping a teenage boy would stop for a girl. Chloe had been blinking hard and her eyesight was almost back to normal. The headlight got closer and she waved her hand for him to stop. The whining of the engine continued at the same pitch; he wasn't slowing. Chloe glanced around quickly and saw no other escape routes: he *had* to stop. Her waving got more frantic as he got closer but he still showed no signs of stopping. He was just a few yards away now and clearly saw her but didn't intend to stop. Chloe grabbed her T-shirt and pulled it up to her chin. She wasn't wearing a bra and the young rider's head jerked round so fast that he lost control of his moped and fell to the ground.

The young rider's helmet scraped on the ground as he turned his head to see the crazy naked girl. Chloe ran towards his moped with her breasts still exposed and bouncing wonderfully. She pulled the bike up to its wheels and pulled her T-shirt down again.

Chloe turned to the boy. "Thank you." She rode off as fast as the bike would take her.

The boy looked after her and said, "No...thank *you*".

Chloe headed for the countryside and abandoned the moped when she heard the police closing in on her. She ran around the woods for a long time evading the cops by climbing trees and hiding in ditches. Knowing police procedures helped a lot. Eventually she came out the other side and onto some rocks. She listened intently and heard the police far in the distance. It wasn't safe enough to try to make her way home yet; she needed to find somewhere to wait until the police got bored. She spotted a small cave and made her way over the rough surface. At the cave's mouth she lit her lighter and looked inside. She saw a sword with a jewel-encrusted handle, a gold amulet with a huge turquoise-coloured stone in the centre, the remains of a suit of armour that a museum would pay a bundle for...oh, and a skeleton. She quickly climbed in and put her arm around her benefactor. She took the amulet and hung it around her neck. Maybe tonight wasn't going to be a total bust.

Despite the cold and uncomfortable ground, Chloe got to sleep quickly. She had strange dreams of blood and wars and monsters…vampires, maybe. Chloe usually only had nightmares about bank managers and she was really scared but she didn't wake. She was dreaming for so long and with such clarity that she developed an understanding of her surroundings. Even though she knew what she was seeing was a dream she still couldn't wake from it. Images of knights fighting swarms of vampires were gruesome to watch but she couldn't close her eyes or turn away from what her mind was projecting. She began to panic that she had somehow slipped into a coma and couldn't wake up. Anything was preferable to this; she even hoped the police would find her and wake her. Then the graphic battles faded into blackness and there was nothing but Chloe and darkness. This was just as unnerving, if not more so. She screamed into the void and a man appeared beside her. He wore a long robe and had long hair and a scraggly beard. Chloe couldn't speak. He put his hand on her forehead and closed his eyes. Chloe could see the concentration on his face. His hand moved slowly down her face and down her neck. Chloe couldn't move. His hand continued down her chest and over her left breast and stopped over her heart. Chloe felt a tingling in her chest. She saw light between the old man's hand and her chest. The light grew brighter and so did the tingling until it washed over her in an orgasmic wave.

Chloe shot upright as she woke. She was panting heavily and looked around the cave and got her bearings. She retraced the path of the old man's hand over her breast to her heart. Something was different about her though she didn't know what. She shuddered as the last of the ecstatic feeling dissipated. "Jesus," she finally said, "That guy really knows how to grope a girl."

There was a little light outside and she guessed it must be near dawn. She dropped the amulet inside her T-shirt and lifted the sword—she would come back for the armour later. As she was walking home she realised it was getting darker; it wasn't dawn, it was dusk. She couldn't believe that she had slept all day and checked her watch. It was almost six o'clock…on Tuesday! She had slept for two days. At least that explained why she was so hungry. She walked quickly back to town taking every shortcut she knew. She was almost within sniffing distance of fried chicken; she just needed to cross the graveyard and go two hundred yards up the street.

She was halfway across the graveyard when she stopped. She looked behind her at a crypt—there was something about it; she felt drawn to it. Somehow she knew; there was a vampire in there. The compulsion to go and fight it was as strong as…as the pull of mass-produced lukewarm chicken that was waiting just round the corner. Chloe was so hungry. Surely no one would expect her to fight on an empty stomach. She made a decision: her calling could wait until she had eaten. A man flew over her head. Chloe ducked behind a tombstone. He landed outside a crypt and went inside. Chloe felt her heart start to race and walked towards the crypt. "What the hell are you doing, Chloe?" she mumbled to herself. "This is a bad idea. Why don't I go and get chicken, fries, a side of coleslaw and a large Sprite. The chances of not being killed in a fast-food restaurant must be at least ten, maybe twenty percent better."

Still, she continued to the crypt because it felt like this was her responsibility; she was *supposed* to kill this vampire. Her time in the police had been mostly routine and boring. She had no 'stories', no interesting collars, no celebrity cases, in short: nothing exciting. She had always wanted that action-packed lifestyle that *Charlie's Angels* had promised her when she was young and now she just might get the chance.

Chloe peeked in through a gap in the door and saw the vampire lighting candles. When he had finished he threw a kick into an unlit part of the crypt. A muffled groan assured him it had found its target.

There were two of them. Shit.

Chloe was almost sick with fear but she couldn't run, no matter how much she wanted to right now. She would find a way to kill both of them. She had to. She listened to what they were saying.

"Come on, get up," said the dark-haired vampire, pacing around impatiently.

From the shadows a young, good-looking blond man stepped into the light. "What time is it, Kaaliz? Can't you let

122

me sleep a little longer? I feel really weak and tired," he pleaded.

"You're just adjusting, George," Kaaliz replied. "Have you thought of a new name yet, by the way?"

"Oh yes, I've been thinking about that. I rather fancy myself as an Andrew. Something very regal about it I've always thought."

"You're missing the point. You're a vampire now, you got to have some kind of cool vampire name like mine," Kaaliz said loudly.

"To be quite honest, I don't understand your name. What does it mean anyway?"

"I don't fuckin' know—who cares? It sounds cool." Kaaliz shook his head impatiently, then pointed at George and said, "I mean it: pick a cool name or I'll have to pick one for you."

George nodded humbly.

"Now," Kaaliz continued, "are you strong enough to come out to feed or do you want me to go and get you something?"

"Well I really don't know what normal is anymore, having no heartbeat kind of throws you off being able to gauge your own health, don't you find?" He smiled but Kaaliz didn't see the joke.

"Can you fly?" Kaaliz asked.

George looked nervous and put his hands up above his head. He didn't move. He looked at Kaaliz and started flapping his arms hopefully.

"No, that's not how you do it," Kaaliz scolded. "Just concentrate and imagine yourself floating away from the floor."

George clenched his eyes and shot straight up in the air like a rocket and smashed his head into the roof of the crypt. He fell to the ground in a heap.

Kaaliz winced and shook his head. "Are you all right?" he asked, trying to control his rage.

"I suppose I shouldn't be," George replied, "but I think I am." He rubbed his head and smiled, showing Kaaliz his fingers had no blood on them. "Maybe it's just as well, I've always had a bit of a phobia about heights."

Kaaliz was choking back his anger. "OK, you stay here and I'll go and get food."

"Do you think I might have some tapioca for dessert?" George asked timidly.

"Goddamnit, will you stop thinking like an old man! Look at yourself. You're young again, and you always will be," Kaaliz screamed.

"I'm just rather partial to tapioca is all," George mumbled.

Kaaliz turned and stomped toward the door.

"Oh, er, Kaaliz, old boy, do you know what time it is?" George asked.

"Why?" Kaaliz answered, infuriated. "Who fuckin' cares? You're immortal now, time doesn't mean shit anymore."

"I just wondered if I'd missed *Countdown*."

Kaaliz raised his finger quickly to an inch from George's face. "You mention *Countdown* one more time and I will cut your fucking head off." Kaaliz walked quickly to the door and stopped. "I'll get you something to feed on and then you go south and make as many vampires as you can and tell them to do the same." He turned to the door.

Chloe saw him coming and ducked around the side. She watched him walk outside, slam the door and fly upwards. He disappeared quickly. Chloe was amazed by how fast it moved.

Chloe crawled back round to the door and listened. She heard George inside ranting about 'quarter finals' to himself. He was obviously upset that he was going to miss his favourite anagram-based TV quiz show. This was her chance to strike. Her heart was beating like an over-enthusiastic bailiff on a door. Her hands were sweating. The sword was slippery. She wiped the handle and then her hand on her T-shirt, and refreshed her grip. This was it. She kicked the door and ran in.

George turned to her. "Hello there."

Chloe was thrown—she should have thought of something cool to say. Actions speak louder than words. She held the sword up.

"Ooh, collecting for the amateur dramatics are you?" George asked innocently.

"Ah, no," she finally said, "ah, sorry about this, but I, kind of, have to kill you." She smiled apologetically.

"Ooh, gracious," he said, like someone had just got a nine-letter word on *Countdown*. "Why is that then?"

"Well, you're a vampire," she said.

George looked blankly for a moment and then a little jolt caused him to speak, "Oh yes, so I am."

"Well, I've been given this mystical quest to destroy vampires." She put the tip of her sword on the ground and leaned on it. "I think," she added. "It was all very confusing with the montages and the blood and screaming, but…no, I'm pretty sure that's what the gist of it was: kill vampires.

"That sounds like a very important job. You must be a very clever girl."

This was not going how Chloe had expected. Instead of a blur of kickboxing and blood, this was more like visiting relatives. She half-expected him to offer her some toffee.

"Go on then. I don't mind really. This vampire lark—it's not all it's cracked up to be, is it?" He opened his white shirt and exposed his boy-band-quality chest. "It is the old stake in the heart, isn't it?"

"Er, I haven't got a stake—it'll have to be decapitation." She felt like a real rookie—imagine forgetting a stake.

"I was always confused with Dracula and The Wolfman. The Wolfman was silver bullets, though, wasn't he?"

Chloe nodded.

"Have you ever killed a Wolfman?"

Chloe shook her head.

"Oh well, never mind, you're still young."

"Aren't you going to put up a fight?" Chloe asked.

"Oh no need for all that nonsense, I don't want to get you in trouble with your boss. Besides that Kaaliz fellow, who, by the way, uses the most terrible language—you must promise not to listen if he says anything nasty—he said I would develop this bloodlust, he called it, but I haven't. To be honest, the whole silly notion of running around biting people seems rather rude to me."

Chloe didn't know what to do. Yes, he was a vampire, but he was just like a nice old guy wrapped up in a sexy, young package. "Wait a minute," she said and walked to the door and looked outside. Maybe she could make him promise not to kill anyone—a nice old /young guy like him would probably keep his word. She walked back in but as she pushed the door closed, a rusty shard of metal on the latch sliced her palm open.

125

She sucked air through her teeth. "George, do you have a handkerch…"

George flew at her and slammed her into the flimsy wooden door. The sword dropped from her hand. She punched at his face, but it had little effect. She drew her knee up between his legs—which got his attention. His hands rushed to his throbbing groin. She pushed him back and kicked him in the head. She glanced at the ground for the sword but couldn't see it. George regained his composure and attacked again, pouncing into the air and landing on her. The force of the landing pushed the pair to the ground. They were face to face. Chloe grabbed him under the chin and tried to twist his neck but it was immovable—the most she could do was keep him from biting her. Then she saw the sword at the bottom of the steps into the crypt. She stuck out her left hand, while her right kept his teeth from her neck, but it was out of reach. She tried to encourage the fight to the left, but couldn't move him. What could she do to hurt him? She had to improvise. She brought her left hand back quickly and grabbed his ear and ripped it off. He screamed shrilly. He released his grip as both hands moved instinctively to the right side of his head. He howled again as he touched the raw flesh. Chloe stuffed the ear in his mouth and hurled him backward against the wall. She ran for the sword. She had just picked it up when George struck her chin with the full force of his fist and she crashed through the door and out into the graveyard.

She lay on the ground, dazed. George came up behind her and grabbed her by the ankle. He picked her up and spun her twice, building momentum, and threw her across the graveyard. Her back gave a loud crack as it landed on top of a gravestone. She slid herself off quickly and onto the ground. She wheezed, trying to catch her breath. She knew that fall should have killed her, but still, she didn't feel too lucky. She lay close to the ground.

She watched George levitating slowly upwards. He only made it about ten feet and he vomited and dropped to the ground again. Chloe picked herself up and rubbed at her aching back. George saw her and ran for the gate. Chloe bolted after him.

Chloe caught up with George on Portstewart promenade. She couldn't believe how much energy she had and how strong she'd been when she was fighting in the crypt. George was fast too. His fear of heights was keeping his feet on the ground but he ran up the promenade, pushing people out of his way with ease. Chloe was gaining on him. George glanced behind and saw her closing on him. He threw a woman wheeling a pram to the ground and pushed the pram out into oncoming traffic. George ran off immediately. The young mother screamed from the ground. Two cars coming in opposite directions were skidding wildly under the full strength of their brakes. They weren't going to be able to stop in time. Chloe ran into the street and grabbed the baby. Both cars hurtled towards her; she only had a second. She held the crying baby close to her chest and launched herself into the air. The two cars crushed the empty pram. Chloe back-flipped in mid-air and landed on her feet on the pavement beside the crying mother. The street was silent for a moment, then they erupted in applause and cheering. Chloe couldn't help but smile. She handed the baby back to its mother and looked for George. She saw him but he was quite a distance away. The traffic had come to a standstill. She ran out and pushed a biker off his motorcycle. She revved hard and sped off after George.

Chloe raced up the streets, still slightly hampered by backed-up traffic. She could almost sense which way George had gone and as she rode onto the beach she saw him in the distance. The bike was powerful but it was a racing bike and didn't fare well on sand. Chloe was again gaining on him when she heard a rhythmic chopping sound from above. The police helicopter. How the hell was she going to explain this to the police, especially if they saw her killing George? The spotlight came on her racing up the beach—no escape now. To hell with the consequences, she thought. Her first priority was to stop George. She manoeuvred the bike alongside him and jumped off. She caught him around the neck and the two of them fell to the ground and rolled over several times. George ended up on top. He threw sand in her eyes and lunged at her neck while she was temporarily blinded. Chloe held him away with one hand and ground a handful of sand into his open wound with the other. George winced with the pain but held his grip. The

127

spotlight fell on the fighting pair. George released her and looked up. Chloe punched him in the face and threw him over. She leapt on top of him and punched him again and again, not giving him long enough between strikes to hit back. The sand began to blow all around them as the helicopter got closer.

"This is the police. Cease fighting immediately and put your hands up," the helicopter's speaker instructed.

Chloe looked up briefly through half-closed eyes. The helicopter was low; it would land any second and George would probably kill them. A gunshot sounded and the bullet hit the sand beside Chloe.

"Cease fighting and put your hands up now," the speaker repeated.

Chloe stopped hitting George and stepped to the side with her hands raised.

George had lost his boyish good looks; the sand sticking to his bloody, pulped face made him look more like a gargoyle. "You're going to jail, bitch. That's what you get for trying to do the right thing." He laughed. "But don't worry, justice is its own reward."

The helicopter was just a few feet from the ground now.

Chloe reached down and grabbed George's left arm and left leg. "You know what? You're right," she said, and hurled him into the helicopter's main rotors. Blood exploded everywhere. Chloe got heavily splattered as George was chopped into a thousand different pieces. The helicopter rocked unsteadily as the engine chewed the body. The pilot tried desperately to clear the blood and entrails from his windscreen. Chloe saw her chance and ran to the sand dunes.

Her speed was remarkable. Even after all that fighting she still seemed to be full of energy. Soon the noise of the helicopter was growing faint. She reached the end of the dunes and looked down. If she jumped down about fifteen feet she would land in a field that would take her home in minutes. She readied herself, closed her eyes and jumped off the sand dune. She never hit the ground. She opened her eyes when she was pulled upside down. She was flying through the air facing the ground. She looked up and saw the other vampire, holding her by the ankle. Chloe tried to swing her other leg and kick him but she couldn't achieve the correct momentum.

He looked down at her attempt. He had emotionless eyes. "When I'm ready," he said with cold detachment, "you're going to replace George".

Chloe was scared. George had been inexperienced but this vampire knew his shit. They were flying fast—too fast. Now she understood why George didn't care for heights. She looked down and watched the fields turn to concrete buildings, then to a golf course. The amulet around her neck slipped down and off her head. She shot out her hand and grabbed it in mid-air. It felt warm in her hand. Somehow, she knew what to do.

"Hey fuckhead," she shouted.

Kaaliz looked down and she held the amulet as close to his face as she could. The stone in the amulet glowed. Kaaliz stopped flying and hovered, hypnotised by the light. Chloe started smiling, knowing what was coming. She looked down and realised they were over a town again. Her smile faded—no soft landing. The amulet shot out a bright pulse of light. Kaaliz let go of Chloe and she began to fall. Kaaliz pressed his palms to his burning eyes.

"Sunlight in a stone, you fuckerrrrrrrrr!" Chloe screamed as she fell.

Kaaliz flew away into the night, still holding his eyes.

Chloe landed hard on her leg and heard a loud crack. She passed out and woke some time later. She looked around and saw no one. She listened and heard nothing but the sea in the distance and the low hum of the streetlights. She tasted the blood in her mouth. She felt the cold concrete pressed against her back. She smelled…chicken; fried chicken! Chloe's hunger shouted like a drill-instructor from the pit of her stomach and she tried to stand. Pain shot through her entire body. She looked down and saw half of the bone of her shin was visible, like a little half-chewed chicken wing. Below it was a pool of blood. She had to get to a hospital, quick. She rolled over to crawl. The protruding bone hit the hard concrete. She screamed. This time the pain was sharp, followed by a slow nauseating dullness and then nothing.

"Kaaliz must have left as soon as the sun went down," Claire said, peering into his empty coffin. "I wonder what he gets up to on his own?"

"Never mind Kaaliz," Xavier replied, "what are we supposed to do with her?" He pointed vaguely in the direction of the living room.

"We keep her. That was the original plan, wasn't it? Make as many as possible, remember?" Claire smiled.

"But she almost killed you. Don't you feel any hostility towards her?" Xavier said angrily.

"She didn't do it on purpose, besides, we *were* trying to kill her," she replied.

Xavier hung his head, defeated by logic. "She drank all the sixty-seven as well," he mumbled.

"Do you want *me* to talk to her; give her the old 'Facts of Death' speech?"

Xavier shrugged. "Whatever," he answered. "But drop me outside first, I'm going to go for a walk."

After Claire had levitated Xavier outside and saw him on his way, it occurred to her that he was acting very odd. She had thought he was jealous that she was spending so much time with Kaaliz, and now, with this new-Made, he would see even less of her, but there was something else. 'Going for a walk'? That wasn't Xavier. He didn't go for long ponderous constitutionals; if something were bothering him he'd usually take it out on the first poor mortal to cross his path. As Claire drifted back down from the skylight to the stage, she knew something was different about him—something was wrong.

When she walked into the living room, Dinner was sitting up straight with her hands on her lap like an eager student on the first day of school. "Hi," Claire said.

"Hello," the girl replied. "I would like to thank you for this opportunity, which I realise was not intended, but nevertheless has happened, and I believe I will make a first class vampire and you will never regret giving me this gift."

"You may not think it's a gift after a while," Claire said solemnly. "You may have heard the word 'immortal' before, but now you're going to find out what it really means."

130

The girl's excited, receptive grin lessened until it hovered between joy and sorrow. "I never dreamed this could happen," the girl answered, "all the nights I wished to leave my terrible life, that someone would wave a magic wand and I could start over, with none of the human horrors. I never thought it would ever come true, but now it has I'm determined not to mess it up—it's my second chance."

Claire was shocked at the girl's willingness to desert her life. "Are you sure you can leave it behind so easily?" Claire asked. "When I first became a vampire I missed my mortal friends and family terribly."

"There isn't much worth missing about my life, I'm a…" She corrected herself, "I *was* a prostitute with HIV. I didn't have friends; I had clients, addicts and pimps. As for my family, they haven't spoken to me in years; I don't even know where they are. To hell with them all anyway, because now I'm not dying, I'm not weak, and I'm not scared. To be honest with you, I'm already wondering what score to settle first. I know some real bastards, some real deserving bastards."

Claire gazed at her for a few moments. She looked into the girl's eyes and felt the sadness of her mortal life, but also the retribution waiting to be loosed. Claire smiled and said, "You haven't told me your name yet. We need to know what to call you now that you're part of the family."

The girl's face erupted with joy. "My name," she said excitedly, "it's not very vampire-y, I'm afraid."

"We usually pick a new name anyway; it's good from a psychological point of view, to reinforce the idea that this is a new life. Tell me your old name and we'll see what we can make out of it."

"It was Joan." She winced.

Claire tried hard but couldn't think of a way to incorporate an X, V or Z into her name. "What about a middle name?"

Joan shook her head.

"A nickname?"

"There was my professional name: Miss Tricks," Joan offered.

Claire immediately said, "How about Tryx? T-R-Y-X. That's kind of cute and sexy."

She smiled and answered, "Yeah, that'll do nicely."

They talked for more than three hours. Claire told her all that she had told Kaaliz two nights before, but somehow it was easier with Tryx. Maybe it was just because she was a woman and Claire didn't get that eerie guarded feeling she got from Kaaliz, or maybe it was just that she was a really nice person. Claire hoped that person wouldn't be destroyed when she made her first kill. She had almost been sick seeing Kaaliz desecrate his first kill's body—it was why she was stalling for time now. But Tryx's first time would be different because Tryx was different; she could feel that already. The conversation had stalled. There was nothing left to do.

"So Tryx," Claire said. "Have you picked which score to settle first?"

Tryx smiled wickedly and nodded.

On the other side of town in a small semi-detached house, which was not at all out of place among the others inhabited by drug-dealers, thieves and wannabe gangsters, Dario Lihst was trying to find a couple of beers for the two prospective clients squirming on the sofa. He rarely did this but they looked edgy and he thought they might leave. They were two men in their mid-twenties who looked terrified at the idea of their impending sexual awakening.

The Internet had opened up a whole new client base for Lihst. The two in question had e-mailed Lihst to confirm their appointment and when he saw the eight different fonts and twelve different colours it was written with he had a pretty good idea of what they would look like when they showed up. He wasn't wrong (right down to the Star Trek T-shirts) and had scheduled them both, one after the other, with the same girl between eight o'clock and eight-fifteen. He walked over, smiling inanely, and gave them each a bottle of Albania's top export lager: Puk.

Tammy walked into the living room wearing black lace underwear with a see-through blue nightgown flapping casually around her thighs. The two men on the sofa almost spilled their Puk when they saw her barely restrained chest heaving like a beacon to all men within sensor range. She smiled at their overexcited faces. A middle-aged man shuffled discreetly out behind her, giving Lihst an appreciative nod as he left.

132

Tammy enjoyed her work and she knew that she was the main draw of Lihst's business, but she often thought of going freelance. Lihst was such a stereotype; he adorned himself with chunky gold necklaces and bracelets, and wore large rings on all his chubby little digits (his motto was: women are like gold—the thicker the better). He walked around with his shirt half-unbuttoned exposing his hairy chest and bloated stomach like he was some kind of Latino lounge singer. He thought he was bigtime but even Tammy could see he was a little man going nowhere. Lihst made his way over to her quickly.

"Where the fuck is that dumb bitch?" Lihst spat in an angry whisper.

"Gee, I don't know, Dario, maybe when you kicked her in the stomach last night she took it the wrong way," Tammy sarcastically answered.

Lihst put his hand under her chin and squeezed her cheeks until her mouth curled in a painful pout. "I don't pay this mouth for opinions," he snapped, throwing her head to the side and releasing his grip. He turned and donned his sleazy smile for the two on the sofa then turned back quickly to Tammy. "You've got a few minutes before your next one, haven't you?"

Tammy nodded reluctantly.

"OK," he said, "you take Kirk and Spock upstairs and fire their phasers for them. It shouldn't take long." He gave her several objects. "There's an eyepiece, a metal glove and a communicator—put them on—and you're only to answer to the name Seven." Tammy took the pieces and walked over to the young men.

"Fuckin' nerds," Lihst whispered under his breath.

The door opened and an old man hobbled slowly in and took the weight off his feet in the closest armchair.

"Evening, Mr. Smith," Lihst said, "we won't keep you waiting long." He turned and saw Tammy leading the two young men upstairs as they giggled about 'The Undiscovered Country' to themselves. Lihst went over to Mr. Smith and wrote down his wheezed-out instructions for what his 'girl' should do. The old man then handed over the majority of his pension to Lihst and folded his arms, waiting patiently. Lihst went and sat behind his desk and thumbed through the erotic magazines (for the clients whose engines took a while to warm-up). There was a knock at the door but Lihst had just got comfortable. He was engrossed by an article on a voluptuous blonde named Sunny (the article was titled: Sunny—the bright point of any day; she was 22 and enjoyed beach volleyball, water-sports and being naughty), and couldn't be bothered getting up, so shouted instead. "Come in, everyone's welcome here."

The door opened and Tryx and Claire entered. "Hello Dario," said Tryx.

"Well, look who decided to show up," Lihst said, getting up and throwing the magazine away. "Where the fuck have you been?" He stomped over to Tryx who, uncharacteristically, didn't flinch. "We're gonna get into this later; I'm only sparing you now 'cause I don't want you covered in bruises for the old guy."

Claire looked over at the old man, who tipped his hat at her in that gentlemanly way. "The old guy?" Claire asked, repulsed and deciding that *Pretty Woman* really was far-fetched.

"Oh, Mr. Smith's all right," Tryx said, keeping eye contact with Lihst.

Lihst edged closer to Tryx until they were only a couple of inches apart. "Well, who but the most desperate are going to go near your sorry, diseased ass?" he whispered spitefully.

Tryx gave him a placatory smile.

"What have you done to your hair, you stupid fuck?" he said loudly.

"It's natural; do you like it?" she said calmly.

"No I don't—you're changing it back. Men want to fuck blondes; stupid fucking blondes like you," he said, still failing to elicit fear from her eyes.

"Damn, I guess *I'm* out of luck then," Claire said with mock regret.

Lihst looked over Tryx's shoulder to see who was speaking. "Well, look what you brought," he said, redirecting his anger into whatever passed for charm in his world. He circled Claire slowly, eyeing her hungrily. "Maybe your friend here can do something to calm my temper."

Claire batted her eyelashes innocently and giggled.

"Yeah," said Lihst, hiking his trousers to accommodate the changing shape of their inhabitants. He tilted his head and spoke to Tryx while still looking at Claire: "You get upstairs and get your clothes off. I'll send Mr. Smith up in five minutes. He wants you to call him Mr. Ed during the act, and rub him down with straw afterwards—I think there's still some in the wardrobe from the time that guy wanted the milkmaid in the haystack fantasy."

Mr. Smith clapped his hands together and rubbed them happily.

"Fuck you, Dario, it's not going to happen. Not now—not ever again," Tryx said.

Lihst couldn't believe that one of his bitches would dare disobey him. He turned angrily and began rolling up his shirt-sleeves. "Hey, Mr. Ed, you can work around a few bruises can't you?" He never looked for the old man's response, because he wanted to see the fear blossom in Tryx's eyes.

Her eyes stared back at him, cold as winter, challenging him to make his move.

He was a little unnerved by her courage and decided on one last-ditch attempt to scare her. He raised his fist and showed her the cheap replica-gold that would precede his fist by a fraction of a second. "You see this?" he shouted.

Tryx smiled. "You see this?" she said, opening her mouth and extending her incisors.

Lihst's mouth fell open and he whispered in awe, "What the fuck are you?" He threw a punch at Tryx, which she caught easily and squeezed it in her hand until she heard bones snapping in rapid succession. Lihst screamed and dropped to his knees. Tryx was amazed at how little pressure she had to exert to crush his hand. She looked at Claire for approval; Claire nodded permission for Tryx to indulge herself.

Tryx released the flesh and bone mass that had been Lihst's hand. He brought it carefully toward his chest, sobbing and trying to catch his breath. Tryx strode over and lifted Lihst's cricket bat—his weapon of choice when the girls needed to be 'put in their place'. She walked back and whacked him across the face, taking care not to use all her strength; she didn't want to kill him—yet. He fell backwards and started crying harder as he lay helpless on the floor. Lihst's nose was flattened and blood gushed down his cheeks from his nostrils. He looked up at her and Tryx hit him again. She heard a click and realised she had dislocated his jaw. He tried to plead but incoherent noises were all that emerged. Tryx dropped the cricket bat. She reached down and put one hand on his throat and one on his groin and lifted him above her head. He quickly forgot all his other ailments and tried to release Tryx's grip on his testicles. She hurled him across the room and he slammed into the plasterboard wall and fell to the ground. He looked up and saw the cartoon-like impression the top-half of his torso had dented into the wall. His body was numb; he couldn't move and wondered if the crazy bitch had broken his back. Then he saw Tryx walking toward him and fear impelled him to scurry across the floor. Tryx stood on the back of his neck and halted him. She bent down and twisted his head until he turned over. Blood bubbled from his mouth as he breathed. She looked down in disgust at the twitching, podgy mess. Through the blood and tears she looked in his eyes at the fear and cowardice, naked and obvious now, as he begged for his life without words. But his pathetic whimpers and grunts were lost on Tryx.

"You took my life from me," she said, filled with hate, "now, I'm taking it back." She bit his neck and drank the sweet liquid from the foul container. The blood streamed down her throat and washed away the last remnants of the naïve, submissive girl she had been. She was empowered in a way she had never felt before. The positive energy surging through her was not solely from the life-giving blood she was drinking, but also from the defeat of her jailer. She was liberated from her past now and no one would ever treat her with such contempt again.

She raised her head, still slightly intoxicated from the kill, and looked around her. Claire had a blank expression on her face. The old man had passed out. Two young men stood at the hall doorway wearing nothing but heavily urine-stained boxer shorts. Tammy stood behind them wearing nothing but her bra, pants and Borg prosthetics. No one spoke. Tryx got to her feet and walked to Claire. Claire put her arm around her and they walked silently to the door.

Tammy wanted to say something before she left but everything seemed ridiculous. What do you say to someone you were friends with and who just ate your employer— Thanks? Tammy took note that relief, not disgust, was the first thing she felt. She tried to think of something about Lihst that she would miss...well, she'd think more thoroughly later. Instead, she tried to think of a single *person* that would miss him—and again drew a blank. Business ideas began popping into her head; season tickets for regular customers, loyalty discount cards—the possibilities were endless. Besides, it would be the healthy thing for her to throw herself into work; it would help her get over what's-his-name's death. This was the right thing to do. She had to trust her instincts, and right now they were telling her that the living room would look great in terracotta.

"Are you all right?" Claire asked as they walked from the house.

Tryx nodded. "It just feels weird that I don't have any guilt or regret about killing him. I just feel...satisfied."

"Completely normal for a vampire," Claire answered quickly. She remembered when it had felt normal to her too, but she wouldn't tell Tryx about her condition. "Hey, you want to go shopping?" she asked brightly.

"Shopping? It's past midnight," Tryx said, smiling at the idea.

"OK, so it's not shopping. Technically, I suppose, it's stealing, but we need to get you some clothes—for the new image."

"Yes, you're right," Tryx replied, "I like what you're wearing; maybe I could get something along those lines."

"The Goth image—it's timeless, and, the punters kind of expect it. Shall we?" Claire put her arm around Tryx's waist.

"How come I can't fly?" she asked, putting her arm around Claire's shoulders.

"That bottle you drank was Xavier's blood—he can't fly either. You usually inherit the powers of the vampire who Made you."

Tryx nodded and Claire levitated them upwards. The pair flew to the town centre and landed on Main Street next to

Illusion (the most expensive and exclusive shop in town). Claire flew up quickly to the gavel and ripped the cover off the burglar alarm. The tamper-switch activated and managed to sound the siren for almost a second before Claire tore the speaker out. Claire drifted down to the front door and pushed the handle until the lock gave way. She gestured Tryx inside. Tryx ran in and started thumbing through the rails of designer labels.

Two hours later Tryx was dressed to kill (literally). She had chosen a tight black-lace bodice and a matching loose black skirt, which just covered her knees. On her feet she wore black leather ankle boots. She was just putting on the final item, a light, full-length black coat, as she descended the stairs towards Claire. The coat slid gently on to her svelte body and billowed gracefully behind her as she walked.

Claire smiled: Tryx looked beautiful *and* she had taken her advice. Claire had told her: dark colours are a must, they make you harder to see at night; get something sexy and distracting for her top, most men die easier if they're getting an eyeful; nothing too tight or restricting on the bottom because it impeded running and fast getaways; ditto with footwear—four inch heels may look nice, but try running from a slayer wearing them, and finally a long coat—something which would make her look bigger if glimpsed by a mortal. She had scored top marks on all counts and had accessorised with some tasteful earrings and a silver necklace.

Tryx got to the foot of the stairs and twirled gracefully. "How do I look?" she asked.

"You look amazing, Tryx," Claire replied, without a trace of bitchiness.

"I feel amazing. I don't know if it's the fact that I'll never have to worry about health, or money, or shit-heels like Dario anymore." She wrapped her arms around herself and gently hugged, closing her eyes in peaceful bliss. She opened her eyes and smiled at Claire. "Or, it could just be the Agent Provocateur underwear."

Claire laughed. "Whatever it is—it suits you."

"OK," Tryx said, "next is make-up." She walked towards the cosmetics department, beckoning Claire to follow.

"Tryx, we don't really bother with make-up," she said apologetically.

"Why not?" Tryx asked, stopping in her tracks.

"No reflection in mirrors—makes it hard to put on."

"Oh yeah," Tryx said, disappointed that she wouldn't be able to see how good she looked. Then she smiled quickly. "We can do each other's. It'll be fun," she said, hopping with excitement.

After much giggling, applying, removing, re-applying and searching for the lipstick shade that best reflected their personality, Tryx and Claire left Illusion. They felt fabulous! Before they had applied the most expensive eye-shadow, mascara, blusher, nail-varnish, lipstick and perfume that they could find, they had each covered the marble-white of their skin with tanning mousse and they now looked like they had just come from a two-week holiday in Barbados.

Chloe woke with her face pressed to the rough concrete. She cursed herself for passing out. She looked around the empty alleyway, not sure how she got there. Her memories were like an ill-fitting jigsaw that had been hammered together. Her skin was clammy. She was shivering. Sweat was running down her face. She looked back at her leg; a crimson puddle had collected below her knee. She knew she had to keep moving but she was so tired. She needed help. She had to make it to a phone. She put her arms out before her and gripped the ground. She braced herself for the impending pain. She took a deep breath. She heard girls giggling. Someone was there, at the end of the alley. "Hey. Help me, please," she cried with all her remaining strength. Then the world lost its focus. She felt a sickness in her stomach. Muddled voices were getting closer and the alley began to spin, rocking her with a nauseating lullaby. The last thing she saw was two well-tanned girls reaching down to her, then consciousness slipped away once again.

"Shit. She's in really bad shape," Tryx said, "What do we do?"

Claire couldn't answer right away. Should she tell Tryx what a *vampire* should do, or what *she* wanted to do? Claire was her mentor; she shouldn't display this kind of emotional weakness, but the girl looked so helpless and innocent. At a stretch, she could tell Tryx that whoever did this to the girl would be a more succulent kill, whereas this girl had hardly any blood left and she looked like she wouldn't hurt anyone. Claire walked over and scooped the girl up into her arms. "I'm going to take her to the hospital. Will you wait here until I get back?" Claire said decisively.

Tryx nodded obediently.

Claire flew as fast as she could. The Causeway Hospital was in Coleraine, five miles away. She reached it in a little over four minutes. She dropped to the ground outside the Casualty department and walked in. The nurses sprung from their tea and biscuits and rushed over. They directed her to a cubicle where Claire put the girl down on the bed and stepped back. The nurses fussed in unison around their only admission of the night. Claire backed out of the cubicle and the Ward Sister put a hand on her shoulder and took her over to the reception.

"Now, what's your friend's name?" she said officiously, with a clipboard in her hand awaiting information.

"I don't know her. She was just lying in the middle of the street so I brought her here," Claire replied. "Is she going to be all right?"

"It looks like she's been attacked. You'd better take a seat; I imagine the police will want to talk to you."

Claire nodded and walked to the waiting area. As soon as the Sister was out of sight she ran outside.

She stood in the patients' garden and exhaled deeply, wondering if she had done the right thing. Wondering what she was going to tell Tryx. She levitated slowly upwards but was only twenty feet in the air when pain shot through her body and she fell to the ground. The pain reached around her insides like lightning. She gritted her teeth and held back her screams. The pain stopped. Claire raised herself onto her hands and knees and the pain hit her again. Her left hand lost its strength and she fell face-first into the grass. The pain was scraping up her spine and shooting out to all her limbs. She writhed around in agony until it stopped again. She rolled onto her back and looked up at the stars. Was it going to happen again? She lay there waiting. After a few minutes she sat up, nervously expecting the pain, but it did not come. She got to her feet and cautiously began to levitate. She hovered for a few minutes before deciding she was OK, then raced back to Portrush.

She landed on Main Street but there was no sign of Tryx. She looked around and found their shopping bags sitting outside Illusion. Claire looked up and down the street. Where could she have gone? "Tryx?" she shouted.

From a side street, Tryx was thrown into the air. Her arms were flailing wildly as her body travelled in a large arc across the street and slammed into a wall beside a first-storey window. The top layer of plaster shattered and followed Tryx to the ground. She lay dazed, not noticing Claire. Claire turned to the side street and watched a figure emerge from the shadows. It was a young girl in a tie-dyed dress and bare feet. She marched towards Tryx like a soldier. Claire needed to distract her.

Claire reached out with her psychic abilities and quickly grabbed a handful of information from the girl's mind. "Hey, Lynda," Claire shouted. "Can I help you with something?"

The girl stopped and turned to Claire. "Where's Xavier?" she said coldly.

Claire was shocked, how did she know about Xavier?

"You're not the only one with psychic powers," Lynda answered. "Tell me where he is and maybe I'll let you live."

Claire concentrated and put up a mental barrier in her head to stop Lynda from learning anything else. "You want him: you'll have to come through me," Claire said and flew at full speed towards her.

Lynda raised her hand and closed her eyes. Claire's flight path swerved sideways and she smashed through a shop window, knocking the mannequins down like skittles. The shop alarm started wailing desperately. Claire pushed away the elegantly dressed wooden bodies that were mauling her and brushed the glass from her clothes. She sat up and saw Tryx getting her bearings back on the other side of the street. Between them stood Lynda with her hand on her left temple. Claire concentrated on Tryx.

Tryx, can you hear my thoughts?—

Wow. That's a really weird sensation.—

I guess I must have made some contribution to that bottle of sixty-seven.—

141

Who is this crazy bitch: a Slayer?—

I've never seen a Slayer with powers like that; I don't know what she is.—

What do we do, Claire?—

We have to make our move now. That little display of telekinesis looks like it took a lot out of her. Can you run?—

I think so.—

Meet me halfway, at that tree behind her, and I'll fly us both away.—

Claire, I'm scared.—

Don't worry, I'll get us out of here, I promise.—

Oh my God, Claire.—

What is it?—

Are those Jimmy Choo shoes lying beside you?—

Shit, you're right.—

Do they have them in a five?—

I don't know but there's a black Prada handbag that would be so perfect with them.—

Maybe we should come back later.—

Good point, Tryx. You ready to run?—

Let's do it.—

Claire picked herself up and stepped out of the shop window. She glanced to check on Lynda and saw a stake hurtling towards her. She jumped quickly to the side but it caught her right shoulder and knocked her back into the shop. Claire got up quickly and pulled the stake out. She climbed out to the street again. Tryx was waiting at the tree and Lynda was running towards her. Claire ran and tackled Lynda, sending them both skidding across the ground. Lynda swung her arm round and caught Claire's shoulder and squeezed the stake-hole. Claire screamed and punched her in the face repeatedly until her grip released. Claire got up and ran to Tryx. Tryx moved to her uninjured side and grabbed on. Claire was invisibly torn from her embrace and thrown across the street and headfirst into the iron railings surrounding a church. Lynda opened her eyes to admire her telekinetic assault. Claire's head was bleeding. She kept trying to stand up and repeatedly failed. Lynda walked towards her to finish her off.

"Hey, bitch," shouted Tryx.

Lynda turned quickly and Tryx hurled a bottle of Chanel at her face. The bottle hit the bridge of her nose and shattered, sending perfume and splinters of glass everywhere. Lynda's eyes stung and welled up so much that she couldn't see anything. She screamed in frustration. Tryx ran to Claire and wrapped her arm around her waist. She lifted Claire gently and started off down the street as quickly as possible.

The air began to heat. The ground trembled. Tryx turned and saw Lynda standing with her arms outstretched, her fists clenched and eyes tightly shut. Lynda's face was almost totally covered in blood now, from Claire's beating, the Chanel bottle's cuts and her own rubbing. She opened her mouth and screamed. She unclenched her fists. The shop windows on either side of her exploded, spewing shards of glass across the street. She moved her hands forward slowly and the next two shop windows exploded. As she moved her hands closer together all the shops she pointed at exploded. The destruction was making its way quickly up the street towards Tryx and Claire. Tryx put Claire down on the ground and shielded them both with her coat. They stayed under until the hail of glass passed. Every burglar alarm in the street was now screaming to be heard above the rest. Lynda's campaign ceased and she stood panting deeply. Tryx got up.

"What are you doing, Tryx?" Claire asked groggily.

"Look at her: she's fucked! She's totally knackered and she can't see; I'm going to finish her," Tryx said in furious resolve. Before Claire could object she was marching down the street towards Lynda, lifting an ornamental samurai sword from an exploded shop on the way. She unsheathed the sword and felt the blade; it was blunt but solid. Tryx knew if she hit her neck hard enough with it, it wouldn't matter if it were sharp or not. She closed in on Lynda. Twenty feet. Fury building. Fifteen feet. Tryx tightened her grip on the sword. Ten feet. Vengeance imminent. Five feet. She drew the sword behind her back. A crossbow bolt ploughed deep into her side. Tryx dropped the sword and yanked the bolt from her body. A scruffy middle-aged man was running towards them, putting another bolt in his crossbow.

Suddenly Claire was standing behind her. "Let's go." She winced. Tryx put her arms around Claire's neck and they rocketed up into the night.

After a mile or so, Claire landed on a flat rooftop to rest. She lay down while Tryx paced nervously.

"Is it always like this?" Tryx said, rubbing the rapidly closing hole in her side.

"No," Claire answered.

"What do you think that was all about?" Tryx asked.

"I know what it was all about; I read her mind while you were walking towards her with that sword," Claire said coldly.

Tryx waited almost a second for her to elaborate and couldn't wait any longer. "So, who was she?" she begged.

Claire got painfully to her feet and said, "Let's just say that Xavier has got a lot of fucking explaining to do."

Christian walked towards Lynda who was still poised for an attack from any direction. He couldn't help but admire her stamina. "It's all right, they're gone now," he said.

Lynda still couldn't see, but she recognised the voice from the police station when Christian had pleaded with her to return to Donegal and let him take care of Xavier. She had said she would, to gain her release, but then began searching the dark streets as soon as she had slipped away from her aunt. "In what fucking universe is it all right that they're gone?" she shouted. "They could have led me to Xavier."

"I thought I told you to go home," Christian said, examining her face.

"I'll go home when I get my life back," she snapped.

"I'd better get you to a hospital," he said.

"I'll be all right in the morning," she said, infuriated by her disability.

Christian took a more parental tone, "Your eyes are cut to shit—you're going to the hospital."

Lynda hated being told what to do, but he was right. He took her arm and led her back to his van.

Fifteen minutes later they walked into the Casualty department of the Causeway Hospital. The triage nurse took the beautifully fragranced bloody mess that was Lynda through to X-ray, only pausing to throw an accusing stare at Christian and say, "What the hell's going on out there tonight?" Christian wandered into the waiting area and sat down on one of the uncomfortable plastic chairs.

Time passes slower in hospitals, Christian had always thought. He wondered if Stephen Hawking had examined the phenomena and if there was a reason for it. More importantly, was there a way to reverse the effect? He looked around the walls at the posters: Quit Smoking Now, accompanied by a rather disturbing picture of a cancerous lung; Drinking Wrecks Lives, with a picture of a crying child; Marriage Counselling, showing two hands, each sporting a gold band on their third finger, holding tightly to each other, and an advertisement for the insomnia clinic. The thought occurred to Christian that he could make a storyboard of his life by rearranging the posters and adding one saying: Vampire-proof your house for less!

Although he had intended to leave when he dropped Lynda off, he now found himself resigned to the fact that he would probably be here all night. But Lynda wasn't related to him and she probably wouldn't thank him for staying, so *why* was he still here? The question was quickly answered: she was a part of Carol and when he had looked into her eyes at the police station he had seen Carol looking back at him.

Christian stealthily took a half-empty bottle of whiskey from his pocket and stole a quick drink while no one was looking. He put the bottle back in his pocket as he stood up and raised his forefinger to a passing nurse, hoping she could tell him how long Lynda would be in X-ray. He was ignored in that professional, detached way that only nurses can do. He began pacing.

Pacing was a long-held tradition of friends and relatives who had loved ones being treated under a veil of secrecy by the NHS. Christian thought it might be a secret ploy to make people get more exercise. Keeping them ignorant of the patient's condition, not allowing them to smoke, filling them with coffee and putting posters of every disease that you could possibly get on the walls would be enough to freak anyone into a frenetic pacing spree. But, as with all exercise, it got very boring very quickly and Christian started wandering.

It was a slow night though and there was no entertainment. Usually you could walk into any Casualty department in the country and find at least one drunken nutter who could enlighten you on the unfairness of life, the cruelty of love and top it off with some government conspiracy of silence that only he knew about. Christian looked around the almost empty department and realised, ironically, that *he* was that nutter tonight.

"Hello."

Christian turned to the cubicle directly behind him and saw a young woman with bright red hair peeking out through a crack in the curtains. "Hello," he answered.

"Will you come and talk to me?" she asked. "I'm really bored."

Christian walked in and sat on the corner of her bed, being careful not to disturb her heavily bandaged leg. "How long have you been waiting?"

"I don't know, forever," she replied. "They pumped me up with all these drugs that they said would probably knock me out, but I'm wide awake. My name's Chloe, by the way."

"I'm Christian."

"Who are you waiting for?" she asked, to get the ball rolling.

"My…my wife's daughter," he said.

Chloe winced as she got the lineage straight in her head. "Your stepdaughter?"

"No," Christian mumbled and hung his head. "It's a long story," he eventually added.

"Great," replied Chloe, "I'm a priority case waiting for emergency surgery, so I'll be here for ages."

Christian gave her a heavily censored version of the story where there were no vampires and Carol had died in childbirth. Chloe watched eagerly, like she watched the American talk shows, and saw the real sadness in Christian's eyes as he told the events that had led him here with Lynda.

"So, I don't really know her," he explained. "We're not even really related, but still I feel an obligation to her."

"She's the daughter you should have had," Chloe empathised. "And she's your last link to your wife. I think you should try to build some bridges with her; I'm sure she'd like to know more about her mother," she said, with that reassuring smile that all TV-talk-show hosts wear like a bikini in a snowstorm.

Christian looked at his ragged clothes and neglected personal hygiene. "I'm not much of a role model, am I?" he said.

"You could be," Chloe answered.

"I don't have the time to spend with her; there's something I have to do first—a work thing—and then I could be free, and so could she," Christian said softly. "Maybe then…"

Chloe smiled and nodded.

"So, what's your story?" Christian asked, "and whatever happened to your leg?"

"Hit by a car," Chloe quickly lied. "I don't have a clue how I got here. One moment I was lying in an alley, the next I'm here."

"Maybe you have amnesia," Christian offered.

"Yeah, maybe," Chloe said, not really believing it. "But I can remember most of the things I forget."

"What do you mean by that?" Christian asked.

"I think amnesia is more psychological than physiological. Think about it, people who have amnesia: how often are they multi-millionaires with perfect marriages and perfect health? Never, right?"

Christian shrugged a vague agreement.

"People choose to forget, or ignore, whatever you want to call it, the things in their life that are unpleasant. Obligation is one. That's what I meant when I said I could remember what I forget, because it's a daily chore. Every day I remember what I was and then I look in the mirror and see what I am. Forgetting what I was is the only way to move on."

"And what were you?" Christian asked.

Chloe considered her response carefully and answered, "Important."

"And you're not now?" Christian asked.

"Tonight I tried to be," she said, hanging her head, "but I was just trying to get back something I lost a long time ago, and look what I got for my trouble." She nodded at the bloodstained pile of bandages where her leg resided.

Christian couldn't figure out what the girl was concealing. Her vague description of her accident and her feelings of failure made her sound like she was some sort of super hero Traffic Warden. He didn't press her though, because he realised there were probably a lot of inconsistencies in his story too. Still, he felt something for the girl, not sexual—though she was quite pretty, it was more like camaraderie between kindred souls. He looked at her glazed eyes closing; the drugs were beginning to take her. He leaned into her and said softly, "Is there anything I can do?"

She smiled weakly, touched by the gesture. "Nothing...can do...don't..." Her eyes closed momentarily and then opened quickly. She mumbled, "Need... a saviour." Her eyes closed again and this time she could not re-open them.

Christian's head spun. Xavier? How did she know Xavier? Had he done this to her? Of course he had, probably indirectly because breaking legs really wasn't his style, but nevertheless, she wouldn't have said his name if he hadn't something to do with it. Christian chastised himself for even considering staying here all night when Xavier was out there wreaking God knows what kind of havoc on innocents. Innocents just like this girl. Christian pushed his way out of the curtained cubicle and grabbed the bottle from his pocket and emptied a generous drink down his throat. The Ward Sister approached him with a stern look on her face.

"You'll have to put that away," she commanded.

Christian put the bottle in his pocket and turned towards the door.

"That girl you came in with is ready to be taken up to the ward," she said.

Christian turned and equalled the Sister's authoritative tone. "Watch her. She'll try to leave." Christian moved close to the Sister and whispered with chilling earnest, "Don't let her leave."

The Sister was quite unnerved by his piercing eyes and ninety-percent-proof breath and looked behind her for a porter. She saw one and realised she had back-up and could stand up to this drunk, but when she turned back the automatic doors were closing and the smell that had accompanied Christian was slowly diffusing.

Audrey Wells sat in Portstewart Police Station clutching a very old book close to her chest with both arms. Several empty plastic cups, which had contained a vague approximation of coffee, were stacked beside her chair. Quigg approached her and interrupted her vigil again.

"Listen, maybe you should come back in the morning," Quigg said politely. She wanted to spare the girl the trouble of dutifully waiting all night when Christian Warke was probably lying drunk somewhere.

"He is fairly unpredictable," Audrey said with a thin smile.

"I'll tell him where you're staying if he comes in," Quigg said, gesturing Audrey to her feet and towards the door. "Do you want a car to take you to your hotel?" she added.

"Audrey shook her head. "I'll walk, it's not far." Quigg held the door open for her.

"Be careful," Quigg said solemnly, and let the door gently close.

The night was quiet and still except for a faint breeze carrying the salt air from the sea. Audrey inhaled deeply and felt invigorated by the crisp breath of the ocean she heard roaring in the distance. The streets were empty but still she walked more quickly through the dark sections of the pavement and lingered slightly longer in the intermittent orange spotlights thrown from the street lamps. It was a myth instilled in her in childhood that if she kept her bedside lamp on, no monsters could get her—monsters were scared of the light. The smallest spark and they would scurry back under the bed or to some darkened corner of her room where they were no threat. It was ironic that such a silly childhood notion was true: there were monsters, and they were afraid of the light. The only discrepancy was the light source. Her little bedside lamp which she had put so much faith in and trusted her safety to all through her childhood would not have stopped any real monsters. Not her bedside lamp or the orange bulbs watching over her now could ward off the real monsters of the dark. Her faith was shaken and she hated herself for analysing her sense of security. It was always the same with her: if she found something to hold on to she would examine it and scrutinise it until she decided it wasn't safe. She stopped under a streetlight and stood there for a moment engulfed in the glow of her charlatan protector. The safe stepping-stones of light that would lead her to her hotel no longer seemed like they would carry her. The darkness seemed more enticing, like being indistinguishable in a crowd, whereas the light would point her out to all that were looking.

'The eyes in the night are always watching.' She remembered the line from a book she had read but couldn't remember the story and, more importantly, if the tale offered an opinion on how to survive walking down a partially lit street in a town with a vampire problem. She walked briskly down the street, treating the light and dark with equal distrust. Her pace quickened. She thought she heard footsteps, closing on her. She stopped and clutched the book close to her breasts like a knight's shield and took a pencil from her jacket pocket and gripped it tightly like a lancer preparing to joust. There was nothing but silence. She started walking again and realised it was probably just the echo of her own footsteps...probably. She broke into full sprint now, which was difficult while still clutching the book to her chest, and saw the hotel, welcoming and safe, like a castle with an open drawbridge. She galloped through the gates and into the lobby.

The night clerk raised an uninterested glance towards Audrey; unaware of the drama she had just put herself through. Her heart was pounding against the cold leather cover of the book she held. She knew she wouldn't be able to sleep so she went into the bar and was surprised to find she wasn't the only one who wanted a drink at four o'clock in the morning. There was a very attractive man sitting at the bar, gazing seriously into a glass of whiskey as if it was a crystal ball. His brow was furrowed with concentration and concern as he poked at the disintegrating ice-cubes in his drink before emptying the whiskey down his throat in one. He turned to Audrey, who was standing at the entrance to the bar still trying to slow her breathing down.

"You look like you need a drink," he said.

Audrey walked towards him, glad of the company, and said, "Oh my nerves, do I ever." She sat on the stool next to his and looked for the barman.

"It's the porter who acts as barman at night," he said. He raised himself up on his stool and looked out to the lobby. "I think he's asleep again." He put his hands on the counter and flipped his legs over and landed behind the bar. "What can I get you, Miss?" he said with a barman's courtesy.

"Vodka and lime," Audrey said, smiling at his charm.

"But of course," he said, bowing. He made her drink and refilled his own glass. Audrey drank quickly and coughed on her first gulp, not expecting the vodka to have been favoured so much in the mixture. He raised his eyebrows, looking for her approval—she nodded. He smiled and sipped his own drink.

He lifted a cloth from behind the bar and started wiping the counter in small circles. "So," he said, "you wanna tell me your troubles?"

151

She shook her head lightly, "No. Why don't you tell me why you're sitting drinking at this time of the morning?"

He studied her for a moment and then gave a 'why not?' shrug. "It's nothing more interesting or exciting than self-pity," he began. "I don't want to go into the details, but, let's just say I'm not long for this world."

He said it with the clarity of someone drunk enough to be completely honest. "You're dying?" she said, with the kind of sincerity and concern that you could only believe from a stranger.

"It's one of those things that you never think will happen, no matter how much you see death or think about it—you never think it'll happen to you."

"Isn't there anything…" her words trailed off. She realised the rest of her sentence was ridiculous and she was embarrassed that even the beginning had made it out. As if he, the one with the terminal disease, wouldn't have tried every possible treatment already.

"Everyone's time comes. Mine draws nearer and there is nothing I can do about it—it's a shitty feeling but like I said, what can I do about it?" He downed the rest of his drink and grinned bravely at her.

She could see it now—he didn't look well. His skin was pale, his lips were almost blue and his eyes looked tired, tired beyond the physical; like they'd seen too much. He topped up her glass with vodka and refilled his own.

"So, you ready to tell me your troubles yet?" he asked.

Audrey was resolute and shook her head coyly. This poor guy didn't need to know that apart from all the diseases that could hasten your journey to the grave, vampires were also real and could kill just as indiscriminately. She pursed her lips tightly.

It was only after her lips had been lubricated with nine very strong vodka & limes that she began to open up.

"You know what my trouble is?" she slurred.

"That you're drunk?" he offered.

"Apart from that," she said. "It's that I get caught up in these ridiculous situations because I equate spontaneity and unpredictability with romance. But men, like you…"

"Like me?" he said innocently.

"...like you, no matter what they say, they want a good little wife who'll sit at home and knit booties and shit, and do whatever her man tells her to. You can understand that kind of marriage in the fifties because people were stupid back then; you only have to look at the movies that are considered romantic: *Seven Brides For Seven Brothers*, seven brain dead fuckers kidnap seven women and hold them hostage until they're all brainwashed into marrying them; *My Fair Lady*, I mean, what the fuck! This Rex Harrison dick pulls this perfectly nice girl off the streets and totally changes her personality, looks and demeanour, and then she gets to wed the chauvinist prick—we're supposed to believe that this is what love is? I tell you what: *The Stepford Wives* is a remake of *My Fair Lady*, trust me. Don't you think that people should just let their partners be? Let them grow, without pruning, into whatever they are destined to become?"

He wasn't listening to her like she was a ranting drunk, he was thinking hard about what she said. "Absolutely," he said softly.

"This guy I came over here to see, I mean, what was I, what *am* I, thinking? He's a total disaster, but there's something about him that makes me want to help him, not only with his health, hygiene and social skills, but with his heart. His heart is capable of feeling so much—I know it is—but he won't let anyone past his big macho charade." Audrey slumped down to the counter and rested her forehead on a coaster. "What am I *doing* here?"

"Maybe you should go to your room and sleep it off," he said.

"Easier said than done," she mumbled, almost asleep.

He picked her up in his arms like a child and she instinctively put her arms round his neck. He bundled her jacket and book onto the shelf her stomach was making with his chest and carried her to the front desk. He swung her feet round and kicked the night porter lightly on the side of the head. He sat up with a start.

"This lady's room key, please," he said. The night porter looked at him suspiciously but handed over the key.

He carried Audrey up to her room and laid her on the bed. She rolled over and groaned. He put her book, jacket and room-key on a nearby chair and walked quietly out the door, closing it securely behind him.

As he was riding down on the elevator a tingling feeling began in his left arm and crept across his chest like a thousand tiny insects. This time he knew it was coming, but he was still unable to do anything but mentally prepare himself for the pain. Suddenly, the power left his legs and he fell to the floor. His chest felt like a huge weight was sitting on it. His breath struggled to release. He looked at his contorted reflection in the polished silver doors of the lift and felt his insides were in a similar state: twisted and abnormal. The elevator car shuddered as it stopped and he felt like his bones might shatter. The doors parted before him. He pulled himself forward slightly and the pain gave its final piercing stabs to his body and then it was gone. He lay on the ground, half-in and half-out of the elevator. The doors tried to close on him several times before he found the strength to stand up. He leaned against the wall, straightened his clothes, and walked shakily across the lobby. The night porter looked at his distressed appearance and was again suspicious.

"Good night," he said, hoping it would ease the night porter's mind.

The night porter was still suspicious, but replied, "And a good night to you, Mister Xavier."

behind the mask

Claire and Tryx sat in an awkward silence waiting for Xavier to get home. Claire got up and started pacing again. Disappointment, rage and betrayal all waited impatiently inside her; she yearned for Xavier to get back so the vengeful trinity could question him. If there had even been a shadow of a doubt in that girl, Lynda's, mind...but there wasn't: she was sure that Xavier was her father.

Lynda had looked about twenty. That would mean she was conceived in the early eighties. That didn't make sense. She and Xavier weren't having any problems, they weren't fighting: she thought they were happy. Was it something she had said or done that had driven him into the arms of another woman or had he fallen in love with someone else? More to the point, how come she didn't know he had done it? After over a century with him she could instinctively feel how he felt, if she concentrated she could narrate exactly what he was thinking, there was no way he could hide something this big from her; it was impossible. It had to be a mistake. This Lynda girl might wholeheartedly believe that Xavier was her father, but she was wrong. She had to be wrong.

Claire looked up at the square of night through the skylight. There was still about an hour and a half until sunrise, it would be typical if Xavier stayed out until the last minute tonight. She sat down on Kaaliz's coffin and looked at the worried expression on Tryx's face.

"Damn," Claire said.

"What is it?" Tryx asked.

"We forgot to get you a coffin while we were out."

"Oh," Tryx said, relieved. "Never mind; I'll kip on the sofa." She studied Claire's pensive face and added, "Do you want to talk about whatever's bothering you?"

Claire didn't want to but she felt as if it was going explode from within her if she didn't. "That girl tonight, Lynda, I read her mind and she thinks..." she paused, fearing that in some way saying the crazy accusation out loud would give it more credibility; somehow make it more possible. She looked at Tryx's suspended expression, waiting for her to finish her statement, and said, "...she thinks Xavier is her father." She

155

looked for Tryx's first reaction and was relieved to see sympathy.

Tryx carefully considered her response and said, "Could he be?"

"Before tonight I would have said no," Claire answered quickly. "But I read her and she believes it, and, it's hard to explain, but when someone has been lied to the thought is different somehow. Even if they don't know they've been lied to, *I* usually do, it just feels a little...I don't know—not right."

"And her thoughts didn't feel this way?" Tryx asked, like a counsellor who had seen it all too many times before.

Claire shook her head.

"I don't know what to tell you," Tryx said. "The kind of guys I have experience with are deceitful, selfish pricks—I haven't had a boyfriend, in the traditional sense, since high school."

"I keep thinking 'He wouldn't', and then I think about all those women who have faith in their husbands fidelity right up to the point when they run off with a twenty-two-year-old beautician called Tiffany, and I think, am I just like them?"

Tryx sat down beside Claire and pulled a penknife from her pocket. She put the penknife in Claire's hand and closed her fingers around it. "If you find out it's true—cut his dick off while he's asleep." The two of them laughed hysterically.

The laughter subsided to a smile and Claire said, "I'll keep it in mind." She put the penknife in her pocket.

Tryx put her arm around Claire's waist and rested her head on her shoulder.

Claire appreciated the gesture and it calmed her briefly. The two of them sat there for a few minutes silently enjoying each other's friendship.

Claire broke the silence. "Fuck this," she said through gritted teeth. She turned to Tryx with wavering conviction and added, "I'm not sitting here for another hour and a half, let's go and get you a coffin".

They had just stood up when their exit was halted by a scuffling sound from above. It was Xavier climbing up the outside of the Arcadia. The fire escape had been removed many years ago to stop children from climbing on to the roof of the old dancehall, but enough of the original fittings remained to

156

facilitate an adventurous climber's, or agile vampire's, ascent to the roof. It was how Xavier got in when he and Claire weren't together. There was a similar method on the inside: a ladder to a lighting catwalk above the stage and a rope to complete the exit.

Claire waited impatiently. Maybe it was just the unpleasant confrontation that was coming, but he seemed to be taking a lot longer than usual to scale the structure and get inside. Finally he appeared at the skylight. Instead of his usual jump to the floor, he carefully wriggled in and grabbed the rope and lowered himself onto the catwalk.

Xavier looked down at the two 'tanned' women staring up at him expectantly. He imagined they were waiting for him to comment on how good Tryx looked in her new clothes. He couldn't muster the enthusiasm to pretend he cared. He felt a weakness and vulnerability he hadn't felt in over a century and it was getting worse.

Claire began reading him as soon as he was on the catwalk. She looked deep into his mind, into the places he would try to hide things from her. She found his worry about his rapidly accelerating condition. He had had two episodes similar to the one that had dropped her from the sky outside the hospital. The first happened when he had taken a quick drink from a PE teacher, but there had been steroids in his system that had soured the blood and Xavier had let him go. He had been laughing as the sports educator had run from him with blood running down his T-shirt and urine running down his leg. Then the pain had seized him and thrown him to the ground where it had silenced his laugher and brought back a feeling lost to him: pain. Pain deeper than being hurt in a fight or even from crucifixes, holy water or sunburn. This pain was worse because when it was over he knew it was not the end—it was just the beginning.

The second attack he was hiding had been tonight—and he had been with a woman. Claire's heart sank. In a bar with another woman: for the scorned women of this time that Claire saw on TV, the knowledge that their other half had even spoken to anyone of the opposite sex would have lawyers making space in their bank accounts and judges polishing their gavels. It was only because she loved him so much that she gave him the benefit of the doubt. She extracted every detail of the rest of the story; from the moment this bar-hopping hussy had sat down beside him until its innocent conclusion.

She was again confronted by the contradictory facts. Lynda's truth was real and yet Xavier had not cheated on her. There was no trace of him ever having cheated on her in his head. Even when he had carried that girl to her room tonight there had been no sexual desire for her in his head. As he walked up the stairs with her, a gentle provocative bounce had drawn his attention to the fact that she had nice breasts, but he had no urge to bury his head between them and make raspberry noises. What wife could ask for more than that?

She watched as he climbed slowly down the ladder to the ground and walked towards her. Claire's original plan had been to open the frank discussion by throwing him against the back wall (she even had a spot picked that would really hurt), but now, because of the strength of both contradictory truths, she was treating the whole thing as a mystery to be solved. She was calm and, at least for the moment, objective.

"I'm going to go and watch TV," Tryx said diplomatically, and left the stage.

Xavier looked at Claire—his wife, lover and best friend— and felt like crying. He always imagined they would be together forever. He hadn't seriously thought that they would ever die; they didn't take stupid risks or hold grudges against hunters or slayers; they were quiet killers. Death was now a rapidly approaching reality that he was completely unprepared for. Even human children had some sense of their own mortality; they knew that people die and someday far in the future they would too, but vampires lived with the complete opposite dogma; they believe in eternity on earth. They are abominations as far as nature was concerned and the Vampyre Corpora (if you believe that sort of thing), warned that they were not welcome in the afterlife, which was why they were given the chance of everlasting life on Earth.

Xavier was more troubled about Claire yielding to the disease, possibly before him, than he was about himself. What awaited Claire if neither Heaven nor Hell held a place for her? What tortures could nothingness bring? He would kill himself if she died first: that was an instantaneous decision that needed no further thought. He looked at the soft jade of her eyes and could hardly bring himself to broach the subject, but he had to. He had experienced the pain twice, the second worse than the first, and he wanted to prepare Claire for what was coming.

"I know, Xavier," she said softly. "It's happened to me too."

Xavier hugged Claire tightly and he felt instantly that his pain and worry had halved.

Claire had saved him the awkwardness of trying to communicate everything he was feeling by reading him; she wished he had the ability to do the same. She didn't know how to ask him about Lynda, especially after the genuine feelings of love she had just felt in him, but she had to. She decided not to beat around the bush and hit him hard with a statement that would instantly panic him.

It was a technique the police used in its most basic form. They would show a suspect a photo or piece of evidence and watch closely for an eye to twitch or sweat to break, but she had taken it to a much higher level. She had noticed that a panic-keyword made all relevant information fly like startled game, while the suspect decided what could be revealed and what concealed. Fortunately as soon as the information was brought to the fore she could see everything. She often thought she would make a hell of a detective.

She chose her statement; if he knew anything he would not be able to disguise it. "I met your daughter tonight," she said flatly.

Nothing.

Xavier looked shocked. His shock quickly turned to panicked regret, and finally to shameful resignation.

Still nothing.

"You won't be able to read anything, Claire," he said, seeing the concentration on her face. He pushed his hands through his hair and turned from her. He walked slowly to the other end of the stage.

Claire couldn't understand it; it was such a weird feeling. She couldn't read anything at all in his thoughts—there was nothing—but there seemed to be a lot of nothing, like his mind was bursting at the seams with nothing.

159

"You can stop trying. Turiz cast a Masking Spell for me, so you would never know anything about it," he said, leaning his back against the wall and sliding down to the floor.

Turiz, Claire thought, Of course. He had been a warlock in his mortal life and his powers had excelled when he was Made. She had heard about his success with Masking Spells. He could hide anything from the prying minds of vampires: the location of a lair, where a family with a tasty blood group lived, a mistress.

A mistress, she thought.

So, Lynda's truth hadn't been a deception. Claire expected fury to consume her but there was something on Xavier's face that wasn't guilt or regret, which stopped her.

Xavier looked at her and sighed—he would have to tell her. He exhaled deeply and said, "Come and sit down. I'll tell you all about it."

Claire couldn't feign stubbornness—she felt like a custodian who had access to every room in a building but one, and now that door would be opened. She walked over with a non-committal expression and sat down, cross-legged, before Xavier.

He looked at her and realised that 'sorrys' were pointless before she heard the story, but he would have them standing by for when he finished.

He took a deep breath and began: "May 29, 1980, was when it happened. It was the hundredth anniversary of my mother's death and I went to lay some lilies on her grave. As soon as I arrived I felt a presence, someone watching me from the bushes. I let them think they had the jump on me but their approach was clumsy. She ran at me screaming, with a stake held above her head—I stopped her easily. She was scared, so scared. I was about to bite her when an idea stopped me. You remember how I always went to my mother's grave to think?"

Claire nodded quickly.

"Well, that was the other reason I was there. You had been really depressed for weeks. You remember why?"

"I wanted a baby," Claire said softly.

"You weren't going out, you weren't eating—I didn't know what to do. I went to the graveyard, the girl attacked me, and as I repressed her futile struggles I thought: This is the answer—a surrogate mother. I thought I could get her pregnant and take the baby when it was born. I know I could have just taken a baby from anyone, but this one would be a part of me. The few seconds when I considered it seemed to last for days. In the end there was only one thing that bothered me about the idea: I would have to be unfaithful to you."

"You raped her," Claire said coldly.

"Yes, and that's another thing," Xavier continued. "I've done a lot worse things to a lot more innocent people and none of it ever bothered me, but after that night in the graveyard…everything was different. You must have noticed a change in me around then."

Claire thought hard and realised there had been a distinct change in Xavier in 1980 but she had been so melancholy that she had regarded it with the same disinterest as everything else around her at that time.

"I was calmer," he explained. "The cruelty, the viciousness felt like it had been exorcised from my body. Of course I kept up appearances when I was out with the lads, but when I hunted alone I fed only on those…deserving, I guess your mate Soliss would call them."

"All this time," Claire whispered, "you kept this from me." She was hurt not just by the act, but also from the fact that he had not trusted her enough to tell her.

"The worst is yet to come," Xavier said ominously. "You'll understand why I kept it from you."

Claire tensed and readjusted her posture as if she was bracing for an impact.

Xavier resumed. "I took her wallet, so I would know where to find her and the baby, and left her there in the graveyard. I had to leave; she was crying and it was hurting me. The sound of mortals crying used to be like fairground music to me, but not that night—not hers. She cried weakly for help, not loud enough to carry any distance, but as I walked from the graveyard I could hear her. I started running but I could still hear her. Even when I was miles away I could *still* hear her whimpered cries. I was over fifteen miles away when it finally stopped but I don't think it was the distance—I think she just stopped crying.

"I felt strange. When your physical state hasn't changed in a hundred years you really notice when something isn't right. I was scared; that wasn't normal either. I decided to go and see Galen—remember he was over, staying in Mussenden Temple?

"He was by himself, everyone was out feeding. I told him everything that had happened that night. He was shocked and didn't speak until he smoked half a spliff, then he said: 'You and I will go now and execute this mortal woman.' Well, I tried to explain the situation again but he wouldn't let me speak. He kept saying there were sacred traditions that had to be upheld. He wouldn't go into details; he said I was too immature to know the secrets of the elders. We started fighting."

"You raised your voice to Galen?" Claire asked in disbelief.

"No," Xavier said with a fearful intensity. "I staked him."

Chills crept up Claire's spine like icy talons. Everyone thought an agent of the Ministry had killed Galen, but it was Xavier. Xavier had killed the master of all vampires. It was inconceivable. If any vampire had found out, they would have tracked him down and inflicted the kind of revenge that only the darkest minds can dream up.

Xavier resumed. "After I buried the remains of Galen in the forest I ran to Turiz—thank fuck he couldn't read minds. I gave him a vague idea of what had happened; he seemed suspicious but cast a spell that would hide the events of that night, and all subsequent related thoughts, from all but me. Two nights later he confronted me. No one had seen Galen and I guess he had put two and two together and worked out what had happened. We fought and I overpowered him, but I couldn't bring myself to stake him. I remembered the look on Galen's face and the traitorous feeling in my own mind—I couldn't do it again. I tied him up. He was furious. He said he was going to make sure that we were tortured for the next century by every demon in the country".

"We?" Claire asked, surprised.

"Apparently, my bad is your bad too. So he had to die. I nailed him to the front door of the Ministry—they took care of him. I went back to Turiz's place. I'd watched him closely the

162

first time and managed to cast a spell that masked my association with Turiz, and the sticky end he had come to."

Claire felt a detached delirium, like she was back with the Maharishi and The Beatles and acid was coursing through her veins, making the unreal real. The events Xavier had described might happen in a dream or a movie but not in reality. But when she looked at the conviction in his eyes she knew that they had happened, and like a dream or movie she was powerless to intervene. Killing your own kind was unheard of; it was the worst crime imaginable among vampires. "I can't believe you killed two vampires," she said shaking her head.

"Two to start with," Xavier said, lowering his eyes to the floor.

"There were more?" Claire took a moment to prepare herself and nodded for him to continue.

"I watched her all during her pregnancy. It turned out she and her husband were members of the fuckin' Ministry—can you believe that? At one point I was sure she was going to have an abortion—I had a lot of people keeping track of her and I knew she had been to see the doctor about it. I don't know what stopped her in the end. During those months I tried to forget the guilt of what I had done and concentrate on the child we would soon have.

"The night before she gave birth, I was watching her again. Her husband had moved out—I think she told him that he wasn't the father—and her sister and mother had moved in. I was glad, her husband was an experienced hunter and taking the baby with him in the house would have been very difficult, and now it was just three unprepared women. I left that night somehow knowing that the child would be born the next day. I thought everything was going to work out."

"Who got in the way?" Claire asked nervously.

"Div and Nix," he answered sombrely.

Claire could almost put the rest of the story together herself when he said that. Div and Nix, the Bonnie and Clyde of the undead, were sick fucks by any standards. Most vampires wouldn't associate with them but everyone knew about them. Nix had been the most unsubtle vampire ever. He couldn't hold his rum and frequently passed out beside the body after a kill. This resulted in him being arrested a lot, and on more than one occasion he slaughtered dozens to gain his release before sunrise. On one fateful night, though, he was taken to an asylum instead of jail and there he met Div. She had been locked up in her teens for killing her parents and if she wasn't crazy before, after seven years in an asylum, she was now. Nix found her accidentally while he was making his escape. She was in the Handi-crafts Room and had one of the male nurses tied-up, stripped naked and she was inserting needles in various parts of his anatomy. The story also said she had cut his tongue out to stop him screaming before she began her pioneering work in acupuncture. Nix fell in love with her immediately and Made her that very night. Together, through the decades, their tastes became more and more sick. Every vampire in the land knew their particular penchant: killing newborn babies.

Xavier breathed in deeply and then released it. He was still furious that those two morons had ruined everything. He composed himself and continued, "When I got there the next night I could hear screaming. I ran up to the door and was able to enter without an invitation—I don't know how. I ran to the bedroom and found the four of them. Div had her arm around Carol's neck—that was her name by the way—and was making her watch while Nix beat and clawed at her mother. Div was dressed as a midwife—must have been how they got in. I ran in and grabbed Nix and threw him across the room. Div said they had no quarrel with me; they just wanted the baby. I told her that there was no way they were having the baby. Nix flew at me and I used his own momentum to throw him through the bedroom door. The door shattered and I picked up a pointed shard and put it to Nix's chest. I looked at Div and told her to get the fuck out or I'd stake him. She smiled that fuckin' insane smile of hers. For a moment I thought she was going to leave, then her fist burst through Carol's chest and she started laughing. I staked Nix—that shut her up. She didn't think I'd do it. But I did. And when she charged at me, I did again. I checked on Carol and her mother—tried to help them—but it was too late. The baby wasn't in the house; I guessed the sister had taken it. I took the remains of Div and Nix down to the beach and burned them and then cast another Masking Spell.

164

No one would give a fuck about those two but it could all have led back to Galen and Turiz and…the whole fuckin' mess".

Claire sat in silence for a moment, taking it all in. Then she said, "You never found the baby?"

"I looked for it for about six months, but it was gone. The sister had covered her tracks well and was lying low, wherever she was. I didn't even know it was a girl until you told me." He almost allowed a paternal grin to break on his face, but caught it just in time. He didn't know how Claire was going to react to all this and didn't want his smile to initiate a barrage of abuse.

Claire stood and walked slowly from him. She didn't know what to think. On one hand he had committed adultery and lied to her, but on the other, he'd done it for her, and she knew he genuinely had—it wasn't just a bullshit male excuse. She looked at his repentant eyes and knew she was going to forgive him, but she didn't want him to know that just yet. She would let him worry for a while; it would be a good deterrent if he ever thought of doing something that stupid again without consulting her.

"I'm going out for a while," she said.

Xavier got to his feet quickly. "It's less than an hour until sunrise."

He was worried—Bingo! She turned her head melodramatically and said, "I won't be long. I'll just take a quick fly and clear my head."

She levitated five feet in the air, but then began to slowly move towards the floor again. It was as if gravity had increased and was pushing her down again. She fought to fly but it gently pushed her feet back to the ground.

Xavier looked puzzled.

Claire was annoyed; a brilliant exit ruined. She quickly invented a reason so he wouldn't know the landing had been forced. "Can you get a paper?" she asked.

"Sure."

"OK then." She cautiously concentrated. If she failed to make it through the skylight this time she wouldn't be able to hide her diminishing strength from him. Her feet left the floor slowly at first; still pushing against that unseen force that had

165

grounded her, but this time she overcame it and flew gracefully out the skylight.

Claire gathered speed and flew quickly through the clean skies. The air was cold, but refreshing and cleansing. She flew faster and faster, intoxicated by the freedom and Xavier's revelation. If she hadn't been able to read his mind and know his motives were pure, she may have reacted suspiciously or violently, like mortal women do. But she had no need: Xavier loved her. Everything he had done, even though he had cocked it up like a professional, had ultimately been for her. She put her arms out like propellers and began twirling in the air with her eyes closed. She felt renewed and forgot all about the troubles that were waiting on the ground. She opened her eyes, looked down and saw the funeral parlour. She could get Tryx a coffin while she was here. She swooped down in circles like an eagle and landed outside the roller-door entrance that Kaaliz had had so much trouble with.

The door was up, which was unusual for this time of the morning. Although, undertakers were on twenty-four hour call so maybe someone had died during the night and they had to collect them. She looked into the large empty room and called, "Hello. Anna?"

A moment later a tall, thin man in his fifties appeared from the back room. His face was tired, unshaven, and his eyes bloodshot. "Can I help you?"

"I was looking for Anna." Claire could sense something, something the man was hiding, something that made her nervous, but it was unclear.

"She's in the back. Anna," he shouted over his shoulder. "I'm sure she wouldn't mind if you went on through." He smiled thinly.

Claire looked into his mind. She couldn't feel anything. Her ability had gone. Like her first attempt at levitating that evening, her gift had deserted her at the worst possible time. The undertaker's words had been cleverly chosen: he had as much as told her to go into the back room—but he hadn't invited her. Claire stood nervously at the threshold to the room, trying to size up the man's intentions.

"Aren't you going to go through?" he asked.

Again, no invitation.

"Or maybe you can't." He started towards her slowly. "Maybe you're a vampire."

Claire didn't need her ability to see the hate erupting on the man's face. She looked up to the sky like a child wanting to be lifted by a parent, but she remained on the ground. She couldn't get up into the air. She tried again. The man was almost beside her. He stopped and looked behind her and nodded. Claire spun around and was hit simultaneously by four crossbow bolts. One hit her upper left arm, another hit her right wrist, the third hit her in the stomach and the last ploughed into her chest, just above her right breast. She flew backward with the impacts and leaned against the invisible barrier that marked out the border of the undertaker's property. She hung there for a minute in pain, trying to gather the strength to run.

The undertaker appeared at her left shoulder and whispered, "By the way, you can come in."

The barrier disappeared and she fell backwards to the floor. Her four assassins, all undertakers, closed in on her. Claire looked up at their unforgiving faces, silently asking 'why?' They reached down, each seizing a different limb, and dragged her inside.

in the dark

Xavier was getting worried. Sunrise was only a few minutes away and Claire still hadn't returned. He had been out and got a newspaper (though he didn't know why she wanted it), and had been down to the basement and found a nice bottle of blood: a 1976 Claire and Xavier cocktail they had bottled after an excellent Pink Floyd concert. He hoped it would remind her of happier times and had uncorked it—to let it breath—and left it on the kitchen counter with two of the good Tyrone Crystal glasses. Since then he had been pacing the stage impatiently waiting for her.

He knew she was probably just doing it to make him sweat; if she had been truly angered by what he told her she would have let him know in no uncertain terms straight away. The fact that she hadn't gone completely batshit immediately was a good sign, more than a good sign; it was a positive endorsement of his actions...he hoped. He looked through the skylight at the fast approaching morning and was relieved when a shadow blocked the pre-dawn light as it came toward the opening. Xavier sank to his knees in a pose of supplication, which he hoped was just cute enough to put a smile on her face.

Kaaliz dropped from the skylight to the dance floor and stared at Xavier. "What the fuck are you doing?"

Xavier hurriedly got to his feet again and stared back at the gruff, discontented look on Kaaliz's face. "Nothing, I thought you were Claire." They stood in an uncomfortable silence like two distant relatives at a family reunion. They had nothing to say to each other and they both knew it. Xavier resorted to smalltalk. "So, did you have a good night?"

Kaaliz stared at him for a long time before answering, "No".

"What happened to your eyes? They look burnt."

"Nothing happened my eyes," Kaaliz said angrily.

Xavier suddenly thought of a good topic. "Oh, you haven't met Tryx, the latest addition to the family."

"You Made another vampire?" Kaaliz said with almost a child's jealousy in his voice.

Xavier tried to ignore his obvious disapproval and said, "Yeah, we…" His sentence ended as he felt Kaaliz plunder through his mind like a clumsy cat burglar grabbing indiscriminately for whatever he could find.

"You didn't mean to Make her; she was a kill that you fucked up," he said coldly.

Xavier stared back at his malevolent glare. There was something about Kaaliz that he didn't trust, something beyond what vampires called evil. He tried to disguise his thoughts, just in case Kaaliz took another look inside his head, and changed the tone of the conversation. "She's in there watching TV, why don't you go and say hello?"

"Where's Claire?" he asked (though by the tone it almost sounded like a demand).

"She's not back yet," Xavier answered.

They stared at each other in a silent stalemate.

The awkwardness ended as they felt the familiar chill of night leave. Even inside the Arcadia they could both feel the air change, the temperature rising a few degrees was all it took to instil menace and danger in the air. The sun was up, and Claire wasn't home.

Christian woke with a start, banging his head on the rear-view mirror, with the words still echoing in is head: SAVE HER CHRISTIAN. That phrase was becoming commonplace in his sub-conscious but it was the new phrase that it was being alternated with in the dream that gave him pause for thought: SAVE YOURSELF. He wiped the sweat from his forehead with his arm, and then the windscreen, which was thick with condensation. He had spent the whole night driving around the empty streets looking for vampire activity; looking for Xavier. He had ended up parking in the East Strand Car Park and the gentle lapping of the sea on the shore had put him to sleep. He felt his coat pocket and brought out the remains of last night's whiskey and downed what was left—just to take the dryness out of his mouth. He threw the bottle into the back of the van where it clinked loudly and then slid comfortably to rest among its own kind. Christian took a fresh bottle from the box behind his seat and put it in his pocket. He tried to comb his fingers through his greasy matted hair but gave up after two attempts and patted down the worst bits with a light coating of spittle instead. He decided he should go to the police station and see if there had been any developments at their end. He put his hand on the keys and then patted himself down, looking for a cigarette. He was out of them, but he was pleasantly surprised to find that someone (definitely not him) had left almost an inch on a butt in the ashtray. He lit it up and started the van—now he was ready to face the day.

Quigg hadn't arrived when he got there so he took the opportunity to go into the Officers Tea Room and helped himself to their coffee, biscuits and cigarettes (that he assumed were for everyone because they were in an unlocked locker).

Quigg burst into the room half an hour later and said, "The Ministry just got a call from Hughes Funeral Home— they've caught a vampire. A guy named Davis called us and said you'd want to get over there".

Christian leapt to his feet and ran to the door, roughly pushing Quigg with him. As the two of them marched up the corridor Quigg was babbling irrelevant details about when it was caught and how it was being restrained but Christian tuned her out; he didn't care. This vampire they had caught either *was* Xavier or it was someone who would tell him where Xavier was. As they neared the door, Audrey walked in wearing dark sunglasses.

"You're a hard man to find," she said with as much charm as her hangover would allow.

Christian was about to push her aside when he recognised her. "It's you, Angela."

Audrey smiled. "Well, yes and no." She held the book up and peered over the top of it at him. "Express delivery service, twenty-four…" Christian pushed past her and outside. Audrey shrugged at Quigg and said, "I guess he's not a morning person".

"No, he's just an ill-bred arsehole," Quigg replied.

Quigg and Audrey walked outside and watched Christian load his coat with equipment: two guns, one a .38, the other an electric stun gun; spare crossbow bolts; three wooden stakes; a crucifix and a large hunter's knife. He walked across the car park to the women with his crossbow in his right hand.

"Let's go," he demanded.

"Can I come?" Audrey asked hopefully.

Quigg answered quickly, "I don't think that's a good idea, Miss Wells. This could be very dangerous."

"Have you read that book?" Christian shouted from the other side of the car.

Audrey nodded. "Cover to cover. It was a very long journey, first there was the coach, then the ferry…"

"OK. Shut up. Get in," Christian barked impatiently.

"Warke," Quigg shouted to halt him. She walked quickly round to his side and whispered, "You can't take a civilian with you".

"She's read the book, she might know something that can help us." He scowled.

"But she could get…"

"Just shut the fuck up and drive the car." Christian stared at her until she complied.

Quigg stomped around to the driver's side and got in. Audrey, who felt like a child with rowing parents, got quietly into the back and Christian slammed his door last and lit a cigarette.

Quigg was furious as they drove to Coleraine. Cutting her down in front of that woman was humiliating enough but the smoking really ticked her off. She had given up recently (two months, nine days, eight hours and seven minutes ago, but who's counting?), and this dickhead reminded her why she smoked in the first place—so she could cope with people like him. How she wished for a smoke now. She would take the headaches, the bad breath, the phlegm and the constant cough for one sweet hit of that stress-relieving nicotine to be coursing through her bloodstream right now. That was it; she *needed* one. Of course there was a problem—she would have to ask *him* for a cigarette if she wanted one. It's a means to an end, she kept telling herself, until she had disguised a sufficient amount of hate as humility. She took a deep breath and turned to him. He put his mud-encrusted boots up on her pristine dashboard. Something resembling the volcanic intensity of Krakatoa erupted silently in Quigg's head.

"Are we going to see a vampire?" Audrey asked nervously.

Christian was inhaling and exhaling smoke like it was an Olympic event he was in training for. "You make it sound like we're going to have tea and scones. We're going to kill a vampire...and possibly torture it first."

Audrey was wary. "I've never seen anyone die before."

"And you still won't. This thing died a long time ago." Christian turned to her. "I'm just going to put it out of its misery." He turned to face forward again.

Audrey was questioning her participation in this outing. What he said was true but if this thing walked like a man and talked like a man, she would find it very hard to see it killed and believe they had done the right thing. She laid the book down on the seat beside her and slid forward in her seat. She was just about to express her reservations and desire to be dropped off *anywhere*, when Quigg spoke.

"OK, we're here." Quigg slowed to a stop outside the funeral parlour.

Christian removed the fresh bottle of whiskey from his coat and took a long drink. His face winced as the whiskey crept around his insides like fire.

Audrey was wringing her hands nervously. The sweat was making them slip and slide in each other's grasp. Her right knee was involuntarily jumping like an old-fashioned Morse code transmitter. She wanted to tell them that she wanted to leave. Christian and Quigg got out and closed their doors. Audrey heard them talking over the roof of the car but couldn't make out what they were saying. Were they discussing her? Her hesitation? Audrey's whole life had been about seeing beyond what everyone else saw. Sure, she had seen things she couldn't explain, but she knew that didn't automatically mean they were bona fide paranormal events. Inside this building was proof. Something few others would ever know truly existed, and even less would see in the flesh. She had to go in. She had to be brave. She got out of the car.

Christian turned to Audrey as her door closed. "Stay with Quigg," he commanded, and walked off towards the open roller-door.

Quigg spotted the fear on Audrey's face immediately. "Just stay close, you'll be fine." She smiled reassuringly and squeezed Audrey's arm lightly.

When they caught up with Christian inside, he was talking to the owner, who told him the vampire was in a back room where they kept coffins. The room had no windows and only one door.

"Show me," Christian said impatiently. The cocktail of whiskey and adrenaline was making him hyper-alert and his heart was beating madly trying to make sure that every part of his body felt it. He stopped outside the door and inhaled, held it, and exhaled. It did little to calm his trigger-happy senses, but he was ready. He took a bolt from the custom made pocket inside his coat and loaded his crossbow. He nodded at the undertaker and braced himself. The undertaker unlocked the door and jumped back quickly. Quigg tensed and moved a step back. Audrey discreetly moved herself behind Quigg. Christian opened the door a crack and pushed the tip of the crossbow through.

The room was dark. He edged forward, opening the door a little at a time until it would accommodate his skeletal physique. He carefully transferred his crossbow to his left hand and felt for the light switch on the wall. He clicked the button down. The darkness remained. He flicked the switch up and down several more times but to no avail. He looked back at the worried faces behind him. He swallowed hard and crept forward slowly.

The room was completely dark except for the triangle of light being thrown from the open door. Christian stayed in the light even though it wasn't sunlight and moved deeper into the room. A loud crackling noise shattered the stillness of the room and Christian tensed, awaiting attack. He looked down and saw he had tread on the glass from broken light bulbs that was scattered across the floor. He also spotted the four blood-tipped crossbow bolts that the vampire had been shot with ahead on the left. It obviously wasn't as badly hurt as the owner had assumed; and it was in here with him. The room was huge. There were too many dark places it could be hiding. He realised he would need a torch to search effectively and started to edge slowly towards the door.

Quigg and Audrey saw him backing up with his crossbow sweeping gently from side to side like the electronic needle on a radar screen. He got within five feet of the door when it slammed shut. The door was impacted loudly from the inside and the noises of a fight ensued. Quigg bounded forward and tried the door but it was secured. She stepped back and rammed it with her shoulder. It moved a little.

Inside the room, Christian was fighting in the dark. The vampire had dropped on him from above and knocked the crossbow from his hand. It had then left him floundering in the dark briefly before striking him squarely on the jaw with both feet. He lay on the ground, dazed, and the creature pounced on him. He grabbed it under the chin and held it away from his throat. His other hand groped frantically at the bulges in his coat until he found his electric stun gun. He flipped the switch and charged it. The vampire's hands closed around his throat and began to tighten. He heard the high-pitched beep of the stun gun, announcing it was ready to use. He buried the two pointed terminals in the vampire's neck and hit it with a full power discharge. The shock travelled through the vampire's neck, down to its shoulders, down its arms, into its hands, into Christian's neck, down to his shoulders and all through his body. The two of them screamed as all their muscles pulled taut. They held there for a few seconds, paralysed in a murderous pose like some piece of modern art that would win lots of awards. The stun gun finished its cycle and their bodies went limp. The vampire collapsed on top of Christian. He had no strength to move it. He heard intermittent thumps getting softer and softer as his consciousness slipped away.

The mood in the Arcadia was uneasy. None of them had gone to sleep and the three of them were in the living room— waiting. Xavier and Tryx sat on the sofa while Kaaliz leaned in the doorway.

"I'm sure she's all right, Xavier," Tryx said brightly.

"What the fuck would you know about it?" Kaaliz said angrily. "You're not even supposed to be. You're a fuckin' mistake, you stupid bitch. You think you know anything about what's going on?"

Tryx glared intently at him and said, "I know as much as you, Edwin."

Kaaliz raced across the room and grabbed her around the throat. Xavier leaped forward and separated the two of them, pushing Kaaliz back towards the door.

"Just cool it, you two," he shouted.

Kaaliz raised his finger and pointed at Tryx. "Don't you ever look at my thoughts again, you fuckin' whore," he screamed.

Xavier remained standing until he was sure Kaaliz wasn't going to attempt a second attack, then sat down. "We're all worried and stressed out but we have to stick together. Claire may have just been held up and couldn't make it back in time; she may have had to duck into someone's attic to wait out the day. But, if she didn't—if she's in trouble—when the sun goes down I want to know where to start looking. Do either of you have any ideas?" He looked at Kaaliz and found the same blankness as always. He turned to Tryx and saw her eyes widen.

"She said she was going to get me a coffin. Does that help?" She smiled at Xavier hopefully.

"I'm going to rest," Kaaliz said loudly and left.

Xavier and Tryx stared after him for a long time, each feeling uncomfortable by his very presence.

"There's something about him I really don't trust," Tryx said.

"I know what you mean," Xavier agreed.

Xavier told Tryx to go to his coffin and rest. He paced the Arcadia dance floor restlessly. When Claire hadn't returned before sunrise his first hope was that it was just part of her 'appreciate what you've got' ploy, but now he feared something worse had happened. She wouldn't have taken it to that extreme. Something was definitely wrong, though he would try to shield the new-Mades from it if he could.

The hours dragged listlessly forward. Outside it was one of the hottest days of the year so far. Xavier heard the joyous cries of children on the beach. Even the damp, cool air inside the Arcadia had become sticky and humid by late afternoon as the sun reached its peak in the sky. Xavier walked into the kitchen and threw water on his face. He pushed the excess from his forehead back into his hair. He was cooled for the moment and sat down at the kitchen table and looked at the newspaper he had bought.

The stories the local paper carried were not exactly the most groundbreaking journalistic exposés. The front page led with JOHN DEAR, a feelgood story about a farmer who had been using the same tractor, which he called John, for the last forty years. Below that story was a picture of a cute little girl on a beach pointing at her plastic bucket and spade, which she held aloft in her other hand. The Caption read: *Eight-year-old Julie-Ann Donaghy enjoys the recent spell of good weather.* "Good thing someone's enjoying it," Xavier said, wiping the sweat from his brow. The next article he looked at did catch his eye.

POLICE 'CONFIDENT' ABOUT CATCHING SEX ATTACKER

Police say the man responsible for the violent sexual assault that occurred on the night of Monday 24, is close to being apprehended. The victim, Anna Hughes, 26, was working late at her family owned funeral parlour in Coleraine. She left around 8:45 to collect dinner from a nearby Chinese restaurant. Police believe the assailant waited for her to leave, overpowered her, and dragged her to the park where she was found the following morning.

A spokesman for The Causeway Hospital reported her condition as 'critical' saying she will remain in the Intensive Care Unit until they are sure she is out of danger.

Her consultant, Doctor Andrew Fleck, said, "It is a testament to this young woman's strength and bravery that she is still alive. Her injuries *are* severe but I believe she has the courage and determination to make a full recovery in time."

The police have issued a warning to all young women in the area to exercise extreme caution when going out at night. They believe the attack was sexually motivated and urge young women in the area not to go out alone.

Sergeant Wilkins of Coleraine Police Station said, "We are working closely with the family and believe we have a solid line of enquiry to pursue. We are confident that we will apprehend this individual in less than forty-eight hours." Sergeant Wilkins would not comment on the rumours that other injuries inflicted on the victim were ritualistic in nature.

Xavier dropped the paper and remembered what Claire had said about Kaaliz trying to attack the girl when she got him his coffin. Her name was Anna, wasn't it? Tryx had said Claire had intended to get *her* a coffin. Xavier threw the table against the wall, breaking two of the legs off. He marched out to the stage.

Kaaliz had gone too far. Xavier didn't mind if Kaaliz endangered his own life—in fact, he kind of liked the idea of the arrogant fucker getting himself into something that he couldn't get out of—but he had led them to Claire. They could be torturing her; she could even be dead because this little fuckwit couldn't keep his dick in his trousers. Claire *would* have told Kaaliz not to mess around with undertakers—they know too much about the dead. Kaaliz had obviously thought he knew better—what a fuckin' moron.

Xavier reached Kaaliz's coffin and threw off the lid. Kaaliz still slept soundly. Xavier grabbed him around the neck and hurled him at the back wall of the stage. Kaaliz only woke up a second before his head smashed into the concrete wall. Xavier strode towards him with not a fraction of his anger sated and grabbed his lapels and fired him to the other end of Arcadia. Kaaliz's back slammed hard against the wall and he dropped to the ground, coughing and trying to catch his breath. Xavier walked towards him.

"Do you know what you've done?" Xavier screamed. He felt Kaaliz's clumsy mind-reading again.

"Bitch deserved it," he said, spitting blood from his mouth. "Your trouble is you're not true to what you are. Why don't you follow your nature—that's all I'm doing. Embrace the evil."

"You're a sick fuck, and it's nothing to do with you being a vampire. You don't care, do you?"

"About Claire?" He got to his feet, brushed himself down and shrugged. "Of course I do. I was looking forward to spending a lot of time with her. That's why she Made me you know—to replace you. She said you were worse than fuckin' useless."

Rage exploded inside Xavier and he had an overwhelming desire to rid the Earth of Kaaliz. Then, the tingling began in his chest. No, he thought, Not now. He stopped his pursuit of Kaaliz, waiting expectantly for the gentle tickling to show its nasty side. Pain shot up his left leg and he fell forward to the ground. His head pulled backwards as a hundred short pains attacked his spine in just a few seconds. He felt like he was being whipped with electricity by an unrelenting attacker.

Kaaliz stared at him in wonder until the attack subsided.

Xavier groaned on the floor and felt Kaaliz again inside his head.

"You're dying," Kaaliz said. A smile broke on his face as he watched Xavier try to lift himself to his feet again. "You're even more pathetic than I thought. Is it any wonder Claire needs another man?"

Xavier used all his fury as fuel to get up. He charged the last few feet and lunged at Kaaliz's head. Kaaliz flew upwards quickly. Xavier slammed into the wall and Kaaliz dropped down hard on his shoulders, knocking him to the ground. Kaaliz stepped forward and began kicking Xavier as hard as he could. Kaaliz landed several really hard kicks to his head before Xavier raised his arms and prevented him getting a good shot, and then he moved to his torso. Xavier hadn't the strength to repel him and eventually his arms fell to his side and he passed out. Kaaliz continued kicking him until his legs tired. Then he

178

flew up to a safe place in the eaves of the roof to wait for the sun to go down. He looked down at the bloody mess he had left Xavier in and chuckled quietly to himself.

heroes & monsters

Christian was stirring. Quigg walked over and kneeled before him. She had succeeded, with the undertaker's help, in breaking the door down and found Christian and the vampire unconscious. She had dragged Christian into a small office just down the hall and laid him on the floor with a couple of coffin pillows beneath his head, then she sat the vampire in a sturdy metal chair and handcuffed her wrists and ankles around the frame.

The undertaker had left around dinnertime after receiving a phone call telling him that his daughter's condition had taken a turn for the worse. Quigg and Audrey had sat in silence for most of that afternoon, watching the vampire closely and occasionally checking on Christian.

Quigg couldn't believe this pretty young woman was a bloodthirsty killer. She looked so innocent, pure and, with her head leaning limply over the back of the chair, helpless. Quigg was reluctant to do anything without consulting Christian, which was why she had been waiting for him to come round. Of course now that he was coming round she wondered what he was going to find to complain about when he woke up. Surely she had done something wrong in his bizarre estimation. She had been wondering for the last hour what it might be: Not killing the vampire? Not calling the Ministry for back up? Not feeding him whiskey intravenously? It could be any, or all, of the above.

The good thing about him being in a heap on the floor was that she was able to take his cigarettes and go to the car to satisfy her longing. She hadn't enjoyed the cigarette at all. It was always the same when she hadn't smoked in a while; the first one was really nasty. But, like all smokers who give up long enough to regain use of their taste buds, she knew that it would get better. After the first pack or so, that's when she would start to enjoy it again. Until then she would just have to endure the foul taste of cigarettes.

Christian turned his head sharply from side to side. Quigg leaned in and was about to put a calming hand on his forehead when his eyes shot open and his fist flew at her face. Quigg fell backwards holding her nose.

"What the fuck are you doing?" she yelled.

Christian looked around quickly at his surroundings and slowly remembered where he was. "Oh. Shit. Sorry."

Blood was now pouring through Quigg's fingers and down her face and blouse. Christian took a hanky from his pocket and offered it to her. Quigg looked at the hanky. She imagined it had been white once, but now it hung in that limbo between grey and brown and was decorated with examples of congealed bodily fluids that she really didn't want to know about. She took her own hanky from her pocket and held it below her nose as she put her head back. Christian stuffed his rag back in his pocket.

"Where's the vamp?" Christian asked when he thought he had shown an adequate amount of concern.

"In the same room where she was. I've handcuffed her to a chair," Quigg answered though the veil of the hanky.

"She? It's female?" he asked, disappointed.

"I'm afraid so."

Christian glanced at his watch. "Look at the time. Why the fuck did you let me sleep so long? When the sun goes down they'll come looking for her. For fuck's sake, Quigg!" Christian rushed out of the room.

Quigg lay back against the wall and pinched the now crooked bridge of her nose. She had known he was going to find something to shout about, and maybe he was even right, but did he have to be such an arsehole about it? She looked out the window and saw the first hints of orange in the sky as the sun made its way to the horizon. Suddenly the reality of her situation hit her. Maybe he was right. Quigg got to her feet and ran after Christian.

She was less than a minute behind him but when she got there it seemed he had already given up on the diplomatic approach and was punching the female vampire repeatedly in the face. Audrey turned as Quigg ran into the room. She looked scared. Quigg could hardly blame her; this felt wrong. She didn't know if it was because the vampire was a woman, or if it was the way Christian seemed to be enjoying pounding her face, but it felt wrong.

"Where is he?" Christian screamed, and landed another punch to the vampire's mouth before she could answer.

"Don't worry," the vampire said, dribbling blood from her mouth. "He'll find you."

Christian hit her again and again. Quigg was growing more and more unsure about Christian's methods. The vampire's face was swollen and bleeding everywhere now. Quigg noticed the vampire's make-up was running off her face on the back of blood streams. She looked closer and realised it wasn't just blood...tears. The vampire was crying. The *woman* was crying. Christian kept on punching. Quigg glanced over at Audrey, who was almost in tears herself. Quigg thought again, This is wrong.

"Xavier, are you all right?"

Xavier slowly came out of the haze and saw Tryx looking down at him with a worried expression on her face. He sat up quickly. "Where's Kaaliz?"

"He's gone," she replied. "He even took his coffin with him." She pointed at the empty stage. "Did he do this to you?"

Xavier got unsteadily to his feet. "Yes, he did, and he'll pay for it, but right now we have to help Claire...if she's still alive." He ran to the ladder that led to the skylight and paused at its base. "Wait here," he said and ran to the kitchen.

Xavier opened the newspaper to page two and scanned down the first column: the obituaries. He found what he was looking for and turned to exit. The wine-bottle of blood was still sitting on the counter, still breathing and flanked on either side by wineglasses. He stared at the glistening little glass bowls perched atop their thin stalks and wondered if they would ever serve the purpose that they were intended for. Would he and Claire ever taste pleasure again? He ran back out to Tryx and the two of them climbed out of the Arcadia.

They dropped the last few feet to the concrete ground and Xavier said, "We have to get to Coleraine as quickly as possible. If we run we'll be there in no time."

Tryx nodded and disappeared in a blur. Xavier had only gone about two hundred yards when he grabbed his chest and started wheezing. Tryx re-appeared beside him in a flash.

"Are you all right?" she asked.

"No, I don't think I am," he answered.

Tryx walked behind him and scooped him up in her arms. "Hold on tight," she said, smiling.

They took off at high speed—not as fast as she could have gone unhindered, but fast enough to get them to Coleraine in less than five minutes. Xavier steered her in the direction of the funeral parlour and they stopped at the end of the street, where she let him down. They stared at the back entrance.

"A big roller-door wide open, this should be easy," Tryx said confidently.

"A big roller-door that we can't enter," Xavier said thoughtfully. "Let's try the front door, and pray for an inexperienced salesman."

"You sound like a man with a plan," she said excitedly.

They walked around to the street entrance. "You do the talking; women are less threatening. Push the buzzer and say *we* are here to view Eleanor Cassidy. It's very important you say *we*, it means that one invitation will get us both in."

"Who's Eleanor Cassidy?" Tryx asked.

"Somebody who died; her obituary was in the paper—this is the funeral home that's burying her tomorrow."

Tryx smiled at Xavier's smart plan and approached the door. Xavier looked up and down the empty streets and gave Tryx a nod to proceed. Tryx pushed the buzzer and waited. The seconds passed slowly. She turned to Xavier nervously; his expression was intense and focussed on the door. Tryx turned back and raised her finger to the buzzer. Just as she was about to press the plastic square again, a voice crackled on the intercom.

"Hello, can I help you?" an elderly woman said.

Tryx stepped close to the small meshed panel and said, "Hello, we're here to view Eleanor Cassidy."

"Are you relatives?" the voice crackled.

Xavier whispered in Tryx's ear, "Grandmother."

"Grandmother," Tryx said quickly. "That is...she was mine."

The intercom was silent for a long time. Too long. Tryx stared at Xavier with a 'what do I do?' look on her face.

"OK," the voice crackled, "you can come in."

Xavier stepped forward and opened the door as the buzz sounded the release of the lock. He and Tryx stepped inside and closed the door. The old woman waddled slowly from a side office with the help of a cane, pushing her glasses from the tip of her nose to the bridge. The old woman squinted, looking them up and down suspiciously.

Tryx smiled nervously. "Terrible business, tragic really."

The old woman swung her cane towards a red button on the wall. Tryx raced forward and grabbed the cane before it connected. She took the cane from the old woman and bundled her gently back into her office amidst a hail of profanities that Tryx thought a woman that age shouldn't know. Xavier joined Tryx.

"We don't have much time," he said. He took Tryx's arm and the two of them ran forward. "Let's find Claire and get the hell out of here."

The first room they came upon was the viewing room. They took a quick look inside and were about to leave when Tryx pointed to an open coffin with the name Cassidy on the trolley. She was a huge African woman with skin like black leather.

"What do you think gave us away?" Tryx smirked.

They ran down the corridor to the back entrance. Xavier heard tiny, unwilling screams—it was Claire. He ran faster towards the sound, getting more and more angry. When he found its source he didn't stop. He sized up the situation en route: Claire was being held hostage and beaten—solution: take a hostage of his own and get them to release her. He ran into the middle of the scene and grabbed a slim, blonde girl around the throat before anyone saw him and backed himself against a wall.

Quigg was the first to spot him and yelled, "Warke!"

Christian ran behind Claire and caught her around the throat, then pulled a .38 revolver from his coat and held it to Claire's head.

Quigg pulled her gun and aimed at Xavier.

"You," Christian said with unrestrained hate.

"Have we met?" Xavier asked.

"He was Carol's husband," Claire mumbled.

Xavier wanted to hold Claire. She looked so badly hurt. "Well, I am sorry about that, but..."

"Shut up! I don't want your pity, I want your blood," Christian screamed. He pushed the barrel of his gun into Claire's temple. "I know this won't kill her but it will turn her into a very attractive egg-plant."

"OK," Xavier said calmly, "Now think about this. It's a stalemate situation. You let her go and I'll let your friend go, OK?"

"Not a chance," Christian said coldly. "You've probably killed thousands over the years—if she has to die, at least she'll be the last. Either way, you're not leaving here alive."

The blonde girl was shaking in his arms. Xavier suddenly recognised her as the girl he had got drunk with at the bar the previous night. He doubted if she could see him through her tears but he wished she could. He wanted to give her a wink and let her know that he wasn't going to hurt her, but she was crying too hard. This guy really wanted him dead and it seemed to Xavier that he didn't care who got killed in the process. Xavier had nothing to bargain with. He would have to try to bluff his way out of this.

"OK," Xavier said, "What if I Make this one and even up the odds a little. How would you feel about that?"

Christian's face dropped. "I won't let you do that," he whispered.

"Then, you let her go," Xavier shouted.

They stared into each other's eyes, looking for a sign of weakness. Neither made a move for a long time, and then Christian slowly cocked the hammer on his gun. Xavier bit his wrist, letting the blood trickle down his arm and held it close to the girl's frantically twitching head. Their eyes locked again.

Christian took the gun away from Claire's head. Xavier relaxed a little and lowered his wrist. Christian turned the gun quickly and shot Audrey in the stomach. The girl fell limp in Xavier's arms.

Quigg spun around and aimed her gun at Christian. "Drop it," she said loudly.

"Stay out of this," Christian replied calmly. He turned his attention back to Xavier. "I told you I wouldn't let you do it."

"Drop that fucking gun now, Warke," Quigg screamed.

Claire started jerking wildly in her seat, screaming through gritted teeth.

"She's still alive," Xavier interjected. "If you get her to the hospital she might be all right."

"Don't listen to him," Christian snarled.

"No, Warke," she said. "He wins this time. Let that one go."

"The fuck I will!" Christian swung his gun around to Quigg. She pulled the trigger first and hit him in the right shoulder. Christian flew backwards and hit the wall. He slid to the ground and slumped over.

Claire's screaming stopped and she fell limply forward.

Quigg turned to Xavier and said, "Do we have trust?"

Xavier nodded at her gun. Quigg put it on the ground and kicked it away from her. Quigg took her keys from her pocket and threw them to Xavier.

"Tryx?" he shouted.

Tryx had been standing in the corridor waiting to make a surprise attack when Xavier and Claire needed it. She had almost rushed in a couple of times but thought better of it. She walked in and Xavier threw her the keys. Tryx ran over and unlocked Claire and helped her to her feet.

"Go," Xavier ordered. Claire put her arm around Tryx's shoulders and the two of them made for the back door. Xavier laid Audrey down and gestured Quigg to come over. She walked towards him bravely and kneeled at Audrey's side. "Keep pressure on it. I don't think you should move her—best call an ambulance, OK?"

Quigg nodded. Xavier ran from the room.

When Xavier got outside Tryx had used Quigg's keys to open her car and was putting Claire in the back seat.

Xavier ran to her side. "Can you drive?"

"Sure, where are we going?" Tryx answered.

"Anywhere but here," Xavier said and jumped in the back beside Claire. Tryx closed the door after him, jumped in the driver's seat and brought the engine to life. She slammed her foot on the accelerator, sped across the funeral parlour's flowerbeds and jumped the car onto the main road. Tryx quickly raced through the streets of Coleraine, her vampire reflexes judging every bend and junction for maximum speed, and out into the countryside.

Quigg had been holding both her hands firmly to Audrey's wound. She thought the flow had lessened a little and carefully removed her hands. There was so much blood. It was dripping off her fingers and running up her arms. She had to phone an ambulance now, while it was under control. Audrey had passed out. Her skin was pale and glistening with a layer of cold sweat, but it wasn't too late—it couldn't be.

"What the fuck have you done?" Christian said, clambering to his feet. He emerged from the shadows holding his gun before him. "You let him get away, you dumb bitch."

"Warke, this woman needs an ambulance, we have to help her. We can find him again," she said, trying to calm the murderous look in his eyes.

"You don't see the bigger picture," he said quietly. "Can you even guess how many people you've killed by letting him go? You're nearly as bad as him."

Quigg started to ease her hand towards the other gun she had in her ankle holster. She felt blood begin to trickle from her broken nose again, but she ignored it. Warke had definitely lost the plot and she would have to take him in. Quigg didn't care what secret agency he worked for; he was going to pay for shooting this woman. "Christian, calm down."

"Calm down? You just fuckin' shot me," he screamed. "I think I have a right to be upset."

Quigg pulled her trouser leg up and lunged for her gun. Christian squeezed his trigger. The recoil hurt his shoulder and the loud crack echoed in his ears. The thin smoke cleared and he saw Quigg doubled over with a bullet hole in the top of her head.

He had just killed a police officer. Even his status as an agent of The Ministry wouldn't get him out of this. They would hunt him down for this. He instinctively took his whiskey from his pocket and drank until he felt the burning inside. The alcohol cleared his thinking. He had to make sure he caught up with Xavier before the police caught up with him. If he was going to jail; he was going there knowing Xavier was dead. Christian glanced at the two women lying in a pool of red on the floor but did not allow sorrow or regret to distract him. He put his gun in his right pocket, his whiskey in his left, and ran out into the night.

just desserts

Lynda poked cautiously at the food on her plate, half-expecting some of it to poke back at her. The shrivelled-up potatoes were stuck firm to the plate by the thin, dry layer of gravy (which she had first thought was the pattern on the plate), next to them sat four green beans (that were brown), and finally a nondescript meat product with its ends curled up rocked gently back and forth in the centre of the plate. She fought briefly with the meat, trying to puncture its surface, but realised she was out-classed and gave up. She put the cover back on her plate, moved it to the side and replaced it with the dessert bowl. They couldn't destroy dessert, could they? After all, with most desserts it was just a matter of taking it out of the fridge or freezer and putting it in a bowl. Surely even the catering staff of the NHS could manage that. Lynda was not hoping for miracles all the same. She held out little hope that cheesecake, Key Lime Pie or Banoffee waited under the metal hood covering her bowl, but strawberry or vanilla ice-cream wouldn't be asking too much—would it? She lifted the cover and revealed two pear-halves floating in their own juice.

A young male Nursing Auxiliary walked past the foot of her bed and she asked, "Hey, what's the deal with this crap—you trying to kill us to free-up beds?"

The young man shook his head and walked on.

Lynda pushed her tray-trolley to one side and lay back in bed. She was thinking about leaving, getting out of here and going to a real restaurant—a place where desserts were delicious and green beans were green.

Her left eye was throbbing painfully. She was sure it was from all the clumsy poking around the doctors had done searching for splinters rather than the impact of the perfume bottle itself. A few painkillers wouldn't go amiss, she thought. But when she had made the same request earlier in the afternoon she was told curtly that she'd get them when they were given to her. Lynda also learned that looking at the nurses with painful longing did nothing to speed up the dispensing process. She finally relented to the truth that the older patients already knew: nurses have their own (frequently

189

interrupted) schedule, and you can only hope your medication will reach you before you die.

The doctor had been amazed with her recovery on his rounds. They had had to remove several slivers of glass from her left eye the night before and now she could see with it, although it was a little blurred. The doctor had said it was the fastest recovery he had ever seen and he was going to come back later to get a full medical history. That was another reason Lynda was anxious to leave. *If the doctor only knew what my father was and why I healed so fast,* she thought, *he might think twice about keeping me here any longer than necessary.*

She turned to the bed next to her as she heard a pleasured moan. The bed had its curtains pulled all the way around and Lynda hadn't seen its occupant. Another satisfied moan escaped through the thin curtain.

Lynda's curiosity could refrain no longer. "If you've got a man in there..."

The moaning stopped abruptly.

"...send him out for some fucking food, will you?" Lynda said.

Lynda heard a shuffling and then the curtain opened a crack.

A pretty girl with crazy red hair and chocolate smeared on her lips, poked her head out quickly and said, "Come on over...and bring a fork." With that she ducked back behind her curtain.

Lynda didn't have to be asked twice—that girl had chocolate. She took the unused fork from her tray and tiptoed over to the next bed.

What she found when she stepped inside the curtain was more than she could have dreamed of—the girl had a Black Forest Gateau on her lap. "I'm Chloe," she said happily. "Tuck in."

"Where did you get this?" Lynda asked.

"Smile at the right porter and you can get anything—I'm getting some fried chicken smuggled in tonight. Sit down."

Lynda sat on the edge of the bed and felt the hard plaster cast below the sheet. "Broken leg, eh?" She scoffed down a large piece of cake. "How did you do that?"

"A car hit me," Chloe quickly said.

"Really?" Lynda replied. "I didn't think many vampires drove."

Chloe stopped mid-chew. She put her fork down where the missing wedge of cake had been. She chewed slowly and swallowed. "How did you know?"

Lynda was making up for a 'healthy' breakfast and no dinner by gorging on the sumptuous dessert. She stopped briefly and wiped her mouth. "I'm a dhampir. You probably don't know what that means, but let's just say what you did last night, I do most nights." She resumed shovelling the cake into her mouth.

"How do you know that?" Chloe said, amazed by the girl's candour and relaxed attitude.

Lynda tapped her temple with the blunt end of her fork. "Psychic FM, one of the perks of the job, so they tell me." She licked the remaining cream from the prongs of the fork and looked at Chloe. "You easily freaked?"

Chloe noticed a playful look in her eyes and smiled. "Not so far."

Lynda held her fork up in front of her face and stared at it intently. Chloe watched in awe as the first prong on the fork bent inwards, the second outwards, the third inwards and the forth curled into a circle. Lynda smiled and said, "Pretty cool, eh?" She then stared at the fork again and the prongs bent back to their original position. Lynda raised her eyebrows quickly twice. "It's magic," she said and plunged the fork back into the cake again. "So who got you, Xavier?"

Chloe was gob-smacked for a few seconds and then got her composure back. She was pleasantly surprised by the girl's attitude and relished the opportunity of talking to someone. "No," she said, shaking her head. "I found these other two; Kaaliz and...George."

"Did you dust them?"

"I got George, but Kaaliz got me—as you can see," she said, with an embarrassed smile.

"Never mind," Lynda said, swallowing. The mass of cake went reluctantly down her throat like a duvet down a laundry chute. Eventually she cleared it and continued. "A vamp smashed a bottle of Chanel in my face last night. That's what all these cuts around my eyes are."

"You've healed really quickly," Chloe said.

"Yeah, another perk of the job. See my feet?" Lynda grabbed her foot and showed Chloe the weatherworn sole. "I haven't worn footwear in two years. I've run over rocks, stones, broken glass, even hot coals—and never got a cut or a blister."

Chloe touched the sole of her foot. It was as tough as leather but smooth to the touch. "That's pretty impressive."

Lynda tucked her foot under her again. "I'm getting out of here tonight, whether *they* like it or not. Do you have any idea where Xavier might be?"

Chloe shook her head. "No, I'm kind of new to this."

Lynda leaned forward. "Listen, I don't know if you believe in such things or not, but I had a dream—it's what brought me here in the first place. I saw where he was sleeping. Now, I've been checking all along the coast of Portstewart, Castlerock and even as far as Ballycastle but I can't find this building."

"What does it look like?" Chloe asked. Lynda had more than proven her psychic abilities and the least she could do was to help her find this Xavier guy.

"It's right on the sea-front. Its windows and doors are bricked up. It's painted a light shade of blue. There's a little beach beside it. It's a big, square building."

Chloe thought hard but the only place that sounded like was the Arcadia. Surely Lynda would have passed the Arcadia if she had been in Portrush at all, but then she hadn't mentioned being in Portrush. It had to be it. She was convinced now and told Lynda, "The Arcadia, at the end of Causeway Street in Portrush".

Lynda's eyes widened. "Are you sure?"

Chloe nodded.

The curtains were cast open and the Ward Sister shouted, "A-ha."

Chloe and Lynda both jumped and then smiled when they saw it was just the Sister.

"I don't believe this was on the menu tonight," she bellowed, staring at the offending dessert. "You two…"

192

"Sister," a young nurse cried from behind, "We have a problem in the ICU."

"Can't you handle it?" Sister barked back gruffly.

"No, I don't think so, Sister," the nurse replied. "It's the girl..." The nurse rubbed her neck at the Sister. Her code was wasted—Chloe and Lynda both understood what she was saying as well. Chloe sat up sharply but pain spiked up her leg and pushed her back into her pillows.

Lynda put her hand on Chloe's arm and said, "Don't worry, I'll take care of it." She got up and marched towards the door with the Sister's objections merely buzzing like flies in the background.

Lynda ran up the corridor to the ICU. Half a dozen visitors were standing outside looking worried. "What's going on," she said to no one in particular.

The three men in the group were all struck dumb and fixated on Lynda. They were silently praising the man, because it really had to be a man, who invented hospital gowns. Making them so short was inspired, but making them from that thin, almost see-through material, was a stroke of genius. And just when you thought he couldn't improve his design he had come up with the opening at the back that you just couldn't close. The three men agreed: it was a work of art.

An old woman with a furry coat and hat stepped forward and said, "These two men in black suits just came in and threw us all out, and then threw the nurses out and locked the doors".

"Stand back," Lynda commanded. The ejected visitors shuffled back a few feet from the door. Lynda threw several high kicks at the doors.

The gown inventor should have received a knighthood.

The lock on the doors yielded and they swung inwards sharply. Lynda strode forward to the two suspicious looking characters leaning over a badly beaten girl's bed. One of them pulled a gun and pointed it at Lynda; the other pulled a small electronic device about the size of a calculator and pointed it at her. Their expressions were blank, hidden behind mirrored sunglasses, but Lynda could tell they were young, in their mid-twenties maybe, and inexperienced.

"OK, guys," Lynda shouted, "What are you doing?"

The one with the electronic gizmo poked furiously at it and said to his partner, "She's a dhampir." His partner lowered his gun and walked to Lynda.

"We are Ministry Intelligence agents, here on official business. This woman was raped by a New Threat, we needed to gather information and a DNA sample from her person."

Lynda looked into his face but saw only herself, reflected in his glasses. She relaxed a little and asked, "Who was it?"

Gizmo-boy spoke up. "New Threat is named Kaaliz, possibly sired by Zigatta-Kaaliz, who is also from this area."

"Nice to see you guys don't take the whole secrecy thing too seriously," Lynda said.

Gun-boy said, "Section twelve, paragraph four, subsection F; Information may be shared with any persons with previous vampire experience, if imparting that information will increase the chances of neutralising the Threat".

"Have you heard of Kaaliz?" Gizmo-boy asked.

Lynda nodded. "There's a girl down the hall, she ran into Kaaliz last night. Maybe you should talk to her."

The two men looked at each other in shock. Gizmo-boy said, "We weren't aware there was an incident last night".

"We have to contain these vampires before they spread," Gun-boy said sternly. There was confidence in his voice, but Lynda thought she also heard fear. "Our latest intelligence suggests there may be as many as five in this area now."

Both agents were too young to have been active in the eighties when the vampire problem was at its height. Lynda's aunt had told her that vampires numbered in the hundreds back then, and this guy was wetting his pants over five?

"Four," Lynda corrected. "Chloe dusted one last night."

"Take us to Chloe," Gizmo-boy said, the sweat breaking on his face as the situation became ever more real.

Lynda sized them up quickly and decided they were more like number crunchers than warriors. She doubted they would last five minutes in a fight, despite their gadgets and guns. Interviewing Chloe would keep them busy long enough for her to get out there and end this thing once and for all. "This way," she said and gestured them to the door. They walked ahead of her and Lynda glanced back at the girl in the bed. Her face was covered in blood-soaked bandages. She was asleep, probably exhausted by her interrogation. She looked so fragile. Lynda whispered to the sleeping girl, "I'll get him. This'll never happen again".

Lynda turned and walked quickly to get ahead of the agents and lead them to Chloe. They walked out the door and down the hall in triangle formation. All three stared dead ahead, not meeting any of the silent, quizzical looks from nurses, patients and visitors.

The trio marched into the ward and Lynda said, "Chloe, these nameless Ministry-types would like to talk to you about last night." The two agents veered left to Chloe's bed. Chloe looked worried. "It's OK; they know. You can tell them everything." Chloe nodded and relaxed. Lynda didn't stop and walked on to her own bedside cabinet and brought out her dress (that the hospital had kindly laundered). She pulled her gown over her head (and noticed how easily it came off—good design).

Gizmo-boy froze at the sight of her perfect, rounded breasts. He was reminded of the first time that he had seen a real ghost; other agents had told him they existed and were incredibly exciting to look at, but he didn't believe it until he saw for himself. He had heard the same thing about women's breasts—people he knew had seen them and been impressed—however he had always held a healthy scepticism. But he wasn't too proud to admit when he was wrong. The legend was dispelled forever as the truth defied gravity before his eyes. The unsubstantiated rumours and sightings were true. Breasts were a very real phenomenon that deserved further investigation. He made a mental note to try to study them up-close in their natural environment in his spare time. But, like a shaky amateur video clip of a ghost, this sighting was maddeningly brief. All too soon her dress dropped down and shrouded the mystery once again.

Lynda ignored the stares of Gizmo-boy and walked to the other end of the ward, giving Chloe a thankful nod as she passed. She stopped at the drug-dispensing trolley and pulled the door until the lock gave. The Sister stepped forward but when Lynda threw a freezing glance at her, she stopped in her tracks. Lynda grabbed a bottle of painkillers and walked out.

The whole ward was silent until the patter of Lynda's bare feet on the hard floor faded in the distance.

Gizmo-boy's device squealed in his hand and everyone jumped. He read the display and turned to his colleague. "One of the sentry-sensors has registered a Threat."

The two agents got to their feet in unison. Gun-boy turned to Chloe and said, "We'll have to document your experience at a later date."

Chloe shrugged. "OK."

The two agents marched out.

Although Xavier had said nothing, Tryx chose the picnic area in Castleroe Forest to hide out. She drove the car through the police tape that cordoned off the area and came to a stop at the river's edge. Xavier looked outside and remembered the killing of the couple that had, in some way, been a precursor to all of this madness. His attention returned to the inside of the car as Tryx flipped on the interior light and turned to check on Claire. She looked badly hurt. Xavier had been doing his best to clean off some of the blood but in the light he saw how poor his efforts had been. Blood was trickling out of her face in at least a dozen places and the wounds weren't closing. Claire was unconscious but Xavier didn't want to talk in front of her anyway. He nodded Tryx to meet him outside and gently slid Claire's head from off his lap and onto the seat. He edged sideways and got out.

Tryx had already lit a cigarette (from the pack she found on the dashboard) by the time he gently closed the door.

"I didn't know you smoked," he said.

"I gave it up years ago," she replied, looking across the river. "But I guess I was still a smoker at heart. I only gave up because of the HIV—I didn't need another shortcut to my grave." She exhaled with delight. "I bided my time, and now I'm me again." She turned and saw Xavier's worried face. She glanced at the car. "Is she going to be all right?"

"I don't know. Her wounds aren't closing, or they're closing too slowly for me to see. Either way, we need to do something to help her."

Tryx puffed quickly. "Anything you need—just ask."

"OK," Xavier said. "Do you know the magic shop in town?"

Tryx nodded.

"I need you to go there and get a few things: Bay leaves, Myrrh and Olive leaves. Can you remember that or should I write it down?"

"No, it's OK, I'll remember. What are you going to do with those things?"

"It's a very potent medicine I can make with those things and a few others I have back at the Arcadia. Hopefully it will speed up Claire's healing."

Tryx flicked her cigarette into the river. "I'll be back in no time."

"Tryx," Xavier said softly, "there will probably be a lot of police and Ministry hunters out tonight—be careful."

Tryx appreciated the concern and grinned. "I will be." She disappeared in a blur. Xavier stared after her for a moment, as a parent must do watching their child go off to war. He hoped she would be careful.

Tryx looked cautiously at the end of the street where Triple Hex, the magic shop, sat in darkness. Sirens were screaming in the distance and she imagined every police officer in the area was looking for them. She was nervous about approaching the shop; surely this would be an obvious place for the police or the Ministry to stake out—it was the only magic shop in the area. Plus, she felt something—a new emotion that she couldn't define. It was almost like paranoia without the doubt. She wished she had more experience with her vampire traits. The street was eerily quiet, maybe too quiet, but she had to get the herbs to help Claire. She would go in fast and grab what she needed; there was no time to disable the alarm. Hopefully, by the time anyone responded she would be long gone. The air was still, as if the world was holding its breath in expectation. Tryx raced at the shop and didn't stop. As she neared the door she turned her shoulder towards it and used her incredible speed to smash it open.

By the time the alarm had started to squeal, Tryx was already behind the counter and had found the Olive leaves. She looked behind her at the shattered door hanging off its hinges. No commandos dressed in black were rushing in...yet. She turned back and scanned the little wooden drawers that housed all the shop's herbal reserves and found the Bay leaves. She turned again to the doorway with 'that' feeling growing again, but it was still empty, as was the street outside. She quickly examined all the drawer labels from top to bottom but couldn't see Myrrh anywhere. She punched the cupboard under the counter and defeated its lock. The cupboard was filled with books on Black magic, Curses and Hexes. Behind them were the more potent elements for spell-casting: bat-wings, chicken blood, frog's eyes, crocodile tears and…Myrrh. Tryx grabbed it quickly. She thought it seemed out of place with the other macabre ingredients but it didn't matter. She stuffed the herbs into her pocket and made her way to the door. Again 'that' feeling warned her. Only this time it was stronger, almost physically pushing her away from the door. Tryx looked to the back of the shop—there was no back door. This was the only way out. She braced herself and walked out.

The street was empty but 'that' feeling inside her was practically screaming as loud as the alarm. She had to get out of there fast—she didn't know why but she knew she was in danger. She turned to run and was dropped on from above. Her assailant landed on her back and pushed her face-first into the ground. Tryx expected the familiar click of handcuffs to close around her wrists, but instead she was grabbed by the hair and her forehead slammed into the hard, brick ground. Her assailant got up and Tryx wearily rolled herself onto her back and looked up. Kaaliz was smiling down at her.

"Hey, bitch," he said. "Doing some shopping?"

Tryx tried to form a coherent sentence but failed. Her head was dizzy. "Help…Claire…help."

Kaaliz grabbed her by the throat and hurled her across the street. She slammed hard into a metal security door and dropped to the ground.

"I guess Freud might call this sibling rivalry," he said, walking towards her twitching body. "But I really don't believe all that shit—I just don't fuckin' like you." He leaned down, grabbed her hair and threw her back across the street. Tryx flew through the shop window of More Than Gardens and landed awkwardly on a pile of wrought-iron furniture that was displayed in the window. The glass cut her badly and she was bleeding and aching all over.

Kaaliz opened his hand and looked at the clump of Tryx's hair that had remained in his hand when he threw her. He smelled it deeply and then blew it off his palm to the ground. "Only the strong survive, whore," he shouted, approaching the shattered window. "And you just haven't got what it takes...not by a long way."

Tryx leaped from the shop window and struck Kaaliz in the face with a spade. He staggered backward about ten feet and tried to hold his balance. Tryx marched towards him, blood smudging her face like war paint, and raised the spade behind her head. Kaaliz had just got his composure back when the sharp edge of the spade plunged into his stomach. He bent over, gripping his mid-section and feeling the blood slipping over his fingers, but he was determined not to fall down. Tryx positioned the spade under his head and brought it up hard on his face. Several of his teeth flew into the air and he finally fell backwards to the ground.

"I should kill you," she screamed. "But I think I'll leave that pleasure for Xavier." She dropped the spade to the ground.

Kaaliz gently touched the jagged shards protruding from his gums. "You fuckin' bitch. Look what you've done to my teeth!"

Tryx leaned down and faced him. "If you have any sense you'll leave here. Go far, far away and don't come back." She stared into his cold eyes with an unflinching resolve, then turned and walked way from him.

Kaaliz was badly hurt. All his instincts told him to lie where he was until he felt better, but his rage was a lot more powerful than his instinct. That whore wasn't getting away from him. With the little strength he had left he pulled himself to his feet and lifted the spade. He hovered just above the ground and flew at Tryx. He broke the spade in two like it was a pencil. Tryx heard the snap and spun around. Kaaliz dropped the metal part of the spade and pointed the splintered end at Tryx and charged.

Tryx tried to jump out of the way but he was too fast. The shaft of the spade plunged into her chest and punctured her heart. Quickly the world closed in around her and then there was nothing.

Kaaliz fell to the ground beside Tryx. The spade handle protruded from her chest like a grave marker. He was surprised by how quickly she had died and vowed not to let the same thing happen to him. He ran his hands over the wound in his belly. It was deep, but the blood of a few teenage lovers would close it in no time. But how was he going to bite them? That crazy whore had smashed his teeth. He raised himself up to a sitting position and looked at the shop window of More Than Gardens. A hand-held pitchfork with three sharp prongs caught his eye. That would be a fun way to get the blood flowing. Just like old times, he thought. He got to his feet and hobbled over to the window, holding his stomach as he went.

As he was about to pick up the fork he felt two sharp pricks in his back. He turned his head and saw two metal spikes buried in his back with wires leading from them. He followed the wires back fifteen feet and saw they were attached to a small electric gizmo in the hand of a young guy in a black suit and mirrored glasses. Another young guy, dressed exactly the same but pointing a gun at Kaaliz, stood beside him.

The guy lowered his gun and said, "Hit him."

Kaaliz was almost amused and a smile cracked his face.

The other guy activated his gizmo and Kaaliz was hit at once with enough voltage to drop a rhino. But it didn't drop him, not immediately anyway; his arms shot out to his sides and shook violently, his legs trembled beneath him but did not give way until the device had been turned off. Kaaliz fell to the ground, just barely conscious, but unable to move any part of his body.

The agents approached him cautiously and manacled his hands and feet. Kaaliz watched with drowsy interest as one of them put Tryx's body in a plastic bag and zipped it up while the other ran off and came back driving a large black van. The driver of the van got out, looked all around and opened one side of the van's back doors. The two of them carried Tryx's body and put it in the back of the van.

Kaaliz wondered why they hadn't killed him. He weakly shouted, "What are you going to do to me?"

The van's driver opened the other back door of the van and revealed a cage. The two of them walked over to Kaaliz and bent down.

Gizmo-boy whispered, "We've got a nice lab waiting for you. They're going to cut you, burn you, poison you and God knows what else until they find out what makes you tick".

Panic hit Kaaliz and he tried to struggle but his muscles were still limp from the shock. One of the men took his feet and the other took his shoulders and they marched him over to the van and threw him in the cage. He lay curled in the foetal position on the metal floor of the cage. He heard the door of the cage being locked behind him and then the two doors of the van closed, and he was in darkness. The internal light came on briefly as the two agents got into the front of the van. Kaaliz looked at the black plastic bag that held Tryx's body and wished he could swap places.

blue building

Christian leapt through a gap in the hedge and into the ditch as the police car approached. The wound on his shoulder sent a spike of pain through his body and he gripped it hard. The bullet had gone straight through and he had burned both ends closed with his lighter. He looked inside his shirt and saw a small trickle of red in the centre of the blackened patch of flesh, but it was not enough to worry about. As the police car drew closer he put his hand on the gun—just in case he might have to use it. The car passed without slowing and he relaxed his grip. He was up to his ankles in mud and the hedge had scratched his face in several places, but none of that concerned him. He had to think. He sat down on the muddy embankment and put his hand in his pocket, swapping the gun for his whiskey. He drank several measures worth and replaced the cap. Where would Xavier go? It was the same question he had been asking himself for the last twenty years but now he *had* to answer it; time, and probably the majority of the police force, was against him.

He was making his way down the Coleraine-to-Portrush road. It had almost been instinct to head for Portrush, but when he thought about it he decided it was just because that was the place he had encountered the two female vampires. He peered through the hedge as another pair of lights appeared in the distance. He crouched down and watched the dim circles of light grow in intensity until they filled his whole field of vision, then just as quickly they became red squares shrinking in the other direction. He wasn't even going to try to hitch—he didn't know who he could trust. The road was dark again in both directions. He climbed through the hedge and back out onto the road.

He resumed walking as fast as he could. He squeezed again at his coat pockets, on the off chance that he had forgotten to check one and he really did have cigarettes on him. He was sure he had, but another search still yielded nothing.

He had been walking about a mile when a car appeared quickly behind him. He hadn't seen it coming because of a sharp corner that he had just passed. He turned just as the headlights momentarily lit him up like a flash from a camera.

Even though it was brief it seemed it was long enough for him to be recognised. The car skidded to a stop in the middle of the road. Christian spotted the blue lights spinning on the car's roof and jumped the wire fence at the side of the road and scurried into nearby bushes. He sat there breathing hard and listening to the subtle, natural sounds of the night. A loud click was out of place, as was the following slam. They're out of the car, he thought. His hand moved to his gun and pulled it out. He heard a light thud—someone landing on the grass after jumping the fence. His breathing quickened until he was almost hyperventilating. He took a deep breath and jumped to his feet. He fired the four remaining rounds in the vague direction of the last noise he had heard. Three of the flashes from the gun illuminated a figure close to him, but the fourth did not. He had got them. He blinked his eyes a few times until they adjusted to the darkness and then he made out the slowly squirming form of his pursuer on the ground. He walked over quickly, keeping the empty gun trained on them the whole time.

He slowed as he got closer, and stopped completely when he saw the face of his supposed hunter. "Lynda?" he said in disbelief.

"Yes it's me, you stupid fucker," she screamed. "What the fuck did you shoot me for?"

Christian looked at the bullet hole on her left shoulder and was glad it wasn't anywhere more fatal. "Well I…Why are you driving a police car?"

"It's not a police car," she whined, rising to a sitting posture. "It's the Doctor-on-call car. I nicked it from the hospital."

Christian looked over and saw that the bright fluorescent letters painted up the side of the car confirmed what she said.

"I'm fine, by the way," Lynda shouted sarcastically.

"Oh, yes, are you?"

Lynda shook her head. "Just help me back to the car. There should be something in there to stem the blood flow."

Christian put the gun away and helped Lynda over the fence and back to the driver's seat of the car. There were two large bottles of Irish Spring Water on the passenger seat.

Christian unscrewed the top of one of them and used it to clean Lynda's wound.

"Go easy with that," Lynda said, wincing with pain. "I bought that water at the hospital shop and got the chaplain to bless it before I left—they could come in handy."

He found some bandages and gave her wound a competent field dressing (his Ministry training wasn't completely forgotten). He considered giving his own wound a sterile dressing but decided it would waste too much time. "That should hold you over until you get to the hospital," he said.

"I'm not going to the hospital. I know where Xavier is."

"Where?" Christian said urgently.

Lynda considered her answer carefully. "I can't drive with my arm like this. I'll show you where if you take me along, and I don't want to hear anything about me being too..."

"Fine," Christian interrupted. He helped her shuffle over to the passenger seat. He slammed the door and turned the key. The engine roared at first and then calmed to a purr. "Where?" he asked again.

Lynda looked at the desperation in his face and was hesitant, but then she thought, If I'd been chasing this vamp for twenty years, maybe my nerves would be shot too. "Portrush," she said.

The car raced forwards, slamming Lynda back against her seat and reopening the wound on her shoulder. She gritted her teeth to cage the pain and looked at the flat square bandage under the strap of her dress. She saw a dot of blood had made its way through the thick cotton. The dot soon grew to the size of a penny and she turned away from it, praying it would be all right until she, or Christian, took care of Xavier. She had to take her mind off it, so she asked him a question that had been bugging her. "If you thought I was the police, why did you shoot at me?" He was silent for a long time—so long she thought he wasn't going to answer, but then he did.

"Xavier got away in a police car earlier on tonight," he answered. That much was true at least, he thought. She doesn't need to know the rest—not now.

Lynda wasn't satisfied with his answer. When he was dressing her wound she had noticed his coat was loaded with stakes and an electric stun gun, so why would he use a handgun, the most ineffectual weapon in his possession? Her psychic powers would usually give her at least an intuitive feeling on whether or not to believe him but she wasn't getting anything. She turned and looked out the window at the darkened countryside speeding past, trying not to notice the bloodstain on the bandage had doubled in size.

Xavier had soaked his handkerchief in the river before getting back into the car. He slid himself under Claire's head and shoulders without waking her and cleaned the blood from her face as best as he could. For all the blood on her face, the cuts were mostly superficial. He was more concerned about the wounds he found on her body that looked like arrow-holes. The amount of blood that had dried on her dress suggested that she was even more badly hurt than she looked.

When he was sure that everything had stopped bleeding he sat there for a long time just looking at her chest rising and falling. She was strong. She would survive—she had to. He couldn't imagine life without her. He brushed her sticky, blood-matted hair from her face and secured it behind her ears. Through the swelling, bruises and blood he still saw the girl he had fallen in love with one hundred and seven years ago.

Claire stirred and opened her eyes. "Are we safe?"

"For the moment. Tryx has gone to get the ingredients for Trellinar." He leaned close to her. "You're going to be all right."

Tears ran from her eyes. "I don't think so, Xavier. When he shot that girl back at the funeral parlour I felt the pain. Like before, only much worse; I thought I was going to die there and then."

Xavier tried to think of an argument that she would believe, but he knew there wasn't one. "You have to hold on," he said desperately. "Maybe the Trellinar will help with whatever else is wrong with us too."

Claire smiled and ran a finger down his cheek. "We're dying, Xavier. I don't think anything can save us."

Xavier lifted his wrist and picked off the scab that had formed. "Here, drink from me."

Claire looked at the blood trickling down his arm. "No, I can't. I feel really bad, Xavier." She turned quickly from him and vomited on the floor of the car. She rolled back and looked at him with tears running horizontally across her left cheek. "It's too late," she whispered.

Xavier wiped the sick from her mouth and said, "You rest. Tryx will be back soon and you'll be OK. I've got a bottle of the '76 breathing in the kitchen for us—remember the Floyd gig? Yeah, you're going to be all right. You'll see." He watched her eyes reluctantly close. He feared they might never open again and went back to watching her breathing.

It was a good deal later that he noticed Claire shuffling uncomfortably in her sleep. He put his hand under her and found she was lying on a book: *The Dead and the Living* by Ezra Moorcroft. He opened the book and began to read.

Xavier was engrossed in the book for most of the night. Occasionally he would look outside for signs of Tryx or glance at Claire, but he quickly returned to reading. The book was revealing things to him about vampires that he had never heard before. He had read the chapter on The Dhampir and understood now why Tryx and Claire had been attacked and how they had been overpowered. He also understood why Galen had been so adamant about terminating the pregnancy.

The chapter he was now in the middle of was entitled Diseases of the Dead. Xavier had found their symptoms and was reading as fast as he could, looking for a cure. He looked at the sky and realised he didn't have time to finish before the sun came up. He put the book down and opened the car door lightly.

Claire woke up and groggily said, "What's going on?"

"I don't think Tryx is coming back," he answered.

"We have to go and look for her," Claire said, trying to sit up.

"We can't; there isn't enough time before sunrise." Xavier slid out of the car and laid Claire's head gently down on the seat. "Maybe she's back at the Arcadia waiting for us," he said hopefully. He closed the door gently.

Claire had lost her power to read minds but she could still read her husband. Xavier didn't believe what he had just said; he thought Tryx was dead, and though she was reluctant to admit it, Claire knew he was probably right.

Xavier got into the driver's seat and closed the door. It had been a long time since he had driven a motorised carriage. He had learned when they first came out but the novelty had worn off sometime during the First World War and he hadn't driven since—the principle was probably still the same though. He started the car and put it in reverse. He released the clutch and the car hopped backwards in fits and starts. Claire was sick again on the back seat. "Sorry, honey, I'm a little out of practice," he said. He managed to get the car into first gear (with some grinding), and drove out to the road. When he got to the higher gears less control was needed and he stopped gripping the steering wheel like a fearful adolescent having his first lesson. He took the back roads, which, although harder to negotiate, were empty at this time of the morning and far from any roadblocks that might be up.

His thoughts returned to what he had been reading in the book. Even though he hadn't finished the chapter, he thought he knew where it was going. Could it be possible? As soon as they got back to the safety of home he would read it all. He felt something inside him that he hadn't felt for a long time— hope—and he couldn't stop a slight smile breaking on his face. But he refused to let himself get carried away with the notion so he didn't tell Claire. He would tell her when he was sure…and only then.

Xavier looked back at Claire; her skin was pale and sweaty, and sick was dribbling from her mouth. He put his foot down and the car received a sudden jolt of acceleration. They raced on towards Portrush.

becoming

Xavier parked halfway down Causeway Street and carried Claire. It would be safer to park further away—if someone found the car during the day it wouldn't take much deduction to figure out where they were—but he hadn't time before sunrise. Claire was drowsy and barely awake. When they got to the base of the Arcadia it took all her strength to hold on around his neck as he piggybacked her up the wall. Sweat was running down Xavier's face as he climbed. He was weak but this was the last obstacle; he could rest when they got inside. As he neared the skylight he realised he had forgotten to lift the book from the back seat of the car. He threw a quick glance at the sky—he didn't have time to go and get it; sunrise was imminent.

He took Claire by the arms and lowered her inside. The catwalk was still a few feet below at his maximum stretch. "Are you ready, honey?"

"Go on," she said bravely. Xavier released his grip and she dropped onto the catwalk and fell on her back against the rusty metal floor. The amount of blood she had lost during the night had made her so fragile that a little fall like that actually hurt. She looked up and saw Xavier descending the rope quickly to her side.

"Are you all right?"

Claire nodded. "Just get me to my coffin and I'll be fine."

Xavier put her arm around his shoulders and walked her over to the ladder. She again put her arms around his neck and he piggybacked her down.

Xavier was panting hard at the base of the ladder so Claire took her weight off him and managed to stand upright on her own. Xavier stretched his tired arms and said, "Well...home, sweet...home".

"You might have tidied if you were expecting company," Lynda said, appearing from stage-left.

Christian appeared from stage-right. "It doesn't matter— I'm going to make a bigger mess." He spun a stake in his hand and threw it to Lynda, who snapped it from the air. Christian reached into his coat and drew another.

208

Xavier looked at Claire and then all around the room. They were trapped. "That's the Slayer that knocked the shit out of me a few nights ago," he whispered.

"No, it isn't," Claire said. "That's your daughter."

Xavier looked closely at the girl: his daughter, standing unsteadily before him, clutching a stake. She was beautiful, or at least she would be on any normal day. But right now her wound was giving her the same complexion as her father and her posture was frail and tired. He was worried first, and that surprised him. She was hurt and he felt he should help her, even though she was holding a stake undoubtedly meant for his heart. Then he felt pride. She was strong and courageous; she had come here to kill him even though she was under the weather. A lot of other girls would have phoned in sick—but not his daughter. He looked into her dark, abused eyes that had seen too much.

Lynda swayed from side to side then blinked rapidly and fell to the ground. Xavier stepped forward instinctively.

Christian pulled out his electric stun gun and shouted, "Ah! Stay right where you are."

"But she needs help," Xavier replied.

Christian glanced over at Lynda. "She'll be fine until I deal with you two." Christian walked towards them, stake in one hand, stun gun in the other.

Xavier turned to Claire. She shook her head slowly and tears welled up in her eyes. She looked so sick and her expression said she just wanted the pain to be over. Xavier nodded, took her hand and turned forward like he was bravely facing a firing squad. Claire's hand went limp in his and she slumped to the ground. He bent down to her and Christian kicked him in the face, sending him ten feet backwards and into a wall.

Xavier coughed and spat blood from his mouth. He saw Christian coming towards him again and pleaded, "She's dying, just let me be with her at the end."

"No," Christian said immediately. "In fact, I think I'll beat the shit out of you, tie you up and make you watch as I torture her for every last second of her life."

"Thanks, but no thanks," Claire said.

Christian turned his head and saw her on the ground behind him. Claire snapped open the blade of Tryx's penknife and drove it hard into his foot. He screamed as it ripped through his shoe, cracked bones and snapped ligaments. He threw his weapons from him, dropped down and pulled it out quickly. He stood up, adjusting his weight to rest on his good foot and grabbed Claire around the throat. He pulled her up to his eye-level and slammed her back against the wall.

Claire was close to passing out but something caught her eye. She looked behind Christian, to where Lynda was lying. "What the...?"

Christian swung his head round instinctively and saw a mist above Lynda. He released his grasp on Claire and she slid down to the ground. The mist became denser, forming into the shape of a woman. Christian was in awe at the sight. Subtle colours followed, giving the figure its final characteristics. Christian recognised his wife immediately. "Carol?" he said softly.

The apparition was speaking but no words were audible. Her face was twisted, like she was struggling to maintain her appearance. Her mouth moved, silently screaming.

Christian listened intently until the words slowly faded in.

"Help her, Christian!" the ghost screamed.

The cries got louder. The same phrase being repeated, getting louder every time. Christian covered his ears and screamed, "No!"

He turned his back on the ghost and glared at Claire, slumped on the floor. "You're doing this. You're inside my head. Get out of my head," he screamed and kicked her in the chest with his injured foot. The kick hurt him as much as her and he fell against the wall. He got his breath back and turned to where Lynda lay—the ghost was gone. "Your mind tricks don't work on me, vampire. You'll fuckin' pay for that with your blood," he spat.

Xavier charged at him and punched him as hard as he could on the nose. Christian's eyes filled up and he swung blindly until he caught Xavier a punch on the side of the head. The two of them stood, crouched over, holding their faces. Xavier regained his senses first and charged again. This time he grabbed Christian off the floor and pushed him through to

210

the kitchen. Christian's back slammed against the wall and Xavier punched wildly at his face and torso.

Christian put his hand in his pocket and felt the bottle of spring water. Xavier spotted the bullet hole on his shoulder and began punching it. Christian ignored the pain and concentrated on undoing the bottle-top slowly with one hand. The cap eventually fell from the bottle and Christian pulled it up and squeezed it in Xavier's face. The water covered Xavier's head and he screamed and dropped to the floor with his hands over his face.

Xavier was on the ground before he realised that the water wasn't burning him. He had been conditioned for so long to fear someone throwing water at him that it had been reflex to expect pain. But there was no pain. He screamed to keep up the façade that Christian had got the better of him. He peeked through his fingers and saw Christian finish off a bottle of whiskey and toss it aside.

"OK, fucko," Christian said, blinking the last of the tears from his eyes. "I'm gonna show you pain like you never imagined."

Xavier scanned the kitchen from behind his fingers and false whimpers, looking for a weapon. He spied the broken table; the legs were quite heavy, maybe he could use one of them as a club. Could he reach them before this psycho caught him? He would have to—it was his only chance. He turned to see exactly where Christian was.

Christian was leaning on the counter. "You're going to be screaming in pain for the rest of your worthless life, vampire— you think about that." Christian laughed and absently reached back and grabbed the bottle of '76. He took a long drink from it.

Xavier's hands dropped from his face and his eyes widened. Christian stopped drinking and looked at the bottle, then at Xavier's shocked expression.

Terror washed over Christian. "That was... blood?" he whispered.

"I'm sorry," Xavier said softly.

"I have to kill you before it..." Christian's body began to spasm and he dropped to the floor. He felt the vampire blood inside him, creeping like snakes around his insides. His

211

screams echoed around the concrete walls and became less and less like human noises and more like a helpless animal caught in a trap.

Xavier got to his feet and ran out past the writhing, screaming thing on the floor that was not yet vampire, but was no longer man. He reached Claire and saw she was still breathing. He shook her gently. "Claire? Can you hear me?"

Claire's eyes opened. "Xavier?"

"Can you walk? We have to go," he said, glancing over his shoulder at the kitchen.

"Where can we go?" she asked weakly.

"Do you trust me, Claire?" he asked.

She smiled thinly and ran a finger down his cheek. "With my life."

"Good," he said quickly, "because that's just what I'm asking you to do." He lifted her up and carried her to the ladder. She held on around his shoulders as he climbed up the rungs.

Christian was screaming like a newborn in the kitchen.

Xavier got to the top and helped her across the catwalk to the skylight. The square opening, illuminated by light, evoked a fear akin to standing before the gateway to hell. Claire threw him a scared, questioning look.

"I'm almost positive about this," he said, resting her against the handrail.

Xavier grabbed the rope and climbed up. He was almost at the top. He saw the sunlight picking out the frayed strands on the rope. He reached up and put his hand into the light. His hand felt warm and he almost pulled it back, but it was gentle warmth—and it didn't burst into flames. He put his other hand above it and it was bathed in harmless sunshine too.

Christian's screaming stopped.

Xavier turned to Claire and outstretched his hand. "Quickly!" he shouted.

Claire grabbed his hand and Xavier pulled her up to his level. She climbed onto his back and held on. Xavier resumed climbing and crept out onto the roof of the Arcadia and collapsed. They were both exhausted and breathing heavily. Then a sight they had not seen in over a century momentarily distracted them from their ailments. Xavier put his arm around

Claire and they watched the remainder of the sun rise. Tears were running down both their faces, not only from the emotion but also from eyes that hadn't been exposed to such brightness in a long time.

"Are you all right here a minute?" he asked.

Claire nodded and asked, "Why?"

Xavier looked at the skylight. "I can't leave her down there with him."

Claire looked proud. "Go. Get your daughter."

Xavier kissed her and climbed inside the skylight.

When he dropped onto the catwalk he looked down. Lynda was still lying in the same place, though a pool of blood had formed around her left shoulder. He looked around but couldn't see Christian. He ran across the catwalk and slid down the ladder. He hit the floor and spun quickly—still no sign of him. He walked cautiously towards Lynda, trying not to make a sound. When he got close to her she looked as though she might already be dead. He crouched down beside her and pushed two fingers beneath her jawbone until he felt her pulse. He looked around again at the dark, suspiciously empty, room. He lifted Lynda and threw her over his shoulder and made his way slowly to the ladder. Christian's stun gun was still lying on the floor. Xavier nervously bent down, picked it up and put it in his pocket. He continued to the ladder.

The ladder creaked loudly as he climbed but still no vampire emerged. He reached the top of the ladder and ran across the catwalk. "Claire?" he whispered at the opening.

Claire appeared and reached her hands down.

Xavier climbed onto the handrail of the catwalk and passed his unconscious daughter to his wife. Claire took her under the arms and Xavier pushed from below until she was out. Xavier reached for the rope to climb out. From the darkness below Christian flew at full speed and punched him in the face. Xavier fell backwards onto the metal walkway. Christian landed on the catwalk so hard that the whole structure shook.

Xavier looked at the young, fresh-faced vampire that stood before him. Christian was now in perfect physical shape and probably had both he *and* Claire's powers. Christian grabbed Xavier and lifted him above his head then slammed him down hard on the metal floor face-first. Xavier lay there aching all over. Christian paced back and forth quietly humming the melody of *Shine On You Crazy Diamond*, waiting for his quarry to regain his strength. Xavier cradled his throbbing ribs and rolled over. He stared up at Christian.

"Funny how things change, isn't it?" Christian said, strolling proudly across the catwalk and back again. "I always said if this happened to me I'd walk right outside into the sunlight."

"Do you want a hand up?" Xavier said.

Christian smiled. "No. I don't think so. I've never felt so fuckin' alive," he screamed. He calmed and looked down at Xavier. "So you understand why I can't have you or your bitch daughter telling Ministry types where I am."

Xavier pulled himself slowly to his feet using the rope. "I won't say a word, promise," he said sarcastically.

"That's very comforting. Of course, I *will* have to kill you all to make sure you keep your word." Christian opened his arms and grabbed the handrail on either side of him. "Come on, I'll even give you first punch, anywhere you want."

Xavier jumped up onto the rope. He pulled the stun gun from his pocket and pressed the terminals to the metal handrail and turned it on.

Christian howled as the electricity invaded his body. The muscles in his hands contracted, gripping the handrail tighter. Xavier held onto the rope until the stun gun had delivered its full charge. Christian dropped to his knees and peeled his charred hands from the rail. He glared at Xavier. Xavier shinned up the rope. Claire grabbed his hands at the top and helped him the last few feet. Xavier was almost out when he felt a hand tighten around his ankle. He turned and saw Christian weakly hanging on.

"You'll never escape me," Christian rasped. "As soon as night falls, you're fuckin' dead—all of you."

Xavier quickly raised his ankle, grabbed Christian's hand and pulled him upwards. The sun hit Christian's face and it began to blister. He screamed and tried to wriggle free. Claire reached in and grabbed his other arm. Christian pulled backwards hard and noticed how weak Claire was. He pulled her wrist close to his mouth. Xavier pulled as hard as he could but Claire's wrist still edged closer to Christian's fangs.

"Christian."

Christian turned and saw the apparition of his wife standing on the catwalk, looking up at him. Tears were running down her face.

Christian focussed on her as if he was trying to remember a dream. His grip relaxed.

The ghost's gaze moved to Xavier and she said, "Save her."

Xavier shot a glance at Claire. The two of them heaved together and pulled Christian outside.

Christian rolled down the pitched roof squealing. He burst into flames just before he fell off the edge. He tried to fly back upwards for a few seconds until his heart exploded out of his chest. He dropped to the ground where his cries stopped abruptly and the fire consumed him.

By the time Xavier had carried Lynda down, there was nothing but ashes where he had fallen. Xavier turned to check on Claire's progress. She was only ten feet from the ground when she blacked out and fell. Xavier laid Lynda down and ran to her side.

new lives

Claire awoke slowly. Her eyes were not used to such brightness and all she could see was white light all around her. She heard soft, comforting voices but couldn't see the kindly souls offering her reassurance. Even though she was disoriented and didn't recognise where she was, she felt strangely safe. This was where she belonged. The overwhelming brightness began to lessen. As her eyes adjusted, shapes began to form in the whiteness surrounding her. Squares and rectangles came slowly into focus until they formed familiar objects: a cabinet, a bed, a chair and a window. The window held her attention because of a dark figure silhouetted against it, staring out.

"Xavier?" she asked weakly.

He turned immediately. "You're awake." He walked over and sat in the chair. "Here, put these on." He handed her a pair of sunglasses and she put them on.

The sunglasses relaxed her eyes. She looked at the room again and realised she was in hospital. It was a private room with its own en suite bathroom and TV. She looked at the window again. The blinds were open and a shaft of sunlight fell on her bed. She reached cautiously forward and put her hand into the beam. The warmth gently tickled the hairs on her hand and she smiled.

Claire turned to Xavier and said, "How?"

Xavier leaned forward and held her hand in the sunlight. "In a nutshell—we're human."

Claire brought his hand close to her face and pressed it to her cheek. His skin was warm. "I don't understand any of this, Xavier."

Xavier gently drew back his hand and produced a book from under the bed. "Well, thanks to Mr Moorcroft, I do." He opened the book and flipped to near the back. "This guy spent his whole life researching all the myths and legends around vampires, trying to find a scientific explanation for their cause. He came to the conclusion that vampirism is a supernatural virus. When you drink a vampire's blood you contract that virus, but—and here's the big but—the virus attacks the humanity or the soul, whatever you want to call it. With the soul disabled, the more primal instincts are given free reign to control the individual's actions. There is that symbiosis of good and evil like we thought, but they don't reside in separate bodies, they both exist in the same body—everyone's body. The struggle isn't a global one; it's a personal one. When the vampire virus invades the host it gives evil the upper hand.

"But, Moorcroft documents a case recorded in the sixteenth century where a vampire reverted back to his human form. It was a monk that was Made, and he ran amok in a local village for nearly a month before he was stopped. It was the other members of his Order who finally caught him, but they didn't kill him. They chained him up in the basement and preached to him daily until his soul began to fight the virus. Moorcroft likened it to taking a course of medicine; eventually the monk was cured.

"Moorcroft's theory was: if the soul was strong, filled with love and compassion, that it could build immunity to, and eventually destroy, the virus."

"You think that's what happened to us?" Claire asked.

Xavier nodded. "We just weren't quite as pure as the monk, so where it took him eight weeks to conquer the virus, it took us over a hundred years."

"So all those pains we felt," Claire said, intrigued, "that was our humanity trying to resurface?"

Xavier nodded. "And now it has."

Claire lay back in her pillow, trying to take it all in. They were human. She would never have to kill again. A calm came upon her that she had either never known or had forgotten long ago.

"You want to see something?" Xavier said, grinning.

Claire nodded and he reached into the bedside cabinet and held a mirror up in front of her face. Claire hadn't seen her reflection in one hundred and seven years. Xavier got up and tilted the blinds as she took her sunglasses off. Apart from the bruising and swelling, which wasn't as bad as she thought it would be, she looked the same as she had in 1894. Tears of joy trickled down her face.

"Remember her?"

"I do now," she replied. She touched the scabs on her face. "How long have I been here?"

"This is the sixth day. I brought you and Lynda here when you fainted outside the Arcadia. She was in Intensive Care at the start but they moved her to the ward a couple of days ago."

Claire whispered, "She's not out there, in the same ward as me, is she?"

"No," Xavier answered, "She doesn't even know how she got here. We're the only ones who know what really happened. I heard on TV that the police are conducting a nation-wide manhunt for that Christian Warke guy over the deaths of those two women at the funeral parlour."

"Two," Claire said. "He must have killed the police-woman after we left." A chill went up her spine as she thought about it.

"I've looked in on that undertaker's daughter, Anna, a few times. She's out of Intensive Care but she's in a wheelchair. I don't know if it's permanent."

"What a mess," she said softly. "What about Lynda, is she OK?" she asked anxiously.

"Yeah. I've been checking on her discreetly. She's going to be all right, but she doesn't know we're here and I think we should leave it that way."

Claire relaxed. "I guess we were just lucky they didn't put us in beds next to each other."

"Not really luck. You see," he whispered, "you're in the gynaecology ward."

"Why?" she asked quickly.

Xavier smiled. "Because you're pregnant."

"Fuck off!" she almost screamed with delight. She smiled and put a hand on her stomach and gently rubbed, trying to feel her child.

"That's just what I said. When I brought you in they were quite worried about that arrow hole in your stomach, so they ran their scans and whatever and then this doctor came out and reassured me that the baby was going to be fine."

Claire chuckled happily. "And did you take it like a man?"

"Oh yeah, I threw up on him," Xavier said.

Claire laughed loudly; pushing tears from her eyes, and put her other hand on her stomach. She laced her fingers together and thought of the baby growing beneath them. "What did he say to that?"

"He said, 'Never mind, Mr Ford, you wouldn't be human if you weren't a little nervous about parenthood.' He was the first person to call me human—I kinda liked it."

"Mr Ford?"

"Yes, and you're Mrs Ford. It was the first thing I could think of when they asked for a name—I got it off the car we drove here in."

Claire exhaled deeply. She took Xavier's hand. "What do we do now?" Panic hit her hard. "Where do we live? What do we do for money?"

"Relax," Xavier said confidently, "I have it all worked out. I went back to the Arcadia and got all my 'crap'—I think you called it—from the basement."

"It is crap," she said with a smile.

"It may be crap, but it's antique crap. Old shields and broadswords are going for a bundle at the moment."

"And what about the Star Wars action figures and spaceships?" she said, smiling.

"Those are still in their boxes—they're collectors items." He smiled at her. "Anyway, I've put out some feelers on the Internet and I think we'll have enough to be very comfortable," he said smugly.

Claire leaned over and kissed him. "Well, aren't you clever?"

"Aren't you glad we didn't give it to the Salvation Army?"

"So, Mr Ford," Claire said, "do we buy a little house with a little garden and a white picket fence and live happily ever after? You, me and junior?"

Xavier leaned in and kissed her. "Sounds good to me, Mrs Ford."

The doctor entered the room, gazing at his clipboard. "I see you're awake—how are you feeling now?"

Claire looked at Xavier and answered the doctor: "Like I've been asleep for a hundred years, and now I'm awake and ready for anything."

"I'll be the judge of that," the doctor replied in his typical, cautious tone. "Now, Harrison, if you could just step out while I examine your wife."

Claire looked at Xavier with a surprised grin.

Xavier leaned in and kissed her cheek. He whispered, "Xavier isn't exactly a normal name—it was the first thing I could think of."

"You seem to be on the mend, Betty," the doctor said.

Claire mouthed the word 'Betty?' at Xavier.

Xavier shrugged and backed out the door, smiling.

Claire giggled quietly to herself as he left.

There were two scruffy-looking guys blocking the doors to the ward as Xavier tried to exit. One was carrying a large fern, while the other appeared to have a sword wrapped up in a bin-bag.

"Man, this is the wrong ward, I'm telling you," said Dave.

"We've been walking around this place for two hours," replied Dave.

"Why did you bring that with you? You look suspicious."

Dave tried to conceal the sword under his coat. "The red-haired girl said not to put it down until we gave it to her."

"Excuse me, man, have you seen a red-haired girl?" Dave asked as Xavier passed.

"No, sorry. Ask a nurse," Xavier said and walked out.

Dave stopped the first nurse he saw. "Can you help us? We're looking for a girl, our next-door neighbour, and close personal friend."

The nurse smiled, happy to help. "Certainly. What's her name?"

Dave looked at Dave and met the same blank stare he was giving.

Xavier walked down the corridor still staring out the windows at the sun every chance he got. He took the lift to the first floor and looked out a window at the gardens, bathed in sunlight and bursting with colour. He was so distracted he didn't hear the patter of bare feet coming up the corridor. He glanced away from the sun for a moment, because even with his sunglasses on, he still wasn't used to the sky being so bright. He saw Lynda stomping towards him with a middle-aged woman in tow. She hadn't seen him yet. Xavier quickly pushed through the doors to the stairway and ducked down. He watched the pair pass. When he was sure they were far enough away he peeked out and caught fragments of their argument.

220

From what he could pick up, Lynda was leaving to finish what she started, and the woman—Aunt Janice—was arguing that she wasn't up to it, especially since she no longer had Christian to back her up. The conversation was cut off as the lift doors closed. Xavier ran to the end of the corridor and gazed out the window just above the entrance. He looked down and a few seconds later Lynda came stomping out with her aunt still tottering behind her, pleading. Xavier felt sorry for his daughter, but he knew the best thing was to stay out of her life. In time maybe she would abandon her quest for vengeance and have a normal life.

Just outside the entrance Lynda stopped abruptly and looked at the ground. Her aunt stopped behind her. Xavier stared at Lynda, and though he could only see the back of her head, he felt something was wrong. She was laughing, or crying, or maybe both. She turned to her aunt and Xavier saw she was laughing, with tears running down her face. She opened her arms and her aunt ran to her and hugged her tightly. It was hard to tell what was going on because he couldn't hear what they were saying, but Xavier thought that somehow Lynda's aunt had managed to talk her out of her crusade. He looked down on the two women embracing and he knew his daughter would be all right—though she should get someone to look at that cut on her foot.

Afterword

I'd like to thank everyone at Black Death Books for taking a chance on an unknown author with some weird stories about vampires in Northern Ireland and for five very happy years together.

And thanks to all the readers who have spread the word.

You keep reading, I'll keep writing.

P.H. 25/08/09

Lightning Source UK Ltd.
Milton Keynes UK
15 December 2009
147549UK00001BA/160/P